W9-BKS-600

THE GIFTED

Other Joanne Kilbourn Mysteries
by Gail Bowen

Kaleidoscope
The Nesting Dolls
The Brutal Heart
The Endless Knot
The Last Good Day
The Glass Coffin
Burying Ariel
Verdict in Blood
A Killing Spring
A Colder Kind of Death
The Wandering Soul Murders
Murder at the Mendel
Deadly Appearances

THE GIFTED

A JOANNE KILBOURN MYSTERY

GAIL
BOWEN

McCLELLAND & STEWART

Library and Archives Canada Cataloguing in Publication

Bowen, Gail, 1942–
The gifted : a Joanne Kilbourn mystery / Gail Bowen.

ISBN 978-0-7710-0998-3

I. Title.

PS8553.08995G49 2013 C813'.54 C2012-908527-8

Published simultaneously in the United States of America by McClelland & Stewart, a division of Random House of Canada Limited, P.O. Box 1030, Plattsburgh, New York 12901

Library of Congress Control Number: 2012956228

Cover art: apple © Artlosk | Dreamstime.com;
blood © Shaik Dawood .K | Dreamstime.com;
paper background © Aliaksey Hintau | Dreamstime.com
Series design: Terri Nimmo

Typeset in Trump Mediaeval by M&S, Toronto
Printed and bound in the United States of America

McClelland & Stewart,
a division of Random House of Canada Limited
One Toronto Street, Suite 300
Toronto, Ontario
M5C 2V6
www.mcclelland.com

1 2 3 4 5 17 16 15 14 13

For Joanne Bonneville,
with love and thanks for the gift of her enduring friendship

CHAPTER

1

As my husband, Zack, slipped into the roomy yellow silk pyjamas that would transform him from a Saskatchewan trial lawyer into Rex Stout's brilliant, food-loving, orchid-growing detective hero, Nero Wolfe, he was one happy guy. Zack has been in a wheelchair since he was seven years old. His costume options are limited, but he loves Halloween and he loves parties and that night we were on our way to a Halloween party. After he finished dressing, Zack watched approvingly as I zipped the fly of the slick vintage suit that would change me from a retired academic into Wolfe's tough, street-smart, confidential assistant and legman, Archie Goodwin.

"You make a very fetching Archie," Zack said.

I bent over and slid a fresh Phalaenopsis aphrodite into Zack's breast pocket. "Nero Wolfe has always been on my top-ten list of men I'd like to know carnally," I said. "I am now speaking not as Archie Goodwin but as the woman in your life."

"We'll leave the party early," Zack said. "I never say no to an intriguing possibility."

The top floor of our building on Halifax Street is divided into two condos. One belongs to Zack's law partner, Margot Hunter, and her stepson, Declan; the other belongs to Zack, me, our soon-to-be fifteen-year-old daughter, Taylor, our two dogs, and Taylor's two cats.

Both our families have a small table for deliveries outside our front doors. That night there was a padded mailing envelope on our table. I picked it up and looked at the address label: "Joanne Ellard Kilbourn Shreve," I said. "I haven't used my birth name in thirty-five years."

"Who's it from?" Zack said.

"Ben Bendure – the filmmaker who did *The Poison Apple,* that documentary of Sally Love's life." I opened the envelope and slid out the contents: two DVDs and a letter addressed to me. I scanned it quickly. "The DVDs are of material that didn't make it into the final cut of the film," I said. "Ben says he'll be eighty next month, his health is failing, and he thinks Taylor should have the footage of her birth mother."

Zack moved his chair closer to me. "What do you think?"

"Since Taylor still refuses to watch *The Poison Apple,* I think getting her to look at these DVDs will be a hard sell."

Zack's eyes searched my face. "But you think it's worth a try."

I nodded. "I do. Sally's been dead eleven years, but there are always new posts about her on the Internet and Taylor faithfully checks *them* out. I wish she wouldn't. It's impossible for Taylor to get a fair picture of Sally from the comments people make about her mother online. Sally's a polarizing figure. People either love her because she never allowed anything or anyone to get in the way of her art or hate her because she used people and when they didn't have anything more to give her, she walked away."

"Taylor may have inherited Sally's single-mindedness

when it comes to her work," Zack said, "but our daughter has a tender heart."

"I know," I said. "And that's what worries me. She could be damaged so easily. Taylor's trying to figure out who she is. The one thing she's clear about is that she doesn't want to be 'a skank' – as she says – like her mother, using sex to fuel her art. Sally did do that, but there was so much more to her. I wish Taylor would be open to learning about Sally as a whole person."

"And you think the material Bendure sent might help Taylor gain some perspective."

"I do, and to be honest, I could use a little perspective myself. The more Taylor's life focuses on her art, the more I realize I'll never be able to give her what Sally could have given her."

"That's bullshit, Jo. From what you've told me, Sally never had any interest in being a parent."

"But she understood Taylor's mind," I said. "Sally would have known instinctively what to do with a daughter who'd inherited her talent. I don't."

Zack squeezed my hand. "You're doing a great job, and Taylor loves you. Stop beating yourself up. Remember what Archie Goodwin says, 'All that really matters is a dance, a chase, a fight, and a kiss.'"

I put the DVDs and the letter back in the padded envelope and placed it on the table. "I'll sign on for the dance and the kiss," I said. "Now we'd better make tracks. When Mieka called, she said our granddaughters are chomping at the bit to go trick or treating, but they won't set out till we see their costumes."

The party we were attending, a forty-fifth birthday celebration for Lauren Treadgold, the wife of Zack's longtime poker buddy Vince, was being held at the Open Skies

Country Club, a world away from our condo in the city's Warehouse District. Our area is part of an urban renewal project called The Village. The developer's mandate is to replace the wilderness of rattrap houses, abandoned factories, and condemned buildings with a pedestrian-friendly neighbourhood of mixed-income housing, small shops, and green space.

Officially, our district is "an area in transition," but the transition is just now inching towards our building. Surrounded by construction hoardings, mud, earthmovers, and the behemoth machines that every day upheave the past to make way for the future, our family lives in a kind of no man's land. Until The Village is a reality, 325 Halifax Street, like the other expensively restored warehouses in our quarter, is a fortress protected against the violence of drug dealers, gang members, addicts, and street warriors by a fifteen-foot security fence topped with razor wire.

As we drove through the railway underpass at Saskatchewan Drive, I stared at the gang tags and wondered about the thought processes that would lead a person to stand in a dark, dank tunnel and spray-paint a wall. Seconds after we emerged from the tunnel something hit the hood of our car.

I yelped and Zack tightened his hold on the steering wheel. "Jesus Christ, what was that?" he said.

"I don't know," I said, my voice shaky. "It could have been stones or chunks of concrete. Someone on the overpass must have thrown them at us."

"Call the cops," Zack said. "If kids are throwing stuff into traffic, they could cause an accident."

As I picked up my cell and hit 911, I tried to count the number of times I'd called emergency services since we moved to 325 Halifax. Counting the wandering souls I saw threading their way through traffic stoned or drunk; toddlers still in diapers, alone and shivering; fights where there was blood; and women and children who'd clearly been beaten, my average must have been close to once a week.

When I broke the connection, I turned to Zack. "The police are dispatching a car to the underpass; they have our contact information, and tomorrow we'll call the station and get the case file number for our insurance."

"Then I guess we just carry on," Zack said.

I could feel the tension gathering in the back of my neck. "Zack, I'm never going to get used to this."

Zack gave me a quick sidelong glance. "You shouldn't get used to it. None of us should. I'll bet you a hundred bucks that whoever threw that rock or whatever it was is about thirteen years old. He's pissed off because it's Halloween. Halloween is supposed to be fun, but for him, it's just the same old shit, so he picked up the weapon at hand."

"And if the police catch him, he'll be in serious trouble."

"Yeah, and my guess is that it won't be the first time that kid has seen the inside of police headquarters."

"Sometimes I wonder if Racette-Hunter is going to make a bit of difference," I said. For several months Zack and I had both been deeply involved in the creation of a centre that would address the needs of a downtown community feared and rejected by many in our city. "Do you really think a community centre is going to change anything?"

Zack was gruff. "Don't go there, Jo. We have to believe that we can give people the tools they need to build a decent future. If we stop believing that, we might as well just hand that kid a bag of rocks and smashed-up concrete and tell him to have a nice life."

As we moved towards our old neighbourhood, the tension in my shoulders relaxed. In the south end, shops and homes were festooned with orange lights and decorated with witches, skeletons, and the other talismans our ancestors believed would deliver them from ghoulies, ghosties, long-legged beasties, and things that go bump in the night. This was a world I knew.

When we turned onto my daughter Mieka's street, a wave of nostalgia washed over me. Mieka is a single mother. After her marriage ended, she and her girls moved back to Regina and into the house in which Mieka and her brothers had grown up. Zack and I had just married and retrofitted a one-storey house across the creek. For years Old Lakeview had been my neighbourhood, and driving down the tree-lined streets brought back memories of taking my own children trick or treating on nights when the air was sharp with the scent of wood smoke and the sidewalks were slick with wet leaves.

It was a chilly night, but Mieka, her partner, Riel, and the girls were standing in the doorway waiting for us. Zack opened the door of his hand-controlled car, grabbed his wheelchair from the back seat, snapped it together, and transferred his body from the car to the chair. When Madeleine and Lena saw him, they came running. After three years, he was still their star-spangled, candy-coated, chocolate-covered top banana.

Lena, who was six, pointed to the sky. "Granddad, did you see? There's a misty moon."

"The werewolves will be tap-dancing tonight," Zack said.

Lena's voice was filled with wonder. "Really?"

Madeleine, at seven, had long since taken Zack's measure. "That's just one of Granddad's jokes, Lena. There's no such thing as a werewolf."

Zack put his forefinger to his lips. "Shh. Can you hear that?"

Madeleine and Lena cupped their ears and listened. "Hear what?" Madeleine whispered.

"That tapping sound," Zack said.

Lena's eyes were huge. "I can hear it. Granddad, do you think it's the werewolves?"

"Consider the evidence," Zack said. "A misty moon, a mysterious tapping sound, and" – he sniffed theatrically – "a definite tang of werewolf in the wind." He turned to Riel. "Surely you can smell it."

Riel, who appeared a little tired and on edge, raised his hand in a Halt sign. "I never take sides in fights about werewolves."

Mieka slid her arm around Riel's waist. "That's why I love you," she said. "Now let's go inside so Mum and Zack can see our costumes in the light."

Madeleine and Lena had been discussing potential Halloween costumes since August. Madeleine had finally settled on Elphaba, the misunderstood girl with the emerald green skin who grew into the Wicked Witch of the West. Lena had chosen to be Elphaba's friend Glinda, the beautiful, bubbly blonde who became the Good Witch of the North. As they pirouetted for us in the front hall, it was clear their choices had been inspired.

After Zack snapped a dozen pictures of Elphaba and Glinda and a dozen more of Elphaba and Glinda with Mieka, who was Dorothy, and Riel, who had dressed as the Scarecrow, I dropped the chocolate cats we'd purchased into the girls' trick-or-treat bags. Riel took the bowl of Halloween candy outside and placed it on a chair by the door, and Madeleine and Lena taped the cardboard sign they'd made to the chair back. The sign's message was unequivocal: *Help Yourself But Think Of The Next Kid.* Mieka locked the door, the girls took off, and we adults trailed along.

Riel was quick to notice the damage to the hood of our car. "What happened here?" he said.

"When we came out of the railway underpass, somebody threw something at us," Zack said.

Riel bent to examine the hood of the Volvo more closely. "I guess when you take a car this expensive for a spin in North Central, you're asking for it."

Mieka frowned. "Mum and Zack could have been hurt, Riel."

"And I'm glad they weren't," Riel said. He turned to Zack and me. "I really am glad you're okay." He reached under his scarecrow's hat and pulled out a handful of straw. "You'll have to forgive me. I don't have a brain – just straw."

Zack's jaw tightened, but he didn't respond and the moment passed. When the girls joined us and breathlessly produced the homemade, absolutely-safe-to-eat candy apples that Mieka's neighbour and my old friend, Jean Van Velzer, had given them, we exclaimed over the artistry of the apples and said our goodbyes.

There were many children in Mieka's neighbourhood, and that night they all seemed to be darting across the streets with only fleeting attention to oncoming cars. Zack was wholly focused on his driving, and neither of us spoke till we were out of the residential area.

"Thanks for not getting into it with Riel," I said.

"No point," Zack said. "He's not going to change his assumptions."

"I know," I said. "I wish he'd do something about that chip on his shoulder, though."

"So do I," Zack said. "But it isn't going to happen, so we might as well get used to turning the other cheek."

We exchanged a quick look of commiseration, then Zack leaned forward and put on a Bill Evans CD, and my thoughts turned to Riel.

I'd been the first member of our family to meet him. Until Riel Delorme dropped out of the master's program at the university, he had been my student. I liked him. He was smart, idealistic, and deeply committed to transforming the lives of the poor and dependent in our city. Like his hero, Che Guevara, Riel believed that the only way to change a society that he thought was fundamentally corrupt and racist was revolution, and it wasn't long before Riel abandoned his studies and became involved with radical politics. He became an urban warrior, heading up a loose coalition of gangs, social activists, and the dispossessed to oppose the Village Project. Rumour had it that he'd also developed a fondness for cocaine. Margot's late husband, Leland Hunter, the developer behind the project, was Zack's client, so, in the public eye, we were associated with it as well.

The clash between the factions was corrosive for both sides, and I was relieved when Riel dropped his opposition to the project and joined forces with Leland. Riel had been clean for two years. He was a valuable link to the community, and Leland came to like and respect him.

From the first, Mieka's relationship with Riel was serious. The physical attraction between them was electric, and Riel was genuinely fond of Madeleine and Lena. When Mieka broke the news that she and Riel had fallen in love, she had quoted Antoine de Saint-Exupery: "Love does not consist in gazing at each other but in looking outward together in the same direction."

For a while it had seemed that all of us were looking outward together in the same direction. After Zack took over as CEO of the Racette-Hunter Centre, he and Riel saw each other daily. As a member of the Racette-Hunter working team, I had come to value Riel's understanding of the complex politics of North Central. He was the project's community liaison officer, and time and again, he extinguished brushfires of opposition before they had a chance to spread. Professionally, we worked together well.

Personally, life was less rosy. We're a close family, but Riel kept his distance. We saw Mieka and the girls as much as we always had, and I told myself that as long as they were happy, we were happy. However, Riel had been conspicuously absent during what would have been his first Thanksgiving weekend with us all at the lake. When I asked after him, Mieka had been vague and I hadn't pushed it.

I was still wool-gathering when we pulled into the parking lot of Open Skies. The club was festive. The path to the lobby was flanked by blazing jack-o'-lanterns, and the crisp October air was heavy with the mingled aromas of melting wax and warming pumpkin meat. The scent evoked other Halloweens in other years, and seduced by memories, I hesitated for a moment before I went inside.

"Penny for your thoughts," Zack said.

"I was remembering the year Taylor wouldn't let me put our jack-o'-lantern on the compost heap after Halloween was over. She'd helped me carve it and she wasn't about to let it go."

Zack chuckled. "So how long was the pumpkin with you?"

"Almost till Christmas. You know Taylor."

"I do. But now she's grown up and tonight she's at a 'mega-cool party' watching *The Little Shop of Horrors.*"

"She was so excited about that party."

"Well, that blond wig *was* pretty spectacular," Zack said.

"It was," I agreed. "But sometimes I miss the little girl with the braids hunkered down on the front porch with her decomposing pumpkin."

The first half of Lauren Treadgold's forty-fifth birthday party followed the well-worn grooves of every private party at Open Skies. The appetizers were plentiful and tasty, the spirits flowed, and the young players in the five-piece band had the good sense to play tunes that their audience recognized.

When we entered the dining room, Vince and Lauren Treadgold were there to greet us. The party invitation had asked that we come as people, real or imaginary, that revealed our inner selves. The Treadgolds had dressed as Caesar and Cleopatra – an appropriately golden and powerful couple.

There are people on whom the gods seem to bestow every gift. Vince was one of those people. He was a well-regarded orthopedic surgeon who bore a startling resemblance to the actor Ted Danson, tall and fit, with a strong jaw, artfully tousled silver hair, and icy azure eyes.

Lauren, too, was one of fortune's favourites. Whip-thin and elegant with high-planed cheeks and doe eyes, Lauren had appeared on the cover of *Vogue* for the first time when she was sixteen years old. Soon after, she left Saskatchewan for the runways of New York, Paris, and Rome. For the next twenty years, her heart-shaped face and signature hairstyle – a severe, side-parted gamine cut – were a fixture on the glossy pages of international fashion magazines. But as I overheard Lauren ruefully note one night after too much wine, every year, stubborn as dandelions, a new crop of sixteen-year-olds appeared. When offers of plum assignments became few and far between, Lauren retired, came home, and married Vince.

The Treadgolds were always a striking couple, but that night they turned heads. Vince's costume was simple: a belted white linen tunic, sandals, and a laurel wreath. Lauren's white linen caftan was unexceptional, but her turquoise and gold beaded necklace was elaborate, and the rope of twisted gold on her head was studded with turquoise. Her makeup was dramatic: Egyptian cat eyes and blood red lips. The most stunning item of her costume was a golden asp bracelet that wound itself around her wrist and ended at the top of her hand in a hooded snake's head with emerald eyes and a forked tongue.

Although Zack and Vince had been poker partners for more than twenty years, I had come to know the Treadgolds well only recently through their work for the Racette-Hunter Centre. Lauren and Vince had agreed to act as co-chairs of fundraising. In theory, their positions were purely honorary. The Treadgold name on the letterhead would underscore the fact that the multimillion-dollar project was both reputable and worthwhile.

However, the Treadgolds' contribution went beyond the nominal. Vince had worked diligently to get donations from his medical colleagues, and Lauren, too, had taken her job seriously. Zack had been impressed by her creativity and by her sure-footed approach to everything she did. She was not a woman who made mistakes.

"Great party," Zack said. He gazed at Vince and Lauren's costumes. "And great costumes, especially that asp bracelet."

Lauren touched a perfectly lacquered nail to the snake's head. "Vince had it specially made. It's a symbol of the healing arts, but tonight I couldn't resist the Cleopatra connection."

"Because Cleopatra used an asp to commit suicide," I said.

Lauren's eyes lit with pleasure. "I did my research. Cleopatra tested different poisons on people and animals and discovered that the bite of an asp was the most painless way to die."

"Fortunately asps are in short supply in these parts," Vince said. He focused his attention on us. "You two look pretty cool. Who are you supposed to be?"

Before Zack and I had a chance to answer, Georges, the club manager, dashed over, holding a cellphone. "Dr. Treadgold, the hospital just called. They need to speak to you." Georges handed the cell to Vince and then stepped back respectfully to await the next development.

Vince thanked Georges and made his call. After he broke

the connection, he turned to Lauren. "Car accident," he said. "I have to go back to the hospital."

"Can't someone else do it?" Lauren said.

"I'm sorry, Lauren. I'm it. That flu that's been making the rounds has decimated the ranks. I have to be there."

"It's not as if it's the first time," Lauren said coldly, and she turned on her heel and walked towards the bar.

It was an awkward moment, and Zack attempted to smooth it. "Looks like you're sleeping on the couch tonight, Caesar."

Vince's laugh was short. "Not the first time for that either," he said. "I'm sorry I have to go. I was looking forward to spending time with you both tonight. Enjoy your evening."

Not long after Vince left, Kaye Russell arrived. Kaye taught painting and drawing in the visual arts department at the university and since August she had been Taylor's teacher. With her platinum buzz cut and round-rimmed tortoise-shell glasses, Kaye was always an arresting figure. Tonight she was wearing a black-and-white-striped T-shirt, a black leather jacket, tight black jeans, and laceless sparkly gold Keds.

Zack gave her the once-over. "Do I get three guesses?"

Kaye shook her head. "You'd need at least ten. I'm Andy Warhol."

"My money was on Annie Lennox," Zack said.

"Maybe I should have worn my Campbell's Soup can raincoat," Kaye said.

"Nah," Zack said. "People like a challenge. With the raincoat, even I could have identified you."

Kaye laughed and then her eye was caught by a new arrival. "There's Julian," she said. "I invited him, but I didn't think he'd come."

"Julian, the boy who's modelling for Taylor?" Zack said. "Not exactly his crowd, is it?"

"Julian has talked about opening a small art gallery," Kaye said. "I think it's the perfect path for him. I was hoping he could make some connections tonight." She waved, and Julian Zentner started towards us. He'd been modelling for Taylor for a month, so Zack and I were accustomed to seeing him around our condo, always dressed in the shabby casual clothes students in fine arts favour.

But that night he had transformed himself, and as he crossed the floor towards us, every eye at the party was on him. He, too, was wearing a white tunic, and he'd dusted his skin with powder until his body was the blue-white of skim milk. The belt of his tunic was covered with small circular mirrors. It took me a moment before I understood that he had come as Narcissus, the boy in Greek mythology who fell in love with his reflection in a pool and died because he was unable to tear himself away from his own beauty.

Tall and delicately boned, with blue-black ringlets worn long enough to curl on his graceful neck, Julian had enhanced his natural attributes for the party. His startlingly green eyes were ringed with kohl and his sensuous lips were rouged and moistened.

His entrance caused a stir, but when Julian joined us he didn't have the air of a young man who had just completed a star turn. He shook hands politely with Zack and lowered his eyes bashfully as he greeted Kaye and me. "I was afraid that Kaye and Lauren Treadgold would be the only people here I knew," he said.

Zack's interest was piqued. "How do you know Lauren?" he said.

Julian tossed his head. "From work. I'm a server at Diego's, and Lauren's one of our best customers. Anyway, I didn't want to ruin Lauren's evening or Kaye's by trailing around after them."

"You couldn't possibly ruin my evening," Kaye said. "But there are people here that I know you'll enjoy."

"Let me take you around and introduce you," Zack said. "Kaye mentioned that you were interested in opening a gallery. There are a couple of people here tonight who might find that idea appealing."

Lauren was part of a group not far from us. When she overheard Zack's words, she joined us immediately. "Count me among them," she said. "Running a gallery with Julian might be a lot of fun."

"You two know each other from Diego's?" Zack said.

"Celeste introduced us," Lauren said. "It's the only nice thing Vince's daughter ever did for me." Lauren stepped back and gazed thoughtfully at Julian's costume. "The myth of Narcissus has always made me sad," she said. "Something about the death of beauty, I guess."

Julian's voice was low. "You'll never have to worry about that, Lauren."

Ignoring the rest of us, Lauren slid her arm through Julian's. "Let's find a quiet place and talk about that gallery."

We watched as Julian and Lauren made their way across the room and disappeared through the double doors.

"Well, that was smooth," Zack said.

"Too smooth," Kaye said. "Julian's only nineteen. He shouldn't get involved with a woman like Lauren Treadgold. I'll talk to him."

"Be careful," I said. "Julian may be young, but he's an adult. He won't appreciate you telling him what he should do. My kids have taught me not to press too hard. You can lose them."

I was surprised when Kaye's grey eyes filled with tears. "I shouldn't have come tonight. I thought a party might help, but it's just making everything worse."

"Is something wrong?" I said.

"Just the same old ache," she said. "It's been twenty years this week since the accident."

I understood the reference. As a young woman, Kaye had suffered an unthinkable tragedy. Her husband and child were killed in a car accident, and Kaye herself was badly injured. Except for a slight limp that became noticeable only when she was tired, Kaye had recovered physically. Her determination to recover psychologically was nothing short of heroic. Many would have been embittered forever by such a cataclysmic loss, but Kaye poured her energies into the young people who every September entered the university bright with ambition and dreams. Teacher, mentor, and friend, Kaye had changed lives, and her pretty bungalow near the campus was filled with paintings and drawings sent by grateful former students.

I put my arms around her. "I know that nothing I can say will help, but, Kaye, you've given so much to so many. Our daughter thinks you walk on water, and Zack and I agree. Taylor's thrilled about the art she's been making since you began working with her."

The reminder of what she'd accomplished with Taylor seemed to lift some of Kaye's sadness. "Taylor *should* be thrilled. Having two pieces accepted for a major art auction is quite a coup."

"It is indeed," Zack said. "And that brings us back to Julian Zentner. Joanne and I are still in the dark about Taylor's portrait of him. *Two Painters* has been propped up in our living room for weeks, but the portrait of Julian remains shrouded in mystery."

Kaye chose her words with care. "It's possible Taylor believes that you and Joanne might not approve of the approach she took to her subject. I've seen both pieces, and in my opinion, *Two Painters* is a better piece of art. It's bold, and the way Taylor uses space and light on that canvas is sophisticated for a young artist. But *BlueBoy21* is the piece that will get the attention. For a fifteen-year-old to paint a twenty-first-century version of one of the world's most famous portraits took confidence, but Taylor brought it off. *BlueBoy21* is stunning." Kaye's voice grew wistful. "After the auction, life is going to change for Taylor."

Zack was clearly perplexed. "Kaye, I'm not getting this. *BlueBoy21* was a student piece. Taylor told us that herself. She was simply working in a genre with which she was unfamiliar. Why should that change Taylor's life?"

"People – important people – are going to notice her work," Kaye said. "They're going to have ideas about what she should do next."

"She's not even fifteen years old," Zack said. "What Taylor does next is up to her and her parents." He moved his chair slightly closer to Kaye. "And to you, of course."

"Thank you for that," Kaye said. "It's good to know I still have a role to play." Her eyes travelled the room. "No sign of Julian. I'm worried. He can't handle a woman like Lauren Treadgold. He's so vulnerable."

"Julian doesn't strike me as vulnerable," Zack said.

"He tries to hide it," Kaye said. "But Taylor captured his sadness in her portrait of him. His beauty but also his longing."

My mind jumped to the possibility that Julian had been attracted to the artist painting him. "What's Julian longing for?" I said as casually as I could.

"The kind of gift Taylor has," Kaye said. "But he simply doesn't have it. He was in my first-year drawing class last year. He worked harder than anyone, but at the end of term, Julian and I both knew the truth. He came to me and asked for an honest assessment of his abilities." She bit her lip, looking close to tears again. "I gave him what he'd asked for."

Zack winced. "That must have been tough for both of you."

"It was," Kaye said. "Julian knew, of course, but hearing me say the words was a blow. I suggested other paths: sculpture, photography, video, but Julian's dream was to become a great realist painter, and he was devastated. If I had it to do over, I'd equivocate."

"In the end that would be crueller," Zack said. "You did the right thing, Kaye."

Kaye's voice was hoarse with emotion. "I wish I could believe that." She zipped her jacket. "Imagining what Lauren Treadgold is doing with Julian is making me sick. I'm going home." She started towards the door, then turned back. "If you see Julian, tell him . . . tell him he is loved."

CHAPTER

2

After Kaye left, Zack and I went our separate ways. Zack made a beeline for Warren and Annie Weber. Warren had made millions in farm machinery. He was crowding eighty, and Annie was a luscious twenty-something. With a winning sense of irony, they had come as "Daddy" Warbucks and Little Orphan Annie.

I talked to a husband and wife, both surgeons, who were dressed in furs as Dr. Zhivago and Lara; to the Treadgolds' next-door neighbours, who were a little too deeply into character as George and Martha from *Who's Afraid of Virginia Woolf?*; and to three Oscar Wildes, one of whom was Zack's dentist. Zack's dentist was a nice man, but he was no Oscar Wilde, and I was relieved when Ernest Beauvais, the First Nations elder who was advising the Racette-Hunter project, rescued me with a gentle request to have a few words about the mission statement we'd worked on together.

The idea of inviting an elder to be part of our committee had been Riel's. He had recommended Ernest, a bear of a man – tall, big-boned, large-featured, and gentle. It had been an inspired choice. A retired ironworker, Ernest Beauvais was deeply rooted in traditional ways but knowledgeable about the character and skills people needed to succeed in the trades. At meetings, he listened attentively and spoke rarely, but when he did speak, people listened.

That night he was dressed in construction worker's gear. His leather jacket bore the ironworkers' union logo and it was clearly vintage. "I'm guessing your jacket has a history," I said.

"It was my grandfather's," Ernest said. "He was one of the Mohawks from Kahnawake who helped frame New York City's skyscrapers and bridges."

"One of the famed Mohawks who don't fear heights," I said.

Ernest chuckled. "Mohawks have as much fear of heights as the next guy. They've just learned to deal with it. They take a lot of pride in 'walking iron.' My kids are more Cree than Mohawk, but all of them, including my daughters, are ironworkers. I taught them just the way my father taught me and my grandfather taught my father."

"Four generations" I said. "That's impressive."

Ernest nodded. "I've been blessed," he said. "I know that I'm part of something larger than myself. I know that my family has a proud history. I know that the work I do is valued. And I know that my children look up to me. If we can give those blessings to the people who come to Racette-Hunter, we will have done our job."

"We will indeed," I said.

Ernest held out his hand. "I'm glad we're working on this together, Joanne," he said. "Now if you'll excuse me, I have a wake to attend on the reserve tomorrow. It's a long drive, and I'll need to get an early start."

As I watched Ernest move, unrushed, towards the door, someone touched my arm. I turned to see Vince's daughter standing beside me, dressed in a shapeless mid-length skirt, sturdy brown walking shoes, and an ancient cardigan. Celeste Treadgold was a boyishly gangly young woman with wavy hair the colour of butterscotch and deep-set eyes that were the same icy blue as Vince's.

When Celeste returned to Regina after years at boarding school in Toronto and a disastrous first year of university, I was still teaching and Vince had asked me to talk to his daughter about straightening out her academic record. When Celeste and I met for coffee, we chatted easily. Our biographies were remarkably similar. Both our fathers were doctors whom we loved deeply but seldom saw. Both our mothers had chosen a path to nowhere. Celeste's mother committed suicide by driving through a blizzard until she found a spot outside the city where she could park her Mercedes and vanish forever into the snowy fields. When the police found her, she was barefoot and, except for her full-length chinchilla coat, naked. Celeste told me that her dreams were haunted by that image.

My mother was an alcoholic who had no interest in raising a daughter. Celeste and I had both attended the same Toronto boarding school, three decades apart, for the same reason: it was easier for everyone if we were out of the way. But as similar as our histories were, they were different in one salient particular. I had survived relatively unscathed. Celeste had not. She was a very angry young woman, and most of that anger was directed towards the stepmother who had urged Vince to ship his daughter off to a private school more than two thousand kilometres from her home.

After our first meeting, Celeste and I had coffee a few times. We enjoyed each other's company, but we led very different lives, and we were both busy. That night, she greeted me with an endearingly lopsided smile. "Finally," she said. "A familiar face. Who *are* all these people?"

"The usual suspects," I said. "The only surprise guests in our demographic are the shiny new replacement wives."

"The Lauren contingent," she said. Celeste scanned the room. "I'm guessing that Little Orphan Annie falls into that category."

"She does," I said. "Rumour has it that she's a very nice woman and that she's making 'Daddy' Warbucks a very happy man."

"Good for them," Celeste said. "I wish it had worked out that way for my father. Have you seen him?"

"There was an emergency. He had to go back to the hospital almost as soon as he got here."

Celeste whistled. "I'll bet Cleopatra was not one bit pleased about Caesar's defection."

"Understandably," I said. "This is her birthday party."

"Stay tuned," Celeste said. "Lauren will make my father pay. She always does – it doesn't have to be a special occasion."

When Zack wheeled over, Celeste looked thoughtfully at his yellow silk pyjamas, leaned over, touched the Phalaenopsis aphrodite in his breast pocket, then gave me the quickest of once-overs. "Nero Wolfe and Archie," she said.

"Not bad," Zack said.

Celeste's expression was mischievous. "Don't be grudging. That was nothing short of brilliant. Now, it's your turn."

I studied her drab outfit and noticed that one of the threadbare cardigan's pocket was strangely bulging.

"Are we allowed to see what's in your pocket?" I asked.

Celeste reached into her sweater pocket and took out a stone.

"Virginia Woolf," I said.

Celeste examined the rock in her hand meditatively. "My poor, brilliant, tortured Virginia. She needed to make sure she'd drown when she walked into the river." Celeste held out the rock so we could see it more closely. Neatly printed on the stone's surface were the words *Bay Roc Villa.* "This is one of my stepmother's collection of stones from places where she and my father have holidayed," Celeste said. "No thoughts of suicide there. Lauren is not prone to existential angst." Celeste dropped the stone back into her pocket and turned her eyes towards the bar. "Well, well," she said. "Julian came after all. He told me he'd been invited, but he didn't seem keen on coming. I guess the birthday girl pouted until she got her way."

Lauren was standing so close to Julian that her breast was pressing against his chest. When she brushed his shoulder with her lips, Zack made a moue of disgust and took Celeste's arm protectively. "We don't want to watch this," he said. "I think it's time for the three of us to check out the grub."

The appetizers table was decorated with mini-pumpkins, owls, ravens, and tarantulas. Festive, but whatever the season, the club's menu never varied, and although the hot hors d'oeuvres had been tarted up for Halloween, they were comfortingly familiar.

Zack and Celeste attacked the curried prawns simultaneously. When they reached for seconds, Zack turned to Celeste: "Are you okay?"

"No," she said bluntly. "Coming to Cleopatra's party was just one of my pathetic attempts to spend some time with my father and, of course, he was a no-show." Celeste looked to the dance floor, where Lauren and Julian were moving as one – their bodies pressed together, their limbs intertwined. With their raven hair and milk-white skin, they could have been mother and son, and that made the sensuality of their movements all the more disturbing. Finally, Lauren whispered in Julian's ear, and hand in hand they left the dance floor.

Zack's gaze followed them. "What the hell's going on there?"

Celeste laughed the low, husky laugh of the confirmed smoker. "I told you. Payback."

Midweek parties at the Open Skies Country Club took into account the fact that the working days of most guests began early. The formal part of events always got underway at ten. I knew that after the cake-cutting, Zack and I would be making a quick exit, so a little before ten, I headed for the ladies' room.

Lauren Treadgold was in there alone, looking critically at her reflection in one of the mirrors above the sinks. Her private time with Julian must have smeared her elaborate makeup. She refreshed her lipstick with an expert's hand, then she picked up a small container of iridescent turquoise eye shadow and smoothed fresh colour on her lid.

"This party was not one of my better ideas," she said.

"We had a good time," I said.

"But you would rather have been at home with your dogs."

"It was a nice party," I said.

"And you're counting the minutes till it's over." Lauren dipped the tip of her forefinger into the eye shadow and began colouring her other eyelid. "To be honest, so am I. My husband chose the design on the cake. It's an edible icing replica of my first *Vogue* cover."

"I'm sure Vince thought the *Vogue* cover would bring back some pleasant memories for you," I said.

Lauren pivoted to face me. "What woman wants to be reminded of how she looked thirty years ago?" She dropped the eye shadow into her evening bag, took out eyeliner, turned back to the mirror, and traced over the dramatic line from her lower lid to the outer tip of her eyebrow.

"You're a beautiful woman, Lauren."

Her laugh was short and bitter. "Not as beautiful as I was when I was sixteen." She moved closer to the mirror. "I hate getting old."

"It beats the alternative," I said.

Lauren sighed. "I wonder."

At ten o'clock on the nose, servers began distributing flutes of champagne and Georges rolled out the dolly that held Lauren's birthday cake. Glasses in hand, the guests gathered round to admire the cake.

Lauren was waiting at the head table and she wasn't alone. Julian was at her side. Their positioning was eerily like that of a bride and groom. Zack boomed out the first words of "Happy Birthday" and everybody joined in. When Lauren bent to blow out the candles, the play of light and shadow on her face had an odd effect, making her seem strikingly beautiful one second and gaunt and old the next.

After the candles were extinguished, people raised their glasses. There was an awkward moment when it appeared no one had been designated to propose a toast – presumably, Vince had planned to say some words in honour of his wife. Lauren managed the situation by raising her glass in Julian's direction. "To youth," she said.

From the back of the room, a male voice, slightly drunken, yelled out: "And here's to you, Mrs. Robinson." The reference to the woman who famously seduced a college graduate half her age elicited a burst of nervous laughter, but Lauren was not amused. She grabbed the cake knife, made a vertical slash across the icing, threw the knife onto the table, took Julian's hand, and bolted. The scene was over in seconds, but the tension in the room lingered.

Georges called over one of the servers and handed him the knife to finish cutting the cake. Clearly, the party was over.

When I finished my piece, Zack took my plate. "So, Archie, are you about ready to call it a night?"

"I am, Mr. Wolfe. Why don't you arrange to get the car, and I'll see if I can track down our host to thank her for the party."

I circled the room and peeked into the ladies' room, but Lauren had disappeared. Finally, I gave up and came out to the lobby. The valet had brought our car around, and Zack was chatting with Georges.

"I couldn't find Lauren," I said. "Georges, would you mind thanking Ms. Treadgold for us?"

Georges's smirk was knowing. "If she returns, I'll be glad to. Mrs. Treadgold and her young friend left a few minutes ago."

Georges was clearly offering information, but Zack wasn't in the market. He shrugged. "Well, when you see Ms. Treadgold, please thank her for us. Have a pleasant evening."

Celeste Treadgold was standing just inside the front door, waiting for her own car to be brought around. When we joined her, she pulled a pack of Benson & Hedges from her bag. "That was instructive," she drawled, tapping a cigarette from the pack. "Now we all know that if we decide to sneak a quickie, we shouldn't do it at the club when Georges is on duty."

"Are you all right?" I said.

"Why wouldn't I be?" she asked. "I'm not the one being betrayed."

Celeste's words were angry, but there was a tremor in her voice. I touched her arm. "Why don't we have lunch together sometime?"

"I'd like that," she said. There were NO SMOKING signs in every room of the club, but Celeste flicked her lighter brazenly. When her cigarette was lit, she inhaled deeply and blew three careful smoke rings back into the lobby. "These are for you, Georges," she said. "It was a swell party."

When we were settled in our car, Zack put the keys in the ignition and turned to me. "Do you buy Celeste's theory that this thing tonight is payback for Vince leaving the party?"

"I think it goes deeper than that," I said. "Before the cake fiasco, I ran into Lauren in the ladies' room. She was standing in front of the mirror and she didn't like what she saw there."

"She's a beautiful woman," Zack said.

"I told her that," I said. "But in her mind, she's thirty years past her prime."

"So Lauren was angry at Vince tonight, and Julian was right here, available. The perfect storm."

The Little Shop of Horrors party was being held at the home of Taylor's friend Gracie Falconer, and Taylor was sleeping over. When Zack and I got back to the condo, Willie and Pantera greeted us as if we had returned from a long and dangerous mission. Zack and I fussed over the dogs, and then we went to bed and fussed over each other. It was a memorable ending to a memorable evening. After we were through making love, Zack offered me the top of his yellow silk pyjamas and buttoned me up.

Zack and I both like a cool bedroom, so on pleasant nights my last chore of the day is opening the window. When I came back to bed, Zack drew me close. "I've been thinking about Julian," he said.

"Not in the last half-hour, I hope."

"Nope, in the last half-hour, my mind was wholly on bringing pleasure to Archie Goodwin."

"And you succeeded," I said. "So what are your thoughts about Julian?"

"When Kaye said Taylor has the future Julian dreamed of, I thought of this kid in our first year in law school. No lawyers in his family. No kindly small-town lawyer mentoring him.

No reason for him even to consider the law, but he had this burning desire to be a lawyer."

"And he didn't have the stuff?"

"No, he didn't." Zack's voice was deep and intimate. "Jo, the first time I read a law book, I knew that I'd entered a world where everything made sense to me. Every class I took, every law book I read, just affirmed what I already knew: the law was where I belonged. And this kid worked his ass off and kept asking me to help him. I did my best, but he just couldn't get it."

"So what happened to him?"

"He shot another student in our class, and then he shot himself."

My heart clutched. "You don't think Julian would hurt Taylor, do you?"

"If I thought that, I wouldn't be lying here beside you. I'd be making certain Julian was locked up. All the same, I'm glad the painting is finished – for Julian's sake as well as ours. It must be tough for him to stand there and watch Taylor do what he'll never be able to do."

"Luckily, that chapter's closing," I said. "The painting's done. Taylor and Julian live in different worlds. There's no reason for them to continue seeing each other."

"Thank God for that," Zack said. A few moments later, his breathing became slow and rhythmic and before long he was asleep.

I wasn't so lucky. It had been an unsettling evening, not simply because of the tensions in the Treadgold family, but also because Julian Zentner had revealed himself to be darker and more complex than he appeared to be when he came to our home to model for Taylor. Zack's story about the boy in law school whose despair led him to murder and suicide had lodged itself in my imagination. It was a long time before I slept.

—

In Regina, the sun rises at about 7:45 in early November. Willie and Pantera awaken at 5:00 a.m. At the side of our building there's a heated dog run, but the dogs and I prefer the roof garden. It's safe and it's large enough for the three of us to get in some decent exercise before breakfast. As soon as the elevator doors open, the dogs are off, chasing each other around the large outdoor planters that house the garden's evergreens and perennial shrubs.

Willie and Pantera had adjusted to condo life with surprising ease. Five months earlier our family had lived in a solid one-storey home on a pleasantly landscaped lot overlooking Wascana Creek. Its only exceptional features were the accessibility ramps for Zack. We lived the privileged lives of upper-middle-class people, and then in the early hours of a placid June night, someone blew up our solid one-storey home. It was an act of violence as stunning as it was life-changing.

By one of those strange quirks of fate that makes people believe in kismet, Zack and Taylor and I were not in our house by the creek the night of the explosion. Most weekends, we drove to our cottage forty-five minutes from the city as soon as Zack and I came home from work on Friday. But that Thursday afternoon, Zack had decided that our family would celebrate my retirement from the university's political science department by leaving for the lake a day early. It seemed the perfect coda for the official end of my life as an academic. When I went to bed, my mind was spinning the gossamer of summer plans.

The blast that had ripped apart our house broke the shell of safety and comfort we had taken for granted. The explosion was a sobering reminder that the threads that tie us to our lives are fragile, and I had taken the reminder to heart.

Robertson Davies wrote that when fate sends a message, it is spiritual suicide to resist. We had all received the message, and we each chose to interpret and act upon what we had learned in our own way.

I looked past the darkness of our neighbourhood towards the Christmas lights that were already sparkling downtown and thought about the changes in our lives. The essentials were the same. Our lives still centred on family, but we had become active in our new community, an area that a national magazine once described as the worst neighbourhood in Canada. I hadn't been to every neighbourhood in Canada, but ours exhibited all the ugly dividends of poverty: gangs, drugs, violence, alcoholism, prostitution, and hopelessness. So our family set about doing what we could to make our community better.

Zack gave up his law practice for a year to spearhead the building of the new Racette-Hunter Centre. As a trial lawyer, Zack was an expert advocate. He knew how to read people, marshal facts, and argue effectively. The job was large, but Zack had a knack for attracting good people, and the project was moving in the right direction.

Taylor was teaching art in a Kids at Risk program in our neighbourhood, and April's Place, the play centre/café our daughter Mieka and her friend Lisa Wallace were starting for North Central's young parents and their children, would be opening at the end of November.

For my part, in early September I'd finished writing the script for a television special called *For the Common Good,* which tracked the conciliation process between Leland Hunter and Riel Delorme. I still had some final editing to do but nothing time-consuming, so when Ernest Beauvais asked me to come up with a coherent statement of purpose for the new multiplex, I was interested.

Ernest and I settled on three clear goals. The first was to

dismantle the stereotypical ideas Aboriginals and non-Aboriginals had about each other. The second was to convince people outside North Central that the community's largely Aboriginal population shouldn't be written off, that they were a resource that could lift up the community. The third was to convince the people inside North Central that the answer to transforming their lives and their community wasn't government assistance. They themselves were the answer, and that meant accepting responsibility for parenting, for work, for the health of their families, and for the condition of their homes.

Becoming part of our neighbourhood was an exhilarating process, but as I stood on the rooftop, I couldn't forget that our building was still surrounded by that fifteen-foot security fence. We had a long way to go.

November 5 was Christmas card photo day for the people behind the Racette-Hunter project. When Zack came out of our bedroom showered and dressed for the day, he picked up the envelope that contained Ben Bendure's DVD. "This has been sitting on the counter for nearly a week," he said. "We don't have to be at the construction site till nine. Do you think it's time we took a look at it?"

"Sure," I said. "I've been planning to call Ben to thank him. If I could say I'd already started watching, I'd seem more enthusiastic."

"You don't seem very enthusiastic now," Zack said.

"I'm not. There's still a lot of unfinished business in that part of my life."

Zack's dark eyes were probing. "Maybe it's time to finish it."

Zack examined the DVDs and chose one. "This covers Sally's early years."

"The years when she and I were close," I said.

"If I'm lucky, I'll get to see you."

"If I'm lucky, you won't," I said. "I was a lumpy girl with braids. Sally was a beanpole, but she already knew how to light up a room."

Zack slid the DVD into the player and the screen was filled with images that were as familiar to me as the back of my hand. Muskoka chairs, bright with fresh paint, facing a sun-splashed lake. A raft bobbing on the waves. A dark green rowboat with yellow lifejackets folded neatly on the seats waiting beside the dock. I had spent sixteen summers at MacLeod Lake. I hadn't been there in forty years, but when I looked at the dock, I could feel the pressure of the sun-warmed wooden slats against my stomach as I lay face down, peering through the cracks to watch a school of newly hatched catfish swim by.

I took a deep breath.

Always alert to my mood, Zack turned to me. "Are you all right?"

"Nothing life-threatening," I said, taking his hand. "Just blindsided by memories."

The camera moved to the beach and zoomed in on Sally and her father building a sandcastle. Both were tanned, long-limbed, and blond. Both wore swimsuits, and the slope of their shoulders as they bent to their work was identical. Beside them on the beach lay shovels, trowels, spatulas, palette knifes, spray bottles to keep the sand moist, and bowls and buckets to use as moulds and shapers. Des and Sally's joy in each other and in the world they were creating was palpable.

And then I came along. As soon as he saw me, Zack hit Pause. Frozen on the screen was a girl in an unflatteringly fussy bathing suit. One of my braids was coming loose, the skin on my nose was peeling, and I had a bandage on my knee.

I grabbed for the remote. "Zack, hit Play. Please."

"I just want to look at you," Zack said. "Your eyes have

always been beautiful. It's amazing to think that that girl grew up to be the centre of my universe."

"It's amazing to think that that girl grew up to be the centre of anybody's universe," I said. "Now take your finger off Pause."

Zack started the DVD again, but the scene that followed made me cringe. Sally's mother, Nina, had sent me down to the beach to call her houseguest, Ben, and her husband and daughter to lunch. When I relayed the message, Sally glared at me.

"Tell her we don't need lunch," she said.

"But Nina has everything ready," I said. "And the table looks really pretty."

"She does that for you," Sally said. "I don't give a hoot about how the table looks, and she knows it."

When Des spoke to me, his voice was kind. "Joanne, why don't you and Ben go up to the house and have some of Nina's lovely lunch? Sally and I will get something later."

There was a final shot of the father and daughter back at work on the sandcastle and then the scene changed to the luncheon, and my nerves tightened.

The table, covered with a snowy linen cloth that touched the grass, was set for five. There were individual bouquets of pansies in goblets at each place. Nina Love's eyes were violet and her sundress was the shade of her eyes. Her complexion even in summer was pale; her skin seemed translucent and her hair was black, lustrous, and wavy.

"They're not coming," I said. My tone was tentative. I was always afraid of disappointing Nina, but I soldiered on. "Des said he and Sally would get something to eat later."

Nina picked up two of the flower goblets and dumped their contents onto the grass. "No loss, Joanne," she said in her deep, thrilling voice. "You and I will have more chance to talk to Ben."

She removed the dishes and silverware from the extra two places and lay them on the tea-table that held our lunch. Then she raised a graceful arm. "Sit anywhere, Ben. We're having lobster salad, your favourite, Joanne. But first come over here and let me straighten your pretty hair."

The face of the girl who went to Nina glowed with love and gratitude. The sight of it sickened me.

"Zack, I can't take any more of this," I said.

Zack turned off the DVD. "Why don't we move to the couch and neck?"

Zack's arms were warm and strong, and after a few minutes, I was able to talk. "I loved Nina, you know. She was my refuge. Nina always said that Sally didn't want her, and my mother didn't want me, so fate had brought the two of us together."

"A persuasive argument," Zack said.

"I didn't need much persuading," I said. "I wanted to be valued, and here was this beautiful, intelligent, charming woman offering me her heart."

"And she turned out to be a murderer," Zack said quietly.

"Yes," I said. "She turned out to be a murderer, but it took me thirty years to discover that." I stood. "The sun's up. Let's head over to the construction site. I could use some fresh air."

It was a good day for photographs: blue-skied, sunny, and still. Progress on the Racette-Hunter Centre had been rapid. The grading and the site preparation had been completed by early summer. The foundation was in and the framing was almost finished. The contractors were optimistic that the windows and doors could be in place by the end of the year. Zack had promised Margot Hunter that the centre would be open by Labour Day, and it seemed possible.

Making our way across the rutted dug-up site was daunting,

but thanks to Zack's new rough terrain wheelchair, it was not impossible. Being involved in a construction project was bringing Zack the joy of a kid who'd received the entire line of Tonka trucks for Christmas. Most days there was little reason for him to be onsite, but he always found an excuse, and more often than not he invited me to join him to watch the big machines. I had been through the big machine phase with my sons, but Zack's delight was hard to resist, and that fall the two of us spent hours in weather that ranged from brilliant to unbearable watching the building take shape.

It had been Lauren Treadgold's idea to give everyone with a significant involvement in the Racette-Hunter project a holiday gift: a red cashmere scarf and a personalized yellow hard hat. Everyone would also receive a framed copy of an onsite photograph of the group of which he or she was a member.

That morning, Lauren was dispensing the hard hats and scarves from the back of her yellow Land Rover. She was hatless, revealing her signature side-parted gamine cut. Despite her form-fitting leather jacket, careful makeup, and smartly knotted red scarf, Lauren appeared tired. Her cheeks were pink with cold, but her eyes were shadowed and her smile was forced.

I didn't recognize the two men ahead of us in line, but both had the hearty, assured faces of the successful. Both were boyishly thrilled as they tried on their hard hats.

I was uneasy, wondering if Lauren would say anything about her very public disappearance with Julian the night of the party. But as we stepped in front of her, Lauren's expression was tight and unrevealing. "Wonderful day for the pictures, isn't it?" she said. "There's a cameraman from NationTV here, too. He's planning to get some shots of Margot and Riel to use in the documentary about the building of the R-H Centre." She turned towards the open hatch of the SUV to get our gifts. A pair of salukis peered at her over the top of the back seat. "Chill," she said in the no-nonsense tone advised by obedience trainers.

"I didn't know you had salukis," I said, grateful for a safe topic for light chat. "They're gorgeous – and they're admirably well behaved."

"We spend a lot of time together," Lauren said. "Salukis are hunters, so they still run after anything that moves, but Dalila and Darius know how to listen." She turned towards her dogs. "You do know how to listen, don't you?"

The dogs wagged their silky tails in unison. "Great names," I said.

"Vince chose them – Egyptian names for the royal dogs of Egypt."

Lauren reached into the SUV and handed Zack and me our scarves and hard hats. Each of the scarves was tied with a dark-green grosgrain ribbon. It was a handsome, festive touch, and I was impressed with Lauren's attention to detail. I took a quick peek inside my hard hat and saw the inscription with my name and the name and dates of the project.

"This is an inspired gift," I said. "The scarf is lovely, and people will hang on to *these* hats."

"I'm hoping so," Lauren said. "We want our donors to feel an ongoing connection with Racette-Hunter."

She turned to Zack. "The Peyben board is first in line for photos. We're taking the pictures in the area where the front doors to the building will be."

"Very clever," Zack said. He began to turn his chair. "You're doing a good job, Lauren."

"I take my responsibilities seriously, Zack – all of them."

Zack raised his head slowly to meet her eyes. "I'm glad to hear that. Vince has been a close friend of mine for more than twenty years."

"And I'm just his problematic wife," Lauren said.

Zack leaned forward. When he spoke, his voice was low. "I'm grateful for the work you're doing for Racette-Hunter. But if you're going to start playing with a boy who's young enough to be your son, someone's going to get hurt."

I'd expected Lauren to minimize her behaviour with Julian the night of the party. She didn't. All she said was "I know what I'm doing," and her tone was defiant.

Zack continued to watch her face. His gaze seemed to unnerve her, and she moved back, momentarily losing her balance.

"Watch your step, Lauren," Zack said. Then he finished turning his chair around and we headed for the site where the photographs would be taken.

Blake Falconer and Margot were already there, decked out in hard hats and red scarves. When Blake saw Zack and me, he held out his arms in welcome and looked up at the cloudless blue sky. "Couldn't have asked for a more perfect day," he said. "The gods are obviously smiling on the Racette-Hunter project."

Zack grinned. "You know, Blake, in your new incarnation as Little Mary Sunshine, you're a real pain in the ass."

Blake was sanguine. "I like my new job."

"That's a relief," Margot said. She was eight months' pregnant and feeling eight months' pregnant. "As soon as this baby arrives, I'm planning to sweep everything off my plate and load it onto yours."

"Bring it on," Blake said. "I couldn't be happier."

It was tonic to see the transformation in Blake, who, during his time as a senior partner at Falconer Shreve, seemed always to be shadowed by a private sorrow. It had been clear to everyone who cared about Blake that he needed a life change; sadly, Blake's chance for fulfillment came with Leland Hunter's death.

When Leland died, management of Peyben passed to Margot. Believing that Margot's grief and lack of business experience would make her easy prey, the board pushed to change the direction Leland had charted for Peyben. Margot recognized what they were up to and delivered an ultimatum: any board member who was dissatisfied with the initiatives Leland had planned should resign immediately. The board assumed Margot could be brought to heel if they resigned en masse. She called their bluff, hired Blake as CEO, and asked him to select a new board.

To a person, the members of that board were progressive, smart, and wholly dedicated to Margot and to Peyben's interests. One of those interests was the building of the Racette-Hunter Centre, and several board members were also members of the Racette-Hunter working team.

The only paid employees of that team were Riel Delorme and a small support staff. The rest were volunteers. Transforming a city block of slum housing and abandoned buildings into a multipurpose centre that would meet the needs of a diverse and often troubled community was a daunting task, but Zack had used the Swiss cheese approach and broken an unmanageable whole into manageable parts, each headed by someone with special knowledge of the field. Norine MacDonald, Zack's executive assistant, and by his assessment "the second smartest woman he'd ever known," coordinated the various departments. The board members were not people accustomed to taking orders, but they were good-natured as the photographer's assistant, a pixie of a woman wearing a candy-cane-striped toque, barked out instructions about where they should place themselves for the photographs.

Taylor didn't have a class till second period, so she'd come to the construction site with Declan, who, since his father's death, had been at Margot's side learning the business. That morning Declan was nattily dressed in a charcoal grey wool suit, a pale grey shirt, and a red paisley tie. Except for his spectacular dreadlocks, Declan was the very model of a young businessman. As he took his place among the captains of finance, Taylor gave him a conspiratorial wink.

When the photographer was satisfied, his pixie assistant shepherded off the members of the board who were not needed for the next shot and began bringing in the additional members of the working team. Ernest Beauvais motioned me over. "Do you know why Riel's not here?" he asked.

When I shook my head, Ernest frowned. "I was afraid of that."

"Is something the matter with Riel?" I asked.

"I hope not," Ernest said. "But he's hit a bad patch."

Zack wheeled over in time to hear Ernest's words. He was clearly exasperated. "Riel better get out of that patch, pronto," he said. "People are waiting for him. Margot's been trying his number, but the calls are going straight to voicemail."

"I'll call Mieka," I said. "She and the girls were planning to come with him."

My daughter answered on the first ring. "Hi," I said. "The photographer's assistant is assembling people for the picture of the working team. She needs Riel to be front and centre, and he's not around."

Mieka sounded harried. "Could you ask them to rearrange the order of the shots? Riel isn't . . . look, Mum. I'm sorry. We'll be there in ten minutes. Please give everyone Riel's apologies."

The photographer's assistant had just finished getting everyone in place when I relayed Mieka's message to Margot. Margot and Riel had worked closely on the NationTV special chronicling the mediation process. I knew Margot liked Riel, but she was visibly annoyed at his tardiness.

Ernest stepped in. "I'll handle this," he said. He walked over and had a few words with the pixie, and within seconds she was moving the working team aside and replacing them with a crew of onsite construction workers.

"I guess now we just wait," Zack said.

Fortunately, we didn't have to wait long. It was only a few minutes before Mieka, Riel, and our granddaughters arrived. As soon as Madeleine and Lena spotted Zack and me, they charged towards us, clearly delighted to be having an adventure on a school day. Mieka and Riel lagged behind. Riel was wearing blue jeans and a leather jacket that was unzipped to reveal his pressed white shirt and the multicoloured woven Métis scarf tied around his waist. He went straight to Margot.

"I'm sorry," he said. "I had a bad night."

In truth, Riel did appear tired and ill. When she saw him up close, Margot's face softened. "You're here now, that's what matters," she said. She reached out and gave Riel's arm an encouraging pat. "Time to put on our game face. The sooner we start, the sooner we'll finish."

Vince Treadgold had arrived and joined us, too. He and Lauren were positioned together for the photographer and they seemed easy with each other. Despite the tensions that preceded the shoot, the photographs turned out well. So did the clip of Margot and Riel arranging evergreen boughs around the doorway of the centre. That shot would be the final scene of our documentary.

There were several other permutations and combinations of personnel to be photographed that morning, but one was of special interest to Zack and me. We'd arranged to have a photograph taken of the two of us with Taylor and our granddaughters.

The girls were already wearing their scarves, but there was a problem. Unlike everyone who'd been photographed,

Taylor, Madeleine, and Lena didn't have hard hats and Riel noticed.

"Hang on," Riel said. "You girls need hard hats. Racette-Hunter is a Safety First construction site."

Margot, Blake, and Riel handed their hats to the girls, and Mieka stepped in to adjust them so the girls' faces weren't shadowed. "Okay, young grasshoppers," she said finally. "You're ready for your close-up." The photographer, Ivan Schmidt, had a grizzled beard and the meat hook hands, cauliflower ears, and battered nose of an ex-boxer. He had been gruffly efficient with the adults, but he was warm with Taylor and the girls.

We all had fun posing, and when the shoot was over Mieka and Riel stood close as Ivan showed them the pictures. "These are really good," Mieka said.

"The young women are very appealing," Ivan said.

"We think so," Riel said. A strand of Mieka's hair had blown over her forehead. Riel reached out and smoothed it into place. "Mieka, why don't we ask Ivan to take a picture of the four of us?"

The tenderness in Riel's gesture lifted my heart, but my optimism was quickly dashed.

Mieka's face was strained. "Not today," she said. "I didn't get much sleep last night."

Ernest Beauvais had joined Zack and me to look at the pictures. Riel knew that we had heard Mieka's gentle rebuff, and he was clearly stung. "You're the boss," he said.

"That's not true," Mieka said. "We're partners."

For a beat, Riel and Mieka faced each other. Their misery was painful to witness, and Ernest took Riel's arm. But Riel shook him off and walked away. Mieka was crestfallen. Mercifully, during the exchange between their mother and Riel, Madeleine and Lena had been playing tag, well out of earshot. "Mieka, I'll get the ladies moving," I said.

"I'm not in a hurry. Taylor and Declan have already left for school."

"And I have a meeting downtown," Zack said. "Jo, do you want me to hang around and drive you home?"

"Thanks, but I could use some extra time with Mieka and the girls, and I don't want to make you late for that meeting."

"Is it okay if I bring Margot back for lunch?"

"Of course." I bent to kiss him. "I'll say goodbye to Madeleine and Lena for you."

The girls were still sporting their borrowed hard hats when I joined them. "You're going to have to give those back," I said. "They've got Blake, Margot, and Riel's names in them. But Ms. Treadgold's SUV is over there, and she might have a couple that you can have for keeps."

Lauren did indeed have extras, but dazzling as the hard hats were, the girls had eyes only for the salukis. When Lauren saw how taken the girls were, she leashed the dogs and asked Madeleine and Lena if they'd do her a favour and walk them.

She didn't have to ask twice. As Lauren and I watched the girls, solemn with responsibility, lead the salukis in a careful circle, Lauren's face relaxed. "Your granddaughters are good with Darius and Dalila," she said. "If you ever consider a puppy, they're more than welcome to come to our house and give the salukis a tryout."

"Thanks," I said. "I have a feeling there could be a dog in Madeleine and Lena's future. Zack's been talking about it, and once he makes up his mind, he's not easily dissuaded."

Lauren looked away. "Has Zack made up his mind about me?"

"Zack has seen Vince through some tough times in the past. It's natural he'd be concerned."

"And how about you?"

"I like both you and Vince," I said. "But you're starting

down a dangerous path, Lauren. There are other people involved. Please think this through."

Lauren tilted her chin obstinately. "Joanne, I've been taking care of myself since I was fifteen, I've learned to think things through. I didn't fall into the traps so many of the other girls fell into. I never had an eating disorder. I never did drugs. I never slept with people just to get ahead. I learned to take directions. I was always punctual, prepared, and professional – a model model." Lauren laughed softly at her joke. "And I was so busy being the model model that I never had a life."

"But after your career was over, you had Vince," I said.

"Being married to Vince turned out to be just another job. He never really got over Solange's suicide. Neither did Celeste. I truly believed that sending Celeste to boarding school was the best decision for us all. I thought we all needed a fresh start. As you know, that didn't work out. And now, here I am stuck in a loveless marriage with a stepdaughter who hates me."

"You don't love Vince?"

"I thought I did, once. And I like him well enough, I know he's a good man," she said. "But Vince and I both know that all he cares about is his work. I'm like the salukis – something beautiful and exotic that Vince can afford to own. Julian is my last chance for real love." Lauren gave me the winsome smile that had sold hundreds of thousands of fashion magazines. "Wish me luck," she said.

I felt a chill. Lauren had obviously reached the point of no return. "I wish you both luck," I said. I was relieved when Mieka joined us. The busyness of getting the dogs back in the SUV allowed Lauren and me to take refuge in the quotidian. We parted with the usual pleasantries.

As I walked with Mieka and the girls to their car, I noticed that my daughter was chewing her lower lip – a sure sign that she was anxious.

I slipped my arm around her waist. "Is there anything I can do to help?"

"No. Riel's just not thinking clearly. We'd talked about him sitting down with Ernest, but you just saw what happened when Ernest tried to get close to him. I don't know what to do next."

"Well, short-term, why don't I come along when you drop the girls off at school, and we can carry on to Magpies Kitchen? I'll even spring for a couple of their cinnamon buns."

"You're on," Mieka said. "Thanks."

Business at Magpies Kitchen was brisk, but we hit it lucky. A couple was just vacating a table by the window. Mieka gave me a thumbs-up. "My luck is turning," she said.

We ate our cinnamon buns and drank our chai lattes in comfortable silence. When she'd finished her bun, Mieka trailed her forefinger through the leftover buttery crumbs and icing on her plate. She was thirty-three years old. When she licked her finger, I didn't say a word.

Mieka took another lick and shot me a mischievous grin. "You know I don't let the girls do this."

"I know. I also know there are times when cinnamon and sugar are the only solace."

"I appear to be in the middle of one of those times," Mieka said wearily. "Mum, I love Riel. He loves me and he loves the girls, but I don't know what's up with him any more. He has these moments of meanness that come out of nowhere. That shot he took at you and Zack about the Volvo last week was just the beginning."

"There was more later?"

Mieka nodded. "We had a great Halloween. Everybody loved our costumes and the girls made out like bandits. We got home, went through the girls' bags with them, then I took Maddy and Lena upstairs to get ready for bed. While we were upstairs, the second string of trick or treaters came."

"The kids from North Central," I said. "They always wait till the neighbourhood kids are off the street."

"They don't want trouble," Mieka said. "They come here because it's safer and they know that even if they don't have a costume, they'll get candy. Those kids have been coming here so long I never even think about it. I just do what you always did – make sure there's extra candy in reserve and keep the pumpkin lit."

"But this was Riel's first Halloween in Old Lakeview, and he didn't know the drill," I said.

"He figured it out soon enough," Mieka said bleakly. "And then he exploded. I didn't need a lecture. I know it's not fair that our kids get so much and the kids in North Central get so little. I told Riel he was yelling at the wrong person, but he wouldn't stop. He just kept on and on and on. I told him to lower his voice because Madeleine and Lena could hear him. He said they *should* hear him because it was about time they knew the truth about their lives."

"Madeleine and Lena *do* know the truth about their lives," I said. "You've always made certain that the girls know they're fortunate."

"I try," Mieka said. "But I was angry, too, and I was scared. I didn't want Maddy and Lena to see Riel like that – he was crazy, Mum. He said we should sell this house and move downtown to Winnipeg Street so the girls could see what 'real life' is like. I told him to take a walk to cool down. He left and he didn't come home until the next morning."

"But things have been all right since then?"

"It's been tense, but we were both trying, and then last night, Riel blew up again over something he saw on the news. He stormed off. He'd just come back when you called this morning. He said he walked around all night, but I don't know . . ."

Mieka swallowed hard. "Mum, Riel knew how important this photo shoot was. He knew he had to show the Peyben board and all the people connected with Racette-Hunter that he was totally committed and that the project was in good hands. By the time he came home, he could barely stand up. You saw what he looked like when we got to the construction site." Mieka stared out the window. "The situation has become intolerable."

My veins tightened. "He's not hurting you?"

Mieka shook her head emphatically. "You know I wouldn't put up with that. Riel's not violent. He's just . . .. a different person. He keeps apologizing for his behaviour, but it never gets better."

During the time that she and Riel had been happy together, Mieka had radiated the contentment of a woman who knows that she is well and truly loved. That morning as the unforgiving November light poured through the window at Magpies Kitchen, I saw how drawn my daughter's face had become. She was naturally slender, but now she was thin and tense.

"The contractors want me to come over and look at our old house sometime today," I said. "Why don't I go over to the house this afternoon, scope out the situation, then pick the girls up from school and bring them back to Halifax Street for a sleepover."

"That would be a lifesaver, Mum. Riel and I need a chance to talk, and if the girls aren't around, maybe we can sort this out once and for all."

Before we separated, I hugged Mieka hard. "We'll get through this," I said.

Mieka's face was wan. "I know. It's just that this time I really believed I'd found Mr. Right."

When I got back to the condo, a courier was dropping a notification slip into our mailbox. "Great timing," I said to him. "That's for us."

The package from NationTV was expected. Jill Oziowy, the producer of *For the Common Good*, had told me the rough-cut was ready. I made myself a cup of tea and dropped the DVD in the player. I'd been working on segments of the program since early summer, so there were no surprises, but this was the first time the segments had been arranged in sequence and in many ways I felt like a time traveller.

The first shots were of an altercation that took place shortly after the convocation where Leland Hunter had been given an honorary Ph.D. On that June day, so bright with promise, Riel Delorme was just the name of a graduate student of mine who'd dropped out five years earlier. I'd just retired from the political science department. Zack, Taylor, and I were still living in our house on the creek, and I was still anticipating that we would live there happily ever after. Leland and Margot were planning their wedding, and Leland's company was razing crumbling houses and abandoned buildings to make way for The Village.

The convocation was marred by a nasty incident. Two weeks earlier, Danny Racette, a young Aboriginal man who was shadowing the project manager, had been killed when explosives were set off prematurely at a demolition site. Those opposed to The Village blamed Racette's death on workplace negligence. When Leland emerged from the ceremony, the protestors sprang into action, chanting slogans and taunting Leland and his family. Somehow in the melee, Riel Delorme's sign hit Leland's head, causing a nasty gash. Seeing blood, the demonstrators' chants grew uglier and the situation deteriorated until Leland was taken by ambulance to the hospital and the police stepped in.

The confrontation between Leland and Riel was a riveting opening scene for the show, but the passages that showed them joining forces were even more compelling.

After Riel and Leland agreed to participate in the documentary, our local producer arranged for an up-close and personal interview with each man. The segments had been shot simply, using an off-camera interviewer. Leland had long been a friend as well as a client of Zack's, and I had come to know him in the months before his death. We were running partners for a time, and as I watched the rough-cut and listened to him talk about his dream of transforming our derelict neighbourhood into a vibrant community, it was impossible to believe he was dead. "There can be no phoenix without the ashes," he said. The passion in Leland's voice caused tears to sting my eyes.

But it was Riel's appearance that riveted my attention. The man on my TV screen was powerful and healthy, and in the interview he was forceful and confident. As he spoke of the life-changing effect the new centre would have on North Central's children and adolescents, his voice was fervent.

My mind drifted to moments that Riel and our family had shared. The images were sharp-edged: Riel building a child-sized ice cream stand for the girls; Riel's arms around Mieka as they watched the girls swim; Mieka's face soft with pride as Riel presented Margot with a Métis scarf at Leland's funeral.

But there were darker memories. Riel was often scathing about the comfort of Zack's and my life, and he and I had clashed over April's Place. Mieka and Lisa had worked with members of the community to make certain it met the neighbourhood's needs. Riel was usually supportive, but in moments of anger, he dismissed April's Place as a sop to divert the community from pressing for everything that was rightfully theirs.

Whatever his mood, Riel had always been bracingly vital. The man I'd seen at the construction site this morning seemed defeated, a tired grey shadow of the man on my screen.

CHAPTER 3

I'd just finished making a plate of tuna salad sandwiches when Zack and Margot arrived. Margot kicked off her boots, slipped off her coat, and looked dubiously towards the stools ranged around the butcher-block table in the kitchen.

"Why don't we sit in the dining room," I suggested. "Everything's ready. What's your beverage of choice?"

"Milk, please." Margot said.

"Milk sounds good," Zack said.

I brought in a tray with sandwiches, plates, napkins, three glasses of milk, and a bowl of potato chips. Margot bit into her sandwich and made an approving sound. "I was starving. These days I'm always hungry."

"Eating for two," Zack said sagely.

Margot was withering. "Racette-Hunter is paying you a dollar a year for those insights, and Big Guy, you're worth every penny."

Zack raised his glass to her. "I'll take that as a compliment."

Margot and Zack had been sparring partners long before I came on the scene, and I'd learned that there were times when it was wise to change the subject. "How did the meeting with the Webers go?" I asked.

"Very well," Zack said. "Especially because Brock Poitras has become the newest member of the Racette-Hunter working team, and today was his first meeting."

"Brock's name is familiar," I said.

"He played for the Riders," Zack said. "He also has an M.B.A.; he grew up in North Central; and he speaks Cree. Construction of the centre is moving along well. What Racette-Hunter needs now is someone to convince the decision makers that they have to start opening doors for people who need a chance."

"Brock is the perfect candidate," Margot said. "He's done it all. He's high profile, so he'll help with fundraising, and he can brainstorm with business leaders about how to set up internships and mentoring and job shadowing programs for the unemployed or the underemployed."

"Wow," I said. "You were lucky to get him."

Margot sighed. "We haven't got him yet. Brock's on loan from Blackwell Investments."

Zack leaned forward in his chair. "But he doesn't belong there. At Blackwell everybody spends the day hunched over their smartphones waiting for the latest news from Bloomberg. Brock has way too much potential to spend his life staring at a spreadsheet."

Margot had just taken a bite of her sandwich. She waved her hand to indicate that as soon as she'd finished, she wanted to talk. When she was ready, she was even more enthusiastic than Zack. "Jo, if you could have seen Brock with the Webers, you'd know why we need him permanently at Racette-Hunter. It turns out that Warren Weber is a big fan of the Riders, so when Brock made the pitch, Warren was receptive. Brock didn't waste his chance. His argument was cogent and passionate. Warren was writing out the cheque before Brock finished."

"Good news all around," I said. I took a breath. "Riel was at that meeting, wasn't he?" I said.

"Yep," Zack said, "and that was the one fly in the ointment."

"What happened?"

"Well, for starters," Zack said, "despite the fact that Brock's argument was dynamite, Riel nodded off."

"He had a bad night," I said. "Something upset him and he walked out. Mieka said he didn't get back till this morning."

Margot finished her milk. "I'm sorry Riel's having problems," she said, "but it would have been better for everybody if he had stayed at home to catch up on his rest. Having the R-H community liaison officer snore loudly during a colleague's presentation to a potential donor didn't speak highly for our level of commitment."

"He's obviously having an off day," I said. "But he's done good work for Racette-Hunter. I just watched the rough-cut of *For the Common Good,* and it's a powerful piece."

Margot picked up her sandwich. "Did the network include the footage the NationTV camera guy shot today?"

"They haven't had time to edit it," I said. "But I know what you're getting at. Riel looked terrible this morning, but that can be fixed in the edit suite."

"I think the problem might be something the edit suite can't fix," Margot said. "Jo, I hate to even say the words, but is it possible that Riel's using again?"

My stomach clenched. "He's been clean for three years," I said. "Before he moved in with Mieka, Riel promised her the drugs were in his past. He has problems, but he loves Mieka and he loves the girls. When I watched the rough-cut, it was clear that Riel's health has deteriorated, but I can't believe he's using again. Maybe he has a medical problem or an emotional one. Depression and anxiety can wreak havoc."

"I agree he doesn't seem well," Zack agreed. "But that doesn't mean he gets a free pass as far as his work is concerned. When Riel finally woke up during Brock's presentation to the Webers, he asked a couple of questions to which he would have known the answers if he'd stayed awake, then he got up and left. No apologies. No goodbyes. No nothing."

"That's not like him," I said. I took a bite of sandwich. Suddenly it tasted like cardboard, but I chewed dutifully.

"It isn't," Margot said. "So what do we do?"

"Let's work on Joanne's assumption that the problem is medical," Zack said. "We'll urge Riel to see a doctor, and if Joanne's right, Riel can take medical leave until he's ready to work again. I'll talk to him."

"No," I said. "Mieka should talk to him. He loves her. I've never doubted that for a moment. I told Mieka we'd take the girls tonight. She and Riel need some time alone to work this through."

"Fine," Zack said. "But the sooner this is taken care of, the better. Racette-Hunter is on target to open Labour Day weekend. We can't afford any stumbles."

When I called Mieka to tell her that we were all concerned that Riel's health or personal issues were getting in the way of his job, her reaction surprised me. She seemed relieved. "Riel's been insisting that there's nothing wrong – that he's absolutely fine," she said. "If I can tell him that people he respects are concerned, too, he'll *have* to listen, and if he knows his job is on the line, he'll have to do something."

"Make sure he knows we're on his side, Mieka."

"I will. I'm not looking forward to tonight, but whatever's going on with Riel has to be dealt with. I'm relieved it's finally come to a head."

Seemingly, it was a day for decisions. In mid-afternoon, Zack and I drove to our house on the creek to decide whether we were ready to sell. We had asked O'Neill and Son, the contractors, to restore the house to a state as close as possible to the way it had been before the explosion, and they had followed our instructions to the letter. When Zack pulled into the driveway, he was wistful. "Home again," he said.

"Is that how it feels to you?"

"Everything looks just the same," he said. "It's tempting to believe that our old life is just waiting for us behind the front door."

"It is tempting," I said. "But we both know it's not that simple. I think the O'Neills may have an inkling that we haven't completely made up our minds yet. You'll notice the accessibility ramp to the front door is temporary."

"Let's check the house out," Zack said. "Reassure ourselves that one way or the other, we're making the right decision."

As we moved through the silent, empty rooms, I experienced the Alice-through-the-looking-glass feeling that had enveloped me so often during the weeks following the bombing. Everything – even the colours of the paint on the walls – was the same, but nothing was the same. I gazed at the yard. Taylor's old studio was there, but the girl who had made art so joyfully in that light-filled space had found another space in which to make art. We had all moved along.

Our inspection was unhurried. We both wanted to be sure.

When we re-entered the front hall, Zack took my hand. "Well, Ms. Shreve, as an old law professor of mine used to say, we've squared the circle. What'll it be – the comfortable past or the uncertain future?"

"I vote for Halifax Street," I said.

"This was our home," Zack said.

"And now Halifax Street is our home," I said. "Everything's temporary, Zack."

Zack drew me close. "We're not temporary."

I stroked his cheek. "No. We're forever. I'll email the O'Neills and tell them they can forget about the accessibility ramps. I guess the next step is to put the house on the market."

"Nobody buys a house this close to Christmas," Zack said. "Let's wait till spring." He checked his watch. "Perfect timing. We can pick up the girls' stuff from Mieka's and be at their school in time to canoodle awhile in the parking lot."

"It's a Catholic school, Zack."

Zack raised his eyebrows. "Catholics canoodle."

Zack had a dinner to attend that night, so as soon as we got home we lit the fire and while I made the girls hot chocolate, Zack measured our martinis. We sat down and listened to Lena's tales of the latest perfidy of her arch-enemy, Jade, and Madeleine's account of her volleyball team shellacking the team from Holy Rosary. Then the girls put on old shirts and went upstairs to paint in their corner of Taylor's studio.

Except for the fact that Zack wouldn't be with us, it was my favourite kind of evening. Taylor and the little girls and I had pot roast, and after we'd cleaned up, Madeleine and Lena had a bubble bath. Because the condo's master bedroom was on the second floor, it was Taylor's by default. The room was very large and had a northern exposure – a perfect studio for an artist. Taylor recognized its potential, and it became her studio. The second floor guestroom was smaller, but it was still spacious enough to accommodate the king-sized bed Taylor deemed essential for a truly great sleepover. That night when I tucked the girls in for stories, Taylor hopped in with them to listen to two of her old favourites: *A Promise Is a Promise* and *Hide and Sneak*, Michael Kusugak's tales of Allashua, a rash but resourceful Inuit girl. When I started downstairs after lights out, I could hear the girls murmuring about the snow fort they were planning to build at the cottage during the week between Christmas and New Year's, and I sent up a silent prayer that they would remain close throughout their lives.

It had been a long day and I was eyeing Zack's and my own bed when the buzzer from the lobby sounded. Ours is not a welcoming neighbourhood, and even friends who know our security number don't feel comfortable dropping in after dark. Nonetheless, it seemed we had a visitor.

The voice was a man's. "I need to see Zack," he said. Even with the distortion of intercom, Vince Treadgold's baritone was distinctive. I buzzed him in, ran a comb through my hair, and waited.

When I opened the door, I stood aside to let Vince come in. I had never seen him looking anything other than immaculate, but that night he was dishevelled. "Zack's not here," I said. "He's at a dinner. He won't be home for a couple of hours. Can it wait?"

"No," he said. "I just punched my wife, and I need to talk to a friend."

His voice was flat, without emotion. I felt half sick, but I managed to keep my own voice even. "Is Lauren all right?"

He nodded. "She'll have a black eye, but otherwise, she's fine." He sounded as clinical as the surgeon he was, but his tapping foot showed he was anything but calm.

"Let me take your coat," I said. "I'll call Zack."

Vince followed me into the living room and sat on one of the two reading chairs by the window. I dialled Zack's cell, but the call went straight to voicemail. Vince's eyes were on my face. I shook my head and left a message. There was nothing in the etiquette book to cover the situation in which

Vince and I found ourselves. "Can I get you anything?" I said.

Vince's smile was wintry. "A lawyer," he said.

"I'm working on it."

I sat down on the edge of the other reading chair. The rain hitting the windows was soothing, and for a moment Vince and I simply listened. Then Vince began to talk. "I was supposed to catch the 7:30 plane to Calgary – a conference on cartilage restoration. I'd been at the hospital since 4:30 this morning. I had my overnight bag with me, and I called a cab to take me to the airport. Then I got a text from Lauren urging me to come home immediately. When I got there the house was quiet. So I went upstairs to our room to see if Lauren was ill."

"Vince, I shouldn't be hearing this."

Vince's laugh was short and sardonic. "And I shouldn't have witnessed my wife being fucked by another man, but I did."

"I'm sorry," I said.

Vince made a quick gesture of dismissal. He didn't want pity. "Do you know what the real shock was?" he said. "Seeing Lauren, who simply endures sex with me, writhing and moaning as her young lover shoved his cock into her." Vince shut his eyes and rubbed his temples as if to erase the images flooding his brain. "I couldn't move, I couldn't speak. I could only watch. When she reached orgasm, she wouldn't let him stop. By the time she came for the third time, she was sobbing, and he finally pushed himself off. Even then, Lauren wasn't finished. She took his head in her hands and whispered something. He started to move down towards her genitals, and that's when she saw me and screamed.

"The boy – and he was just a boy – got out of bed, picked up his clothes, and sauntered past me. Lauren was angry at *me*. She said, 'What are you doing here? You were supposed to be at a conference.'

"When I told her I'd come because of her text, she just stared at me." Vince stopped and swallowed hard. "My mind was racing. Lauren's text had been sent less than half an hour before I got home. Nothing made sense. Then I had this blinding insight. Lauren had sent the text because she *wanted* me to see her with her lover. When I told her that I knew what she'd done, she slid out of bed, told me she had no idea what I was talking about, and started to walk away. I grabbed her arm and pulled her so that she had to face me. When I saw the contempt in her eyes, something inside me snapped."

The room was incredibly still. Our bouvier, Willie, moaned in his sleep.

Vince stood. "May I use your bathroom?"

His question placed us both firmly back into the world of the commonplace.

"Of course."

As I stroked Willie, waiting for Vince to return, my mind drifted.

Years before I met Zack, Mieka broke her leg skiing. It was an ugly break, and Vince Treadgold had been the surgeon who operated on her. One of the nurses who cared for Mieka told me that I was fortunate that Dr. Treadgold was Mieka's surgeon because he had gentle hands.

I tried not to think about how Vince's gentle hands had struck his wife. My cell rang. It was Zack.

"I got your message," he said. "So what's going on?"

"Vince showed up here about fifteen minutes ago. He found Lauren in bed with her lover. My guess is that the lover was Julian, but whatever the case, Vince hit Lauren and he wants to talk to you."

"What the hell?" Zack said. "Vince isn't that kind of guy."

Suddenly I was very tired. "Zack, just come home."

"I will, but let me talk to Vince first."

"He's in the bathroom – just come now, please."

"Okay, of course," Zack said. "I have to say a couple of goodbyes and wait for my car, but I'll be there ASAP. How are you doing?"

"I'm okay, but I don't know how to handle this. Vince has already told me far too much."

"Tell him to put a sock in it."

"I did."

"Tell him again."

When Vince came out of the bathroom, he looked better. He'd clearly splashed water on his face, his hair was damp and gently tousled, and he smelled pleasantly of Dove soap. I knew Vince was a long-time member of AA, so I made us tea and we returned to our reading chairs in the living room. I tried to steer the conversation to safe territory, but Lauren's presence hovered between us, and we finally gave up and retreated into silence.

When I heard Zack's key in the lock, I met him at the door. "Are you okay?" he said.

I kept my voice low. "I'm fine, but I'm going to take the dogs up to the roof garden for a run and give you two a chance to talk."

Zack removed his scarf and handed it to me. "Keep your neck covered, and wear your jacket. It's raw out there."

The scarf still held Zack's body warmth. "You take good care of me," I said, and then I kissed him and called Willie and Pantera.

The dogs and I stayed on the roof until I saw Vince get into the Mercedes he'd parked in front of our building and drive off.

Zack had more tea steeping when the dogs and I got back. "I thought you might be up for a hot toddy," he said.

"It's been a hot toddy evening," I said. "Can you talk about how things went with Vince?"

"No reason not to. Vince says he told you everything."

"Did he recognize Lauren's lover?"

"No. Seeing his wife actually enjoying sex was enough to devastate Vince." Zack rubbed his eyes. "Jo, why the hell would Lauren have sent that text?"

"I don't know," I said. "She told me she feels trapped in their marriage, but Lauren has never struck me as cruel. Is it possible Vince misunderstood the text?"

"No. He showed it to me. The message came from Lauren's iPhone and it was clear and concise. 'Come home as soon as you get this.'"

"What's Vince going to do?"

"I told him to go to a hotel. I don't believe Lauren's the type to take an axe to Vince in the middle of the night, but violence begets violence, and I figure better safe than sorry."

"I wonder how Lauren's doing?"

"I wonder that, too," Zack said.

"I'm going to call her," I said.

"If Lauren brings charges, as she has every right to do, I'll be representing Vince. I'm not sure calling her is a good idea."

"I'm sure," I said, and I went to the telephone and dialled the Treadgolds' number. I listened as the phone rang a half-dozen times, then turned back to Zack. "No answer," I said. "Do you think Lauren went to the police?"

"I don't know," Zack said. "For what it's worth, after the incident, Vince apparently remembered his Hippocratic oath. He checked out Lauren's eye, made her an ice pack, and told her to get medical help if her vision seemed impaired."

"Take two aspirin and call me in the morning," I said.

Zack poured the tea into mugs and added lemon, honey, and brandy. He handed me my toddy. "You do realize that a good lawyer will be able to get Vince off."

I sipped my drink. "Are you the good lawyer?"

Zack shrugged. "How's your toddy?"

"Nice change of subject, Mr. Shreve. You look beat," I said.

"That's because I am beat," Zack said. "Let's finish our drinks and hit the sack."

Most often when we were both tired, Zack and I just kissed, said good night, and moved in close, but that night we talked. Our topics were inconsequential, nods to the precious normal things in our lives. Zack passed along some intriguing anecdotes from the dinner he'd attended. I told him about Taylor curling up with Madeleine and Lena for stories. When I mentioned overhearing the three girls planning the snow forts they would build at the lake, Zack chuckled. "I'm not an expert on adolescent girls," he said, "but it seems to me that Taylor's more eager than most girls her age to hang on to her childhood."

"It's a good place for her," I said. "I'm sure Kaye has told Taylor what she told us – that the auction is going to change everything for her."

Zack pulled up the blanket. "I'm not exactly thrilled about Kaye's prophecy."

I moved close to him. "Neither am I," I said. "But there's nothing we can do about it, so we might as well just tighten our skates and hope for the best."

CHAPTER

4

The art auction started at seven, so we were planning an early dinner. As I set the table, I was grateful that my enthusiasm for the evening ahead was no longer dampened by concern about Mieka and Riel. Mieka had called in mid-morning with a report about her night with him. They had decided to live separately until they had worked out their problems. The good news was they were both determined to do whatever was necessary to save their relationship. Riel was going to see his doctor and seek counselling, and he would be a frequent and welcome visitor to Mieka's home. It wasn't a perfect solution, but it was a first step, and I was optimistic.

When we sat down to dinner, Taylor was in a strange mood. She was usually a hearty eater and a lively mealtime companion, but that night she picked at her food silently and excused herself before dessert. When she went upstairs to get ready, Zack wheeled his chair close to me. "Is she just nervous about the auction?"

"That's my guess," I said. "But I'll give her a chance to shower. And then I'll see what's up."

Fifteen minutes later when I knocked on the door of Taylor's bedroom, there was no answer. I went down the hall to Taylor's studio. The door was ajar. Taylor was in her robe, her hair damp from the shower, staring at the blank canvas on the easel in front of her.

"Is everything all right?" I said.

She whirled around to face me. "No. Nothing's all right. What if my paintings are no good? So far, the only people who've seen my work are our friends, my teachers, and Darrell. Tonight, strangers are going to be looking."

"Darrell chose to put two of your paintings in the auction," I said. "He wouldn't have done that if they weren't good."

"He's a friend of our family. He's probably just being nice."

"Darrell's a professional art dealer," I said. "And he's agreed to be Racette-Hunter's link to the artistic community. He wouldn't compromise his standards just to be nice. Besides, he cares about you. He wouldn't let you show your work publicly if you weren't ready."

"What if nobody bids on my pieces?"

"They will. I've already told your dad that if we don't come home with *Two Painters*, he'll sleep in the garage for the rest of his life."

Taylor had inherited Sally's wide and expressive mouth. I could gauge her feelings simply by looking at the line of her lips and at how the corners of her mouth turned. Now her lips twitched into the beginning of a smile. "What if somebody bids against him?"

"Then your dad will have to bid more. He always says I never ask for anything. He'll be relieved to know that I can be wildly extravagant when there's something I really want."

"What about *BlueBoy21*? What if people just don't like it? It's pretty conservative."

"Conservative because of the connection with Gainsborough?"

"No, because it's not 'cutting edge,'" Taylor said, flashing her fingers in furious air quotes. "*BlueBoy21* is my take on the kind of art Gainsborough made, especially the way he used warm colours against cold colours to find the true face of his subject. For a lot of critics now, showing the inner life of the subject isn't enough."

"Sounds like you've done a lot of research on this," I said.

"Julian knows a lot about the modern art scene. He warned me that some people might have a problem with *BlueBoy21* because it doesn't make a statement."

"But you still made the painting you wanted to make."

"I didn't have a choice," Taylor said, and I could hear Sally in her voice.

"Fair enough," I said. "Now get dressed. I guarantee there will be heated bidding on your work."

"Because I'm Sally Love's daughter."

"No, because you're Taylor Shreve, and you're already as good as your mother was when she was your age."

Taylor cocked her head. "You've never said that before."

I held out my arms to her, and she folded into them. "You've never been fifteen before, but it's true. I saw your mother's work when she was your age, and you're that good. Now, we'd better get dressed. Your dad will be grumbling."

Taylor held her stomach. "I think I'm going to throw up."

"Maybe wait a few minutes before you put on your new outfit."

Ten minutes later, Taylor swanned down the stairs, luminous in an understated little black dress. For the second night in a row, Zack was in his tux. I was wearing the silvery-lilac silk sheath I'd bought when I was an attendant at a recent wedding. It was too revealing, but Zack loved it and it had been expensive, so I was amortizing. Zack gave our daughter and me an appraising once-over. "I think it's safe to say that tonight, I am the luckiest man in the city."

As soon as Zack started the motor and pulled out of the parking garage, Taylor leaned forward towards us. "There's something I have to tell you about the painting Julian modelled for."

"We're all ears," Zack said.

"I called the painting *BlueBoy21* because the boy in the painting is sad, not because he's wearing anything blue. Actually, he's not wearing anything at all."

I gulped. The title of the painting had thrown me off. I had assumed Julian was posing in costume.

"So *BlueBoy21* is a painting of Julian naked." Zack cleared his throat. "Is he standing behind a plant or something?"

"No," Taylor said. "He's standing in front of a mirror."

"So we get full-frontal Julian," Zack said.

"Mmm-hmm," Taylor murmured. "And you can see his buttocks, too." Her words began to tumble over one another. "It wasn't an easy painting. A boy's body has so many different shades. I always thought a bum was a bum was a bum, but a boy's buttocks are hard to paint, and of course, their genitals are almost impossible – all those folds and the different shadings . . ." Her voice trailed off.

Zack was game. "Well, I'm looking forward to seeing how you dealt with it," he said.

After that we were silent till we reached the entrance to the Hotel Saskatchewan, where the valet parking attendant's presence saved us from further discussion.

We ran into Margot and Declan Hunter at the coat check. Margot was wearing a one-shoulder jersey maxi dress the colour of a holly berry. "That's a great colour for you," I said. "Very festive."

"'Tis the season," she said. She stroked her abdomen. "My little drummer girl is certainly enjoying all the action.

She pounds away every time she hears a tune with a beat."

"She likes it when I play my guitar, too." Declan said. "I am so stoked about meeting this baby."

Like Zack, Declan was wearing a tux. It was a formal occasion, so Declan had tied his dreads back, and he looked boyishly handsome. After the initial round of greetings, he and Taylor paired off and wandered arm in arm into the Regency Ballroom, where the auction was to be held.

"I wonder what's going to happen there," I said.

Margot was watching them fondly. "My fantasy is that in ten years, Taylor's going to look across the hall and realize that the boy in the condo next door is the one she's loved all along."

"Do you really think Taylor and Declan are still going to be living at home in ten years?" I said.

"It's my fantasy," Margot said. "Everything works out the way I want it to."

"Well, why not?" Zack said. "When Taylor's twenty-five, she'll be ready to consider dating, and I approve of Declan." He spotted someone across the room. "Now that we've settled the Taylor–Declan question, there's a guy over there I want to talk to about getting his company involved in our mentoring program."

Margot turned back to me. "We laugh, but Declan's feelings for Taylor are very intense. A couple of weeks ago he checked that documentary about Sally Love out of the library."

"Synchronicity strikes again," I said. "Ben Bendure, the director of *The Poison Apple,* sent me a DVD of some of material that didn't make it into the final cut. Did Declan say anything about the film?"

Margot met my eyes. "He said he understood why it was tough for Taylor having Sally as a mother."

"Did he elaborate?"

Margot shook her head. "He didn't have to. Sally would be a tough act for any young girl to follow."

"Taylor's not just any young girl," I said. "She's a prodigy."

"She is," Margot agreed, "but she's also a virgin. In the documentary, Sally's very open about the fact that when she was fifteen, she was in a sexual relationship with a man much older than her. Even thirty years later, Sally credits that relationship with bringing her to maturity as an artist."

I sighed. "I know. It's not exactly the message Zack and I are trying to give our daughter."

"Not exactly the message Taylor wants to hear, either," Margot said. "She and Declan are close, and Taylor still won't date anybody but him. Declan has told me that Taylor doesn't like boys touching her. Apparently she and Declan have worked out their own rules."

"And Declan dates other girls," I said.

Margot raised an eyebrow. "He may be in love with Taylor, but he's still a seventeen-year-old boy."

The Regency Ballroom was a many-windowed space that had been restored to the grandeur of the 1920s, a time of blazing chandeliers, heavy drapes, and ornately patterned carpets. Chairs had been set up facing the dais where the auction would take place, and a selection of the art was on display around the perimeter of the room.

Margot's eyes swept the ballroom. "Shall we mingle or stroll?" she asked.

"You should probably mingle," I said, "but I'm going to check out the art."

I'd just picked up the brochure about the pieces to be auctioned when someone touched my arm. I turned and found myself facing Vince Treadgold.

I tried not to show my surprise, but Vince wasn't fooled. "The last person you expected to see," he said.

"Maybe not quite the last," I said.

"Zack says I should just carry on with my life," Vince said. "This is an important night for Racette-Hunter. I've urged a number of my colleagues to come, so I figured I should show up."

My stomach knotted. There was a chance that the boy with whom Lauren had been in bed wasn't Julian, but I wasn't optimistic. Vince picked up on my anxiety. "Not willing to be seen with the pariah?"

"You're not a pariah," I said.

"Then let's look at the art."

The first piece we looked at was a star blanket made by a young Cree artist. The pattern was traditional, an eight-point morning star, but the fabrics the artist had used were lush – mostly velvets and satins – and the mosaic of pink, purple, indigo, and gold they formed was as dramatic as a prairie sunset.

"That's a beautiful piece," Vince said.

"The fun of an auction is that you can bid on it," I said.

"Maybe for my office," he said. "I don't think that's Lauren's taste." His laugh was bitter. "Of course, neither am I. Shall we move on?"

My pulse was racing. Only a fraction of the pieces up for auction were on display, and I was praying that *BlueBoy21* would not be among them. Vince was a proud man and having to stand in a public place as friends and strangers stared at the naked portrait of the boy who in all likelihood was his wife's lover would crush him.

The crowd was thick in front of the next piece, a large abstract, so we bypassed it. I spotted Taylor's *Two Painters* a few easels down, and my pulse slowed. It seemed unlikely that Darrell would have put both her pieces on display.

"There's something farther along I want you to see," I said. "I don't know if Zack has told you, but our daughter is an artist."

"I believe he's mentioned Taylor's talent once or twice," Vince said quietly. "Zack's a very proud father."

I thought of Celeste and how she hungered for the kind of love from Vince that Zack lavished on Taylor. "Zack came to parenting late, but he's certainly enthusiastic," I said. Vince and I moved to *Two Painters.* "This is the piece that I'll sell all my pop bottles to come home with tonight. It's of Taylor and her birth mother, Sally Love."

Vince and I stood silently side by side taking in the painting. The scene was an artist's studio, with a floor-to-ceiling window that bathed the subjects in light that was cool, atmospheric, and almost silvery. The artists had their backs to each other. Both were barefoot. Both were wearing denim cutoff shorts and men's shirts with rolled-up sleeves. Their bodies, long-limbed and graceful, had the same lines, although Sally's body was more muscular. Both women had their hair tied back from their face; Sally's blond hair knotted loosely at her neck, Taylor's dark hair in a ponytail. Physically and in their total absorption in the work before them, the kinship between Sally and Taylor was apparent, and yet there was no connection between them. It was clear, despite their proximity, that each woman felt that she was the sole occupant of the space in which she found herself. Interestingly, the painting on Sally's canvas appeared to be complete, while Taylor had drawn only a few preliminary lines.

Vince moved closer. "There was a retrospective of Sally Love's work in Toronto last year. Lauren had to drag me to it, but I'm glad I went – especially now that I've seen Taylor's art. There are some powerful genes at work there."

"And not just from Sally," I said. "Taylor's grandfather, Desmond Love, was a painter, too. I loved his work. Des was a tremendously physical man, and you could feel the energy coming off his canvases."

"What did he paint?

"Abstracts," I said. "I asked Des once what they were about. I was just a dopey kid, but he treated the question seriously. He thought about it for a while, and then he said, 'They're about the magic of paint. I start with a blank canvas and then suddenly where there was nothing, there's colour and movement and life.'" I felt a lump in my throat. "Des died not long after that. He was forty."

"Sally died young too, didn't she?" Vince said.

"She was forty-five."

"She left an impressive body of work."

"Sally was driven," I said.

"When a parent dies young, children often feel the touch of the scythe on their own necks," Vince said.

"You think Sally suspected she might die early?" I said.

"I'm extrapolating from my own case," Vince said. "My father was also a surgeon. He died when he was thirty-eight. As a consequence, I've always been ruthless about time."

"Sally was ruthless about time, too," I said. "That was never easy for me to accept."

"She didn't have time for you?"

"No. There were long periods of time when Sally forgot I existed. More seriously, until Sally discovered that Taylor was gifted, she seemed to forget she had a daughter."

"But you were always there."

"That seems to be my role in life," I said.

Vince's azure eyes were penetrating. "What is it Woody Allen says? Ninety per cent of life is just showing up? I consider Zack my closest friend. I was relieved when you showed up in his life."

"Someone had to stop him from living like an eighteen-year-old with a death wish," I said.

"I'm glad it was you," Vince said, "although I'll have to admit you were a surprise. You were so . . ."

"Ordinary?"

Vince shook his head. "I was going to say 'private.' You're always cordial, but you don't give much away. Anyway, you were exactly what Zack needed."

"And he was what I needed," I said.

"Then you were both lucky," Vince said, and with that, we moved along.

We'd been given a period of grace. *BlueBoy21* was not among the pieces displayed. When Vince ran into a colleague from the hospital, I excused myself and went in search of Zack.

He was chatting with our former premier and my long-time friend, Howard Dowhanuik. Howard was seventy-one, and after a lifetime in politics, he had the battle-scarred, clever-eyed wariness of an old eagle. For the first time in my memory, he was wearing a tux. I straightened his tie. "You're looking very dapper," I said.

"As are you," Howard said. "You didn't used to wear dresses like that when you were involved in politics."

"That's because we were the people's party."

Howard's gaze was assessing. "You look good, but you don't look like you."

"My corduroy overalls were at the cleaners," I said. "So how do you like hobnobbing with the fat cats?"

Howard drained his glass of champagne and plucked another from the tray of a passing server. "The booze is good, and it's free, which leads me to my question. Whenever our party had a fundraiser, tickets were ten bucks a head. Everybody brought food; we charged for the booze, which we watered; and then we passed the Colonel Sanders bucket around for donations. This shindig isn't cheap. Who's paying the shot?"

Zack was sheepish. "My poker club," he said.

"You guys have that kind of money?" Howard said.

"We do," Zack said. "But Joanne's giving me the evil eye, so let's change the subject."

Howard laughed. "Fine with me. There's something I want to talk to you about anyway. Have you heard anything about a hush-hush land deal our mayor and his cronies on city council are involved in?"

Zack shook his head. "No, but I've been pretty focused on Racette-Hunter."

"Everybody's busy," Howard said equitably.

"Everybody's always too busy to pay attention to City Hall," I said. "That's why civic politics is such a magnet for bottom feeders. So what's the land deal?"

"My guess is it's a setup for a bait and switch," Howard said. "Remember that land southwest of Westchester Place that the city bought after the last election?"

"It's designated for two hundred units of affordable housing," I said. "But nothing's happened."

"Something may be about to happen now," Howard said. "Mayor Ridgeway and a group of his affluent friends just purchased a parcel of land in Dewdney Park that could nicely accommodate two hundred units of housing."

Zack sneered. "Bastards," he said. "So Dewdney Park, affectionately known as 'Needle Park,' gets the affordable housing, and Westchester Place, with all those nice shops and promises of green space, libraries, and schools, gets the high-end housing."

My blood pressure spiked. "They are bastards," I said. "The whole point of putting affordable housing in Westchester Place was to keep low-income people from being ghettoized. Dewdney Park already has serious problems. Dumping a group there that is already marginalized will just exacerbate the problem."

"The mayor's right over there," Zack said. "Why don't we ask him a few questions?"

"I'm in if you want me." Howard turned his hooded old eagle's eyes on me. "Joanne?"

"Let's see what the mayor says first," I said. "We're not political, just concerned citizens who've heard a troubling rumour."

"You always had a good ear for these things, Jo," Howard said. "And since you don't need me, I'm going to get something to eat."

When Howard left, Zack moved his chair closer. "Ready to meet the mayor?"

"Not yet," I said. "We have a more immediate problem. Zack, did you know that Vince is here tonight? He wanted to support the auction."

Zack winced. "So he's going to have a chance to stand in a room with his friends while a painting of his wife's naked lover is auctioned off."

"Can you think of a way to get him out of here?"

"Not offhand, but I can warn him. That way, he at least has the option of leaving inconspicuously." Zack rubbed his temples, a sure sign of stress. He was about to make a move to find Vince when the mayor himself, who must have seen us with Howard, appeared beside us.

The wattage of the mayor's smile was dazzling. Solidly built, blond, and sunny, Scott Ridgeway was a man to whom pleasing others came naturally. He held out his hand to me and then to Zack. "I was hoping I'd have a chance to thank you for what has been a mutually beneficial partnering. The Racette-Hunter multiplex will be a jewel in the Queen City's crown."

It was difficult for me not to look at Zack. The city had been a persistent thorn in our side from the beginning. At every turn, they had attempted to block, delay, and bury the project under a blanket of red tape and ancient ordinances. More than once, Zack had threatened to dump a load of manure on the lawn in front of City Hall, but he let Scott Ridgeway's reference to "our mutually beneficial partnering" pass without rebuke.

Though thwarted in his mission to talk to Vince, Zack was all charm. "We're glad you could join us tonight, Mr. Mayor. I hope you brought your chequebook." Zack gestured towards the glowing eight-point star on the blanket behind the mayor. "Hanging that piece in your office where you could see it a hundred times a day would be a useful reminder of our city's diversity."

The mayor beamed. "We already have some Aboriginal art. It was done by schoolchildren."

Zack raised an eyebrow. "Do you have a quota?"

A shadow of perplexity crossed Scott Ridgeway's broad face. "I don't understand," he said.

"I just wondered if the City had a quota on how much Aboriginal art they purchase," Zack said.

"I don't know," the mayor said and he looked crestfallen.

Clearly, Scott Ridgeway was a person who needed to please others. It wasn't much of a leap to believe that he would be easily led. The silence among us grew awkward. Scott Ridgeway blinked first. "I'll get back to you on your question, Zack," he said. "It was nice talking to you both."

When the mayor started to move away, I stepped in front of him. "I have a question, Mr. Mayor," I said. "Tonight I heard a rumour that the two hundred units of low-income housing that the City promised would be built in Westchester Place are now going to be built in Dewdney Park. Is that true?"

Scott Ridgeway's round blue eyes roamed the crowd desperately. He was seeking salvation, but none was forthcoming. "Where did you hear that?" he asked.

"From someone I trust," I said. "Is it true?"

"I can't answer that," he said. He scuffed the toe of his shoe against the floor sheepishly. He knew he was about to disappoint again. "Other people are involved," he said weakly.

"Other people *are* involved," I said. "That's my point. There are families waiting to become part of Westchester Place. Can you imagine what it means for someone who's lived his or her entire life in North Central to be promised an affordable house in a good neighbourhood?"

He surprised me by answering. "No," he said. "I can't."

"Can you imagine what it will be like for the people in Dewdney Park to learn that the city is planning to increase the density of the unemployed and underemployed in their neighbourhood? Dewdney Park is already struggling. Every year when the snow melts, the community association has to patrol the alleys for hypodermic needles and used condoms before the kids start playing there. If the city builds two hundred low-income units there, you'll push Dewdney Park over the edge."

"I can't talk about any of this," he said finally. "I'll get back to you on your question, too, Joanne."

The mayor sprinted off, putting as much distance as possible between him and us. Zack reached over and rubbed my lower back. "Nicely done," he said.

"Why do I feel like a bully?" I said.

"Because attacking Scott Ridgeway was like shooting fish in a barrel. How the hell did he get elected anyway? This is his, what . . . second term?"

"Third," I said. "Did you vote in the last civic election?"

"No," Zack said.

"Then you just answered your own question."

"Okay, point taken," Zack said. "So when's the next election?"

"Next October," I said. Across the room, Scott Ridgeway, smoothly guided by his aide, was glad-handing the well heeled. I drew Zack's attention to the mayor's progress. "That's how it's done," I said. "Mayor Ridgeway cultivates the people who matter. When the election is called, the people who matter fill Ridgeway's campaign coffers and get people who share their vision to vote for him. The people who matter have a lot at stake. They have to make sure the mayor is someone who will serve their interests."

"A lapdog like Ridgeway," Zack said.

"You've got it," I said. "And people who don't vote make winning very easy for them."

Zack was thoughtful. "I'm not the only one who doesn't vote," he said. "I imagine the turnout in North Central is pretty dismal."

"It's abysmal," I said. "Maybe voter turnout is something Racette-Hunter should focus on."

Zack nodded. "Yeah," he said. "Maybe it is."

Just then, Margot stepped up onto the stage, Declan at her side. The program was about to get underway. There was no chance now for Zack to warn Vince.

Privately Margot still found it difficult to talk about Leland without breaking down, but that night her voice was firm. She thanked everyone for coming and then she went to work, explaining that the driving force behind the Racette-Hunter Centre was something she termed "The Brain Gain Initiative." Margot said that before her husband died, he had come to realize that the people in North Central should be treated as their community's greatest asset; they should be given real chances to acquire the skills and confidence needed to lift up their community without wholly relying on government.

She explained that the facilities would be open to all, and that in a very real sense the centre would belong to the people who used it. Everyone paid, but the cost would be on a sliding scale, so people would pay what they could afford. There would be first–rate recreational facilities: an Olympic-sized swimming pool, two gymnasia, and centres for health, fitness, and the performing arts. There would be an infant learning centre and a space for child care. There were industrial arts shops where people in the community could learn trades. But everyone who used the facility would have an obligation to help the next person. If you were swimming, you taught someone else to swim; if you were shooting hoops, you taught someone else to shoot hoops; if you were using the child-care facility, you were obliged to take a shift caring for other children; and so it went. The idea was community building, and that meant responsibility for one another and pride in accomplishment.

In her brilliant red dress, Margot was a compelling figure, but Lauren Treadgold was standing ten feet away and I couldn't keep my eyes off her. She had done her best to hide the damage to her appearance. A leather patch covered her eye, but even skilful makeup couldn't conceal the ugly bruising that had spread to her cheek. Her black silk gown was daringly cut, and she was wearing the stunning snake bracelet she had worn the night of her birthday. Her hand rested gracefully on the back of the chair beside her, and she held her head high.

Zack had pulled his wheelchair up next to the arrangement of chairs that filled the centre of the room, and I joined him there. I'd been looking forward to the art auction for weeks, but as Darrell Bell took the stage and began describing the first piece, a work of silver-stained fused glass, my chest was tight. The piece was superb, but when I ran my eyes down the brochure that listed the items for sale, I saw that

BlueBoy21 was Number 6. I pointed the listing out to Zack.

"I'd better give finding Vince another try. Tell Taylor I'm sorry, but *Two Painters* is Number 33, and I'll be beside you for that."

"She'll understand," I said and made my way to a seat in the middle of the back row.

I saved the seat next to me for Taylor. She slid in, just as the bidding on Number 5 had ended. She wasn't alone. Julian and Kaye Russell were with her. Kaye was in a vintage aubergine gown that flattered her slender figure. Julian was dressed formally in a grey Edwardian-style jacket and a cream vest. There was a creamy rose in his lapel, and as *BlueBoy21* was brought onto the dais and positioned on an easel, Julian plucked the flower from his buttonhole and handed it to Taylor. I had spent years watching Taylor. I thought I was familiar with her every expression, but the quiet joy that lit up her face when Julian gave her the rose was new, and its intensity frightened me.

BlueBoy21 was a large piece, seventy by forty-four inches – Taylor had told us that its dimensions were the same as those of Gainsborough's *Blue Boy.* As the audience took in the painting, there was silence and then a buzz. The nude Julian was close to life-sized, and my first impression was of darkness and light. Julian was standing in front of a pier glass framed in elaborately carved dark wood, painted in burnished browns, densely applied. On either side of the pier glass were large shuttered windows made of that same carved wood. Against the darkness, Julian's flesh was incandescent – light seemed to come through his body the way light comes through fine china. He was flawless. His skin was without blemish and, except for the modest tangle of black pubic hair, smooth. His limbs were almost female in their grace and lack of developed muscle. We were close enough to see the shadings of the buttocks, and in the mirror, the dark pink of the testicles, the pink shaft of the penis, the lighter pink of the penis head. The body was perfectly rendered, but it was Julian's face that wrenched the heart.

He was a person alone with a private sorrow. As *BlueBoy21* stared into the pier glass, his eyes were filled with pain and the knowledge that, perfect as his reflected self was, it would never be enough.

When Darrell Bell began reading the description of the piece, Taylor's face was stone, but a small smile played on Julian's lips. When the bidding started at $5,000, Taylor's hand crept over and touched Julian's. The room was almost silent; a man whom Darrell had pointed out to me as a dealer was standing against the wall, talking on his cell; when the bidding hit $15,000, the dealer raised his paddle. I knew Darrell was surprised, but his face showed nothing. *BlueBoy21* had been intended as an apprentice piece, and it was highly skilled, but it was the longing in BlueBoy21's face as he looked in the mirror that made my nerves twang. In capturing the moment when a human being realizes that the one thing he wants is forever beyond his grasp, Taylor had touched a chord that resonated. She had painted a Blue Boy that reflected the bitter poignancy of our century.

At $17,000, there was a moment of quiet, and it seemed as if the bidding was over; then a voice from the crowd called out $25,000. I knew without turning my head that the voice was Vince Treadgold's. Lauren's hand rose to her throat. *BlueBoy21* was removed from the stage and the next piece brought out.

Taylor's face was pink with excitement. "I can't believe this," she said.

Julian's expression was knowing. "I can," he said. As he brushed Taylor's cheek with his hand, she lowered her eyes. "This is just the beginning for us," he whispered.

Then he said goodbye to Kaye and me and disappeared into the crowd.

Taylor raised her fingers to her lips. She seemed stunned. I was stunned, too – by the amount the painting had brought, and by Julian's words and obvious intimacy with Taylor. In seconds, the axis of our world had shifted. But Kaye seemed oblivious to that. She hugged Taylor to her. "Well, you did it," she said.

Taylor's voice was small. "Now I have to do it again," she said.

"Oh you will," Kaye said, and there was an edge in her voice. "Nothing can stop you now."

The auction continued. Zack joined us. He took both Taylor's hands in his. "I'm still learning about art," he said. "But I know enough to realize how amazing that painting of Julian is. Congratulations."

Taylor coloured. "You didn't mind that the boy in the painting is naked."

"Not a bit," Zack said.

When I bent to embrace him, he whispered, "Poor Vince. I couldn't get to him through the crowd before *BlueBoy21* came up. I don't know what he was thinking, but it must have been Julian he found her with."

"Do you want to go back and stay with him?"

"No, I promised I'd be here with you and that's how it's going to be."

The bidding for *Two Painters* was hot as well. Finally, the field narrowed to two: the dealer on the cellphone and Zack. When the dealer offered $16,000, Zack offered $18,000; after a terse conversation on his cell, the dealer didn't counter, and the piece was ours. When Taylor, Zack, and I exchanged fist bumps, Kaye seemed lost in thought. "I think I'll head for home," she said finally. "It's been a long day."

Taylor touched her arm. "I don't know how to thank you, Kaye. Julian was exactly right for me."

"You were right for Julian, too," Kaye said. "Goodnight."

Zack stayed with us through the rest of the auction. As her contribution to the evening, Kaye had curated a selection of works by young artists and artisans for the auction. Some of the pieces were truly lovely, and Margot and Declan joined us to choose something to take home.

Margot discovered a collection of pursies, small, classic change purses, very feminine and sweet, with soft pink and purple fabric vaginas hand-sewn in the openings. They had the goofy playfulness of happy sex, and Margot bought a baker's dozen of them for female friends. Declan steered clear of the pursies and bought Taylor three triangular silver bangle bracelets, and in turn, Taylor bought Declan a bold black-and-white-striped cashmere scarf. It had been a good night for the Hunters and the Shreves.

It had not been a good night for Vince Treadgold. The lineup to pay for purchases was long. We were still far from the payment table when a female volunteer took Zack aside. They moved out of earshot, and when Zack rejoined us, he looked glum. "What's wrong?" I said.

"It's Vince," he said. "Beth Ann was on the desk when he paid for his purchase. He insisted on taking the painting with him even though she tried to dissuade him. She explained that there were insurance issues, and that the Racette-Hunter Foundation could deliver the piece to his wife first thing tomorrow morning."

"To his wife?" I said.

"Yes, apparently, Vince was firm on that point. The painting was for Lauren, and he's determined to give it to her personally. There was a lineup, so Beth Ann got one of Darrell's people to re-crate the piece. Luckily, in her non-volunteer life, Beth Ann is a lawyer, so she wrote up a waiver saying that if the piece was damaged, the Racette-Hunter Foundation wasn't responsible, and Vince took off with his prize. I should have tried harder to find him, Jo."

"No," I said. "This was Taylor's night. You'll be around to help Vince deal with the fallout when it comes."

"The fallout has already started," Zack said. "Beth Ann is certain that Vince had been drinking. He must have nipped out to that bar off the lobby and ordered a couple of quick ones. Jo, Vince hasn't touched alcohol in fifteen years, and he's been faced with some tough situations, including the night when his first wife took her own life."

"Celeste and I talked about her mother's suicide. Celeste is haunted by the image of her mother barefoot in that snowy field."

"So is Vince," Zack said. "Solange suffered from depression. Vince believed he should have picked up on the signs sooner. And now his second marriage is crashing. Vince doesn't handle failure well. He's in for a tough time."

The line inched along. We paid for our purchases and headed home. Taylor was wearing her triangular bangles. As we drove through the dark city, she kept her forehead pressed to the cool glass of the window in the back seat. The evening had left us all with plenty to ponder.

CHAPTER

5

The Racette-Hunter working team was gathering mid-morning at Margot's for a debriefing about the art auction, so Zack and I had planned a leisurely breakfast.

When the dogs and I came back from our run, it seemed as if the leisurely breakfast was right on target. The porridge was on the stove and a copy of the local newspaper, still folded, was beside my plate.

I unhooked the dogs. "Anything going on around here?" I said.

"Nope," Zack said. "Taylor's still sleeping."

I topped up Zack's coffee, poured myself a cup, and picked up the paper. On page one beneath the fold was a large picture of Taylor standing beside *BlueBoy21*. Without comment, I handed the paper to Zack. He peered over his glasses at the photo. "Nice picture of Taylor," he said. "And the photographer certainly captured Julian's glory. All over the city, kids are choking on their Cap'n Crunch as they get an eyeful of Julian's jewels."

"Kids don't read newspapers any more," I said. "And if someone's offended by Julian's jewels, the paper can argue that it's art."

"True," Zack said, "but a Joe Fafard bronze calf sold for $40,000 last night, and I don't see the calf on the front page."

I stood over Zack's shoulder and started to read the article. The opening sentence got my attention and raised my ire. "Taylor Shreve, the fifteen-year-old daughter of famed artist Sally Love and Regina trial lawyer Zachary Shreve, was the star of the show at the Racette-Hunter Art Auction last night." The piece was long on human interest: "a Grade Ten student at Luther College High School donated a work she'd created and the painting sold for $25,000."

"So you and Sally are Taylor's parents," I said. "I guess that puts me and Taylor's biological father in our place."

"You have every right to be pissed off," Zack said. "I expect our daughter's not going to be any too happy about the reference either."

"She won't be, but she'll be pleased about the photograph and about the attention her work's getting." I filled our bowls with porridge and took Zack's to him. "When Sally donated her fresco to the Mendel Gallery, there were people prepared to run her out of town on a rail. She didn't turn a hair. She was content with the way the fresco turned out, and that was all that mattered."

Zack sugared his oatmeal and flooded it with cream. "Did I ever tell you that I actually saw *Erotobiography*?"

"No," I said. "After three years, you still have secrets."

"Not many," Zack said. "Anyway, I was in Saskatoon on a case, so I went over to the Mendel with some of the other guys to check out the action. Sally's fresco really was something – that big sea of blue with all those penises and clitorises floating around."

"The owners of those penises and clitorises weren't as amused as you are," I said. "They all belonged to people with whom Sally had been intimate."

Zack guffawed. "How the hell would they know? I couldn't

pick out my penis in a police lineup. Now your clitoris is another kettle of fish."

I shook my head. "You really do have a way with words," I said. "Time to clean up our act and call our daughter."

When Taylor came down, she picked up the paper, gazed critically at the photo, and tilted her head. "I wish the light had been better," she said. "You can't see the shadings."

Our refrigerator door is what our younger son, Angus, calls a zonk board, that is, a space for sharing information: photographs, weird tweets, bizarre blog fragments, and party invitations. Taylor went to the drawer where we kept miscellanea, took out a pair of scissors, clipped the photo but not the article, and attached the clipping to the refrigerator door with a magnet from Mr. Electric. Then, without further discussion, she joined us at the breakfast table. "I know porridge is good for me," she said, "but do we have any crumpets?"

Taylor always ate her crumpets over the sink so the melted butter wouldn't drip on her shirt. When she was young, she needed a stool to reach the basin. She didn't need a stool any more, but the sight of her savouring her crumpet while saving her shirt always made me smile. That morning, just as Taylor finished her crumpet, her cell rang. She answered, then half turned away from Zack and me. "I can't talk right now," she said. "I'll call you back." She slipped her phone back into her pocket, put her plate in the dishwasher, and, without quite looking either of us in the eye, muttered, "I'm going to get back to work." Then she raced upstairs.

When we heard the door to Taylor's studio close, Zack said, "So what are the odds that our daughter's caller was one of her BFFS?"

"Minimal," I said.

"Am I right to worry?" Zack said.

"Taylor's almost fifteen. Most girls her age have been giggling on the phone with boys for a couple of years."

"Julian isn't most boys," Zack said.

"Let's hope Taylor realizes that sooner rather than later," I said and began to clear the dishes. Zack picked up his cellphone, hit a number, and listened. After a moment, he turned it off.

"This isn't good, Jo – I've been trying Vince all morning. His cell is off, he's not at the hospital, and when I called the house, Lauren said he hadn't been home at all."

"Do you think he went on a bender after the auction?"

"I'm afraid that's a real possibility."

"Is there anything I can do to help?" I said. "I could call motels and see if Vince is registered anywhere."

Zack shook his head. "If he's drinking, he won't register under his own name. Desk clerks require a financial incentive to cough up information about a guest who doesn't want to be discovered, and that's a transaction that has to be handled person to person. I'm going to take a little drive before the meeting and check out some of Vince's old holing-up places."

"I hope you find him," I said. "For everyone's sake."

I'd just finished making our bed when Ben Bendure called. I hadn't heard his voice since he delivered one of the eulogies at Sally's funeral, but I recognized his rich, rumbling bass immediately.

"Ben, I was going to call you today to thank you for the DVDs. That was very thoughtful."

In his note, Ben had mentioned that he was in failing health, but he still had an ear for nuance. "Very thoughtful," he said, "but you haven't watched them yet."

"I tried," I said. "I couldn't get past that scene of you, Nina, and me having lunch at the lake."

Unexpectedly, Ben laughed. "Even dead, Nina controls us," he said. "I tried to edit out the scenes she was in, but I couldn't."

"Nina was part of our story," I said.

"She *was* our story," Ben said flatly. "She wrote our script; she directed us; she was our star; and she was so damn beautiful, it was almost impossible not to forgive her." He paused. "I loved her, you know."

"So did I," I said.

Ben laughed again. "More fools us," he said. "But I didn't call to reminisce. I saw the picture of Sally's daughter in the paper this morning. She's obviously turned out well. That child lived through a nightmare. It's a miracle that you got her past it."

"She's not past it yet," I said. "Taylor never talks about her life before she came to live with me."

"Does she remember it?"

"She says she doesn't. She never mentions her father, although she lived with him for the first four years of her life, and she never mentions Nina."

"Who was also a big part of her life," Ben said. "Does Taylor talk about Sally?"

"She follows what's said about Sally online."

"Don't we all? She's been dead eleven years, but Sally still fascinates. The travelling retrospective of her work is a hot enough ticket for NationTV to replay *The Poison Apple* in January."

"So the network will be promoting the show during the holidays," I said.

"Good news for me but obviously not for you," Ben said.

"I'm just concerned about Taylor. When she was little, she wanted to hear everything I could remember about Sally. She couldn't get enough information. Once, when she was just five or six, we were visiting friends who owned one of Sally's paintings. We found Taylor standing in front of the painting tracing its lines. She said, 'My mother touched this, and now I'm touching it.'"

Ben's voice was hoarse with emotion. "That must have been very moving."

"It was. But now Taylor won't look at the art Sally made."

"I'm sorry, Jo."

"So am I," I said. "But I don't know what to do about it."

"From hard experience, I can tell you that the worst thing to do is ignore the problem," Ben said. "That's what I did for years after Sally died, and it tore me up. Finally, I decided I had to lay my ghosts."

"So you made the documentary."

"Dealing with all that archival material was pure hell, but it was worth it. When *The Poison Apple* was finished, I was finally able to move along. Of course, by that time I was seventy-eight years old." For a beat he was silent. "Don't let Taylor wait," he said quietly, and then he broke the connection.

The dogs and I had just come down from our second visit to the roof garden that morning when Darrell Bell arrived with *Two Painters*. As he unpacked the crate, I felt a frisson of joy. Before we moved in, our condo had belonged to Leland Hunter. It had been decorated professionally, and the rooms were warm with the colours of Tuscany. One of the design features was a two-storey wall of exposed brick from the original warehouse. We had moved a round scrolled mahogany dining table and chairs close to the windows across from the wall so we could see the city as we ate. The area caught the morning light, warming the patina of the old brick. From the moment I saw *Two Painters*, I knew the piece belonged in that space. After Darrell hung the painting, we stood back and assessed it.

"You have a real prize there," Darrell said. When I didn't respond, he raised an eyebrow. "Buyer's remorse?"

"Never," I said. "That wall has been waiting for that

painting. It's such a strong work. It anchors everything else into place, and it's beautiful. I love the light and the colours, and I love the subjects. I could look at it forever."

Darrell's voice was gentle. "But . . ?"

"Sally and Taylor have their backs to each other," I said. "They're so separate. There's no connection between them."

Darrell shook his head. "There's a link, Joanne. They're both making art, and for them that's enough."

"But it's not enough," I said, and I was surprised at the emotion in my voice. "Sally and Taylor are more than strangers who happen to share a passion. They're mother and daughter. Taylor told me once that making art allows her to see what she's been thinking all along. Look at the empty space she's left between Sally and her."

"Art is about space as well as colour," Darrell said. "Taylor's choice not to fill that space reveals a great deal about her attitude towards Sally."

"I know, and it saddens me. You've probably noticed that we haven't hung any of Sally's work in the condo. Three of the paintings are on loan to that travelling retrospective, but the rest are in storage. It's museum-calibre storage, but it's still storage. Sally would hate that no one's seeing her work."

"I'd be more than happy to sell any or all of Sally's paintings for you," Darrell said.

"Most of them are Taylor's," I said. "They were part of Sally's estate. I keep hoping Taylor will want to have them around her some day."

"She will," Darrell said. "I don't know much about kids, but I do know that Taylor is a person who cares about art and respects the people who make it. At some level, she already knows that it's wrong to allow serious art to be locked away in a vault. She'll come around." He checked his watch. "Now you and I better get to that meeting. Last night at least six people who had art in the show offered their services as mentors when R-H is up and running, and I'm keen to share the news."

Margot was dressed casually in jeans and a lemon cowlneck sweater. As a trial lawyer, Margot's killer red fingernails had been her signature. That morning as she let us into the condo, she held out her hands to me. The daggers were gone. Her nails were close-clipped and without polish.

"More motherly?" she asked.

"The first time you change a three-alarm diaper, you'll realize that short nails are the only option," I said.

Margot laughed. "Zack says seeing me without my killer nails is like seeing Samson after his haircut."

"So Zack's already here."

"He is, and he brought Brock Poitras with him."

"What's he like?" I said.

"In a word – perfect," Margot said. "And Brock hasn't arrived a moment too soon." She lowered her voice. "Zack filled me in on the situation between Vince and Lauren. It's heartbreaking."

"Did Zack have any luck tracking down Vince?"

"No, and he's worried. So am I. The Treadgolds have been good friends to Racette-Hunter. Lauren's inside. Her face is a mess, but she came anyway. I don't know why. All she has to do is deliver a report, and I could have done that for her."

"Maybe she wants to make certain that people see what Vince did to her," I said.

"But we're the only ones who know it was Vince," Margot said. "I overheard Lauren telling someone she'd slipped at the gym."

"Maybe she's leaving the door open for a reconciliation," I said. "Is Riel here?"

Margot rolled her eyes. "Yes, and I wish he wasn't. He looks worse than he did the day of the photo shoot. When

I asked how he was doing, he snapped at me." She stepped aside. "Come in. See for yourself."

For a moment I stood in the doorway of Margot's sun-splashed living room, taking in the scene. The mood was welcoming. Jasmina Terzic, the housekeeper who effortlessly took care of Margot's household and ours, had set out a table with carafes of tea and coffee, bottles of juice and water, and baskets of fresh fruit and muffins. Riel was sitting alone in the corner. I started towards him, but Ernest Beauvais beat me to it. When Ernest moved a chair close to Riel and murmured something that made Riel chuckle, I relaxed and went over to introduce myself to the one person in the room I hadn't met.

Brock Poitras towered over me. He had a black brush cut, tawny skin, and a smile that came slowly but was worth waiting for. His first words to me were praise for my older daughter, so of course I liked him immediately.

"Elder Beauvais tells me you're Mieka Kilbourn's mother," he said. "She's remarkable."

"I agree," I said. "How did you and Mieka come to know each other?"

"As part of Blackwell's initiative to show that it has a heart, the company sent me to deliver a cheque to your daughter's new play centre."

"Actually, April's Place is a community play centre, but Mieka and her friend Lisa Wallace are getting it off the ground."

"Mieka showed me around," Brock said. "I was impressed."

"The grand opening's at noon on November 30. Why don't you come? There'll be bannock and venison stew."

"Then I'm there." Brock pulled out his smartphone and made a note of the event. "Bannock and venison stew are in short supply at Blackwell," he said. "Don't get me wrong. Blackwell is a good place to work, and James Loftus is a great boss, but I've wanted to do something in the community for a long time."

"Now's your chance," I said.

"And I don't want to blow it," Brock said. "I don't want to be the guy who's just there for the photo op. Mieka says you and Zack have been involved with Racette-Hunter from the beginning. If you have any ideas about how I can contribute, bring them on."

I laughed. "Well, you asked for it. Last night Zack and I were talking about getting people in North Central more involved in civic politics. Is that something you might be interested in?"

Brock frowned. "I'm not very political."

"Electile dysfunction," I said. "There's a lot of that going around. Zack didn't vote in the last election. He was complaining last night about the mayor, and I told him that we get the government we deserve."

"Ouch," Brock said. "Time to turn the corner?"

"I think so. The next civic election is eleven months away," I said. "We could get a solid ground operation going by then."

"I'm a rookie," Brock said. "I'll need a playbook."

"I've spent years working in electoral politics," I said. "We can work on a playbook together."

Brock grinned. "Okay," he said. "I'm in."

I touched his arm. "And I'm grateful," I said.

Ernest began the meeting with the same prayer he used at the start of all our meetings: "Great Spirit – Grant us strength and dignity to walk a new trail."

Margot gave a brief overview of the subjects the meeting would deal with. Then she beckoned Brock to join her. "I have some very good news," she said.

Margot's introduction of Brock was fulsome. After she

announced that Brock would be working with them on a six-month secondment, he rose to offer a brief and gracious acknowledgement of his welcome. Riel did not join in the applause that greeted Brock's words.

The individual reports from the various teams were all positive. The auction had surpassed expectations – financially and in terms of positive publicity and patron satisfaction. The on-site Christmas photo shoot had been a success and holiday cards would be mailed out to Racette-Hunter's donors and potential donors the first week in December. The construction of the centre was ahead of schedule, and if all the variables continued to break our way, a Labour Day opening was definitely on track.

As the reports were delivered my focus kept shifting to Lauren. She could easily have come up with an excuse to stay away from the meeting, but not only had she come, she'd positioned herself next to Zack, who was the meeting's chair. Lauren was refusing to be a victim. With a model's instinct, she had chosen a look that would merit attention: a Mondrian print tunic top, black leggings, and tall black boots. Her makeup was careful and her hair was sleek. She had again covered her injured eye with the rakish black leather eye patch, and when she delivered her report on fundraising and development, she held her head high, proud of her success.

After the last report was delivered, Ernest stood to offer a closing prayer. But before he could begin, Riel cut him off. "I have a question for our new committee member, Brock," Riel said. "Exactly what is your function at Racette-Hunter, bro?"

There was no mistaking the antagonism in Riel's voice. Brock was cool. "Joanne and I talked about that before the meeting. We thought that I might approach people in North Central and talk about how they can organize to elect a mayor and councillors who will represent their interests."

"So you'd be doing community liaison work," Riel said, and his voice was tight with anger.

"Something like that," Brock said. "Elder Beauvais is about to say the closing prayer. Why don't we listen, and then you and I can go someplace for coffee and talk?"

It was an olive branch, but Riel didn't take it. He jumped to his feet. "There's nothing to talk about, bro. I may not have an M.B.A., but I'm smart enough to know when I'm being pushed aside."

Riel stormed out of the room, kicking at the leg of the table on his way, startling everyone. I stood, but Ernest Beauvais put his hand on my arm. "Give him a chance to let what he's doing sink in," he said softly. Then Ernest bowed his head and began the prayer.

As we left Margot's, my thoughts were with Riel, but Lauren was waiting outside the door and she, too, had a problem. "Have you heard from Vince, Zack?"

Zack shook his head. "Let's go to our place," he said. "We shouldn't be talking about this out here."

Lauren and I sat on the stools at the butcher-block table and Zack pulled his wheelchair up beside her. She removed the patch from her eye. "I thought this thing might make it easier for people to deal with me, but it's so irritating," she said. Zack examined her eye closely. The black and blue bruising appeared to have spread, and the eye itself was bloodshot. "Have you seen a doctor about that?" Zack asked.

Lauren's laugh was hollow. "Just Vince," she said. "Zack, I had no idea that *BlueBoy21* was a painting of Julian. You have to believe me. Darrell and Kaye handled the art. I saw the names of the artists and the descriptions of their pieces, but except for the star blanket we used in the advertising, I never saw the pieces."

"So Julian was the man that Vince found you with," Zack said.

Lauren's nod was almost imperceptible.

Zack's tone was firm but not condemning. "What you and Vince are doing to each other is brutal. Lauren, Vince was drinking last night."

"He hasn't had a drink in all the time we've been married."

"Well, now he has," Zack said.

"Because he recognized the boy in the picture," she said.

"Yes," Zack said softly. "Another man might have run away when he recognized Julian, but Vince—"

"Was determined to watch me suffer," Lauren said.

Zack was keeping his temper under control, but I could see from the pulse in his neck that it was costing him. "You weren't the only person who suffered last night, Lauren."

"I'm aware of that," she said. "I wish I knew what to do next."

Zack sighed. "That makes two of us. But the first order of business is to find Vince. I tried a few of the hotels he used to stay at when he was drinking but no luck. I also tried the hospital. They were tight-lipped. Were you able to get any information from them?"

"I didn't try," Lauren said. "I was embarrassed to ask strangers about my husband."

"You're going to have to get past that," Zack said curtly. "Finding Vince is the priority."

Lauren removed her cell from her yellow leather over-the-shoulder bag. In less than a minute, we knew that the news was not good: Vince had called the hospital saying he had urgent family business and requesting that his surgeries for the next week be reassigned or rescheduled.

"He's never done that," Lauren said. "No matter what happened, Vince's patients always came first."

"We have to find him," Zack said. "Before Vince joined AA, there were many weekends when all he did was drink. He can't go that route again. There's a private detective agency the firm uses – they're good and they're discreet. I'll call them, but I'll need the licence number of Vince's Mercedes."

"Vince wasn't driving his car when he left the hotel," Lauren said. "He was driving my SUV. He told the parking valet that the painting wouldn't fit in the Mercedes and that he needed the extra room." Lauren wrote down the description and the licence number of her Land Rover and handed it to Zack. "This isn't much to go on," she said.

"We may not need it," Zack said. "It's entirely possible that Vince will call."

Lauren stood. "Don't hold your breath waiting for the phone to ring," she said. At which point, of course, our land-line rang.

I answered. It was Darrell Bell. He was a man of uncommon equanimity, but he sounded agitated. "Jo, there's a situation with the painting Vince Treadgold purchased last night."

"What kind of situation?" I asked.

Darrell's laugh was short. "This is going to sound like something from a bad movie, but I just got a phone call from a man who says he has *BlueBoy21* – more accurately, he said that he has the painting that was in the paper this morning. The one that's worth $25,000."

"Where are you?"

"Still in your building's parking garage."

"Can you come up here? Lauren and Zack and I are at our place."

"I'll be right there," he said.

"So what's happening?" Zack asked.

"Darrell had a call from a man who says he has *BlueBoy21*."

Lauren's voice was even. "What happened to Vince?"

"I don't know," I said.

When Darrell arrived and joined us at the table, Zack pushed his chair back so he could see the three of us. "I guess the first question is how the man on the phone knew to call you," Zack said.

"No mystery there," Darrell said. "He called the Racette-Hunter office and said he needed to get in touch with somebody about the art auction. They gave him my number."

"So who are we dealing with?" Zack said.

"My guess is it's a young guy trying to sound tough. He says if we want to see the painting again, we should call him back and arrange for a meeting place. He also says to bring cash."

"And, let me guess," Zack said, "if we involve the police, all bets are off."

Darrell raised an eyebrow. "So you've seen the movie, too."

"Yep," Zack said. "Give me the tough guy's number. I'll arrange the meeting, but, Darrell, I'd like you to come with me to make sure the painting hasn't been damaged."

Lauren remained composed. "Did this man say how he came to have the painting?"

Darrel shook his head. "All he said was that *BlueBoy21* was in his possession."

"We'll know more soon," Zack said.

He dialled the number Darrell had given him and introduced himself, saying that he was a lawyer and that, as long as no major laws had been broken, he was ready to do business.

When he hung up, Zack gave us the broad strokes. "The guy says he was walking past the parking lot of the Sears discount store a little after midnight last night. He noticed that the hatch of an SUV in the lot was open, so he went over to investigate. He spotted the crate, figured it contained a flat-screen TV, and took it home so it would be 'out of harm's way.' Imagine his dismay when the flat-screen TV turned out to be 'a fucking painting.'"

"He must have been delighted when he picked up the morning paper and discovered what the painting was worth," I said.

"So the SUV and the painting were in the parking lot," Lauren said. "Where is Vince?"

Zack rubbed his eyes. "I don't know."

"There must have been an accident," Lauren said.

"If there was an accident, Vince walked away from it," Zack said. "You would have heard something by now if he'd been injured. And the guy didn't say anything about the SUV being damaged. I don't want to involve the police, but it's your call, Lauren."

Lauren shook her head vehemently. "No police yet," she said. "Let's keep this private."

Zack was sanguine about the meeting in the parking lot. As he pointed out, it was daylight and the Sears discount store was a busy place. I volunteered to go along with Lauren and drive one of the Treadgold cars back. I tried to make my suggestion sound matter-of-fact, but a man in a wheelchair is an easy target and if something went wrong I wanted to be with Zack.

Nothing did. The exchange of cash for the painting was smooth. As Darrell had deduced, the Good Samaritan was young – probably late teens or early twenties – a thin, jumpy Caucasian boy. Beneath his lower lip was the small triangle of facial hair my students referred to as a womb broom. After Darrell had examined *BlueBoy21* and pronounced it unharmed, Zack handed over the second half of the payment. The Good Samaritan couldn't sprint away fast enough.

Darrell slid *BlueBoy21* into the back of the Land Rover. Lauren clearly didn't want to let the painting out of her sight, so I agreed to drive the Mercedes back to her home on Albert Street, where Zack would in turn pick me up.

Zack stopped Lauren before she climbed into the driver's seat. "I noticed that the right headlight of your car is broken."

Lauren seemed distracted. "I'll call and make an appointment when I get home."

"Better sooner than later," Zack said.

Lauren's voice was frosty. "I said I'd call."

"Good," Zack said. "No use letting a small problem become a big problem."

During Zack and Lauren's exchange, Darrell's cell rang. His call was short, and when he broke the connection, his grin was puckish. "Here's where it's fun to be an art dealer. That call was from the guy who bid against you last night. He wants to buy *Two Painters.* Name your price."

"It's not for sale," Zack said. "Come on, Darrell. You know that."

"I do," Darrell agreed. "And I told my potential client you'd never sell, but he insisted that I try."

"And you tried," Zack said. "Look, I don't want to be churlish. Does your client live here in the city?"

"No, in Calgary."

"An hour's flight from here. Tell him to hop a plane, come to our place, have a drink, and look at the painting. We'll even introduce him to the artist."

"I'll pass that along," Darrell said. He jammed his hands in his jacket pockets. "Zack, I know I'm skating on thin ice here, but you know the Treadgolds. What do you think is going to happen to *BlueBoy21*?"

"Beats me," Zack said.

Darrell's expression was cool and amused. "Well, Taylor's professional career is certainly off to a dramatic start."

"It is," I said. "Especially considering that she won't even be fifteen till next week."

CHAPTER 6

Getting the Racette-Hunter project underway demanded time and energy from everyone involved. The art auction had been our major fundraiser, and I had anticipated that after it was over, I'd be able to relax: shop for some fun birthday gifts for Taylor, catch up on my reading, work with Brock on a political playbook for North Central, and sit in front of the fireplace with Zack enjoying life.

However, as Robbie Burns famously noted, "The best-laid schemes o' mice and men gang aft a'gley." Our weekend was miserable. There was no word from Vince. The private investigators discovered that Vince had flown north to Prince Albert on a commercial flight and then seemingly vanished. November is white-tailed deer season in our province and Vince was a hunter. Zack thought that Vince might have rented a private plane and gone to a hunting lodge. Every time I looked at the deepening of Zack's worry lines, I knew that he wasn't buying his own theory, and I was angry. Vince knew that people would be concerned about him. If he was sober, it was unconscionable that he hadn't let someone know he was safe. The only logical conclusion was that wherever he was, Vince was drinking.

The news about Riel was equally grim. When I told Mieka about Riel's anger at the meeting, she'd immediately tried to get in touch with him. She'd left messages and texted, but Riel hadn't responded, and Mieka was anxious.

Monday just after Taylor left for school, my cell rang. Zack and I were still at the breakfast table. It was Celeste Treadgold asking if I could please have lunch with her. It was a simple request, but I could hear the anguish in her voice. It occurred to me that she would have been old enough to remember Vince's drinking and disappearances. The possibility that the cycle had begun again clearly terrified her. We agreed to meet at noon at Orange, a Japanese–Korean fusion restaurant in the Cathedral District. I'd just hung up when Zack's phone rang. He listened for a moment and mouthed Vince's name.

I waited until the call ended. "Is Vince all right?" I said.

"He's fine. As I suspected, he went up north to hunt."

I felt my gorge rise. "Why didn't he call?"

"I don't know. I'm just relieved that he's okay. Jo, I know you're angry that Vince didn't get in touch with anyone, but he's been through hell. Please, cut him a little slack."

"When is he coming home?"

"Not till next week."

"I overheard you asking Vince about what he did after the auction."

"I did, and in a nutshell, after the auction, Vince got scared sober. When he left the hotel, he thought he was capable of driving. Within five minutes, he realized he wasn't. He pulled over, parked, then walked to the Senator – that dive where we have our poker games – and registered for the night. The next morning he made arrangements to fly up north."

"But you must have checked at the Senator."

"That was first place I went, but Vince was already gone by the time I got there. There was a new guy on the front desk. He didn't know me, and the Senator's staff are known for never volunteering information about their guests. Anyway, end of story."

"Not quite," I said. "What about the smashed headlight?"

"Vince doesn't remember hitting anything," Zack said. "He doesn't have the keys to the SUV, so it's a safe assumption he left them in the vehicle."

"And somebody just happened by, took the SUV for a spin, hit something with sufficient force to knock out the headlight, then dumped the vehicle off in the Sears parking lot?"

"That appears to be the case," Zack said amiably.

"End of discussion?" I said.

"Nothing more to discuss," Zack said.

"Then we might as well move along," I said. "Does Lauren know that Vince is okay?"

"No. Vince called the hospital and after he talked to me he was going to call Celeste. But he doesn't want to talk to Lauren."

"That's understandable," I said, "but Lauren *is* Vince's wife. She has a right to know that he's safe, especially since he plans to stay up north for a week."

"Point taken," Zack said. He picked up his cell, hit speed-dial, and left a message for Lauren that was curt but not unfriendly. Then he turned to me. "Good enough?"

"Good enough," I said, but I was still uneasy. "This isn't over, is it?"

"No," Zack said. "I'm sure you noticed that when I asked Lauren if we should contact the authorities, she said, 'No police *yet*.'"

"I noticed," I said. "Do you think calling the police is

Lauren's trump card to get what she wants from Vince?"

"That's exactly what I think," Zack said. "I don't know what Lauren wants, but whatever it is, I don't like the game she's playing."

Zack slid his smartphone into his pocket. "Vince is a helluva poker player," he said.

"Where did that come from?" I said.

"Remember that line from the old Kenny Rogers's song about gamblers having to know when to hold 'em and know when to fold 'em? Vince has always had a sixth sense about knowing when it's time to walk away from the table."

"And you think it's time for Vince to walk away from Lauren?"

"No," he said. "In my opinion, it's time for Vince to run."

The Cathedral area of our city is a fine place to wander on a lazy afternoon. Within a six-block area, you can find pickerel caught that morning in Lac La Ronge, handcrafted silver jewellery, maternity leggings for a groovy mama, a dazzling blue dendrobium orchid, and the funkiest sandals on the planet. You can also eat at one of a half-dozen quiet restaurants with adventurous menus and servers who neither hover nor hurry.

Celeste had reserved a window table, and I was able to watch as she got out of her car, hesitated, lit a cigarette, sucked deeply, then lowered her head against the wind and walked towards the restaurant. As she faced the entrance, Celeste took a long final drag before she threw the cigarette to the sidewalk and ground it out with the toe of her boot.

She was wearing jeans, a pea jacket, one of the crimson Racette-Hunter scarves, and a black toque with ear flaps. When she spotted me, she gave a little wave and came over to the table. "I'm glad you could make it," she said.

She slid into her seat, removed her jacket, and whipped off her toque. "Since my father went missing I've been crazy," she said. "Now that he's safe, I'm still crazy. I'm relieved, but I'm angry at him. What kind of person am I to react that way?"

"A normal person," I said. "Every so often when my kids were little, one of them would get lost. I'd be frantic – imagining the worst. Then I'd find them and all the while I was hugging and reassuring them, I'd be fuming because they'd frightened me so much."

Celeste ran her fingers through her wavy butterscotch-coloured hair. "That happened to my mother and me," she said softly. "I wandered off in a department store and when she found me she was laughing and crying at the same time. I'd never seen anyone do that. She covered my face with kisses, but all the time she was kissing me she was whispering, 'Ne me refais plus ça, chérie. Ne me brise pas le coeur.'"

"You and your mother spoke French to each other," I said.

"Yes," she said. "We always spoke French. It was like a secret language. A secret language, now lost."

There were no words to lessen Celeste's sorrow, and I was relieved when the server arrived with water and the wine list. We both ordered a glass of Argentinian Malbec.

Celeste picked up the menu. "I've never eaten here," she said. "What do you recommend?"

"Well, Taylor likes the okanomi yaki and the tako yaki."

Celeste skimmed the menu and made a face. "Deep-fried squid with cabbage pancakes and deep-fried octopus with dumpling balls? I don't think so. What do you and Zack like?

"We usually order dishes that we can split: gyoza, and yakitori chicken and kushiyaki."

Celeste read out: "Dumplings, chicken, and vegetables on skewers and prawns and scallops on skewers. Sounds good to me."

The server came with the wine, and we ordered our meal. Celeste took a sip of wine. "This is very nice," she said.

"The wine, but also being able to talk with somebody I feel I can trust. Joanne, I've done something."

I raised my hand in a Halt sign. "Celeste, is this something you should be talking to Zack about?"

"Not yet," she said. "If it comes to that, I will talk to him, but right now I just need to get the words out. I'm scared – for my father but also for me. I can't lose him again, Joanne. I know why he started drinking the night of the art auction. He says he's sober now, and I believe him, but it wouldn't take much to push him over the edge. If he starts drinking again, he could lose everything – his medical licence, his reputation, his career – everything he's worked so hard for."

"Zack's concerned about that, too," I said.

"Concern isn't enough," Celeste said. "My father needs to get Lauren out of his life."

Vince's angry account of his wife's passion for her young lover was still sharp in my mind. "Lauren may decide to leave on her own," I said.

"Not until she gets what she wants," Celeste said grimly.

"You seem very certain about Lauren's plans," I said. "Has she confided in you?"

Celeste whooped. "My God, Joanne. You must live in a parallel universe. Lauren and I do not *confide* in each other. We barely speak. My information comes from Julian."

"Julian?" I said. "I *am* living in a parallel universe. Lauren mentioned once that you'd introduced her to Julian. I assumed it was just one of those casual social things."

Celeste's lips curled with amusement. "Nothing about Lauren and me is 'casual,'" she said. "Julian and I work together at Diego's. Lauren was in for dinner one night with friends. I was her server. She spotted Julian serving at another table and she asked me to introduce her. Lauren said she wanted to meet some of my friends, and idiot that I am, I was flattered, so I called Julian over and introduced them." Celeste stared out the window at the mural painted on the side of the supermarket across the street. "As they say, the rest is history."

"Julian and Lauren became lovers that night?"

"Diego's has the perfect setup for assignations," Celeste said. "The restaurant is in a boutique hotel – nothing simpler for a patron to do than reserve a room while she's paying her bill."

"How long ago was this?"

Celeste's fingers thrummed the table and she gazed around the restaurant. "I don't know. Maybe a month ago."

"You never told your father?"

"No. My father knows how I feel about Lauren. I didn't want him to think I was being vindictive or – worse – that I was lying."

"So you let him believe everything was fine."

Celeste drained her glass. "No, I did something that ensured my father would *know* that Lauren was being unfaithful to him."

The penny dropped. "You sent him that text," I said.

Celeste's nod was almost imperceptible. "It was a terrible thing to do. I know that now, but I didn't set out to make trouble. My father had called to tell me he was going to be away for the weekend. He and Lauren have a dog walker, but she doesn't come on the weekends, so I volunteered to walk the salukis. When I got to the house, I saw Julian's jacket in the hall, and I went upstairs to investigate. I heard Lauren and Julian making love. They were having sex in the bed Lauren shared with my father, and I lost it. I went downstairs, and when I saw Lauren's iPhone in the living room, I fired off a text telling my father to come home. Then I took the salukis for a walk.

"I stayed out with them for more than an hour. When I came back, my father was leaving the house. His face told me everything. He said, 'Don't go in there,' and then he took the dogs from me, led them into the house, unhooked their leashes, came back outside, and walked towards his car. He didn't say another word. It was as if I didn't exist."

Celeste's desolation was heartbreaking. I reached across the table and touched her hand. "I'm so sorry," I said.

Celeste's laugh was bitter. "Not half as sorry as I am. I've made so many mistakes."

"When we see people we love being hurt, we get desperate," I said.

"I *was* desperate," Celeste said. "But I think I've found a way to make amends. Last night when I went to work, I told Julian that I knew that he and Lauren were having an affair. I thought he'd shut me out, but he was more than eager to talk. He said his relationship with Lauren was out of control. He had never intended their affair to be anything more than 'a mutually satisfactory arrangement.'"

"Meaning?"

"Julian gave Lauren sex, and she gave him money, but now Lauren wants more. She wants to live with Julian openly, and she believes that my father's assault on her makes that possible."

"Because Lauren can demand the moon, and if Vince doesn't meet her demand, she'll go to the police," I said, still struggling with the idea that Julian had sold himself to Lauren. "So where does the possibility for you to make amends come in?"

"Julian thinks that if my father understands the game Lauren is playing, he will call her bluff, and Julian will be able to slip out of Lauren's life."

"That's a high-stakes move," I said. "Lauren might go to the police anyway."

"Julian says that, given the fact that Lauren has a history of affairs with much younger men, she won't risk it."

"I didn't realize that Julian was one of many," I said.

"Neither did I, until Julian filled me in. Apparently, Lauren's been unfaithful to my father for years. She told Julian all about the other boys. She said she had to stay in the marriage, but she needed a little excitement on the side. In Lauren's eyes, Julian's predecessors were just diversions, but Julian is the real thing. Lauren told him that he's the man with whom she wants to spend the rest of her life."

"But Julian doesn't want to spend the rest of his life with Lauren," I said.

"Julian has other plans," Celeste said dryly.

My pulse quickened. "Do Julian's plans involve someone else?"

"I don't know. All I know is that Julian is anxious to get on with his future and Lauren is standing in his way."

"And Julian thinks that if Vince knows about the other boys, Lauren's only option will be to stay in the marriage?" I said. "You've lost me."

"Lauren likes money," Celeste said. "She's counting on my father to subsidize her life with Julian."

"Through alimony," I said.

Celeste nodded. "Julian wants my father to know about the other boys so he can deny Lauren the kind of alimony she'll demand."

"And she'll be forced to stay in the marriage," I said. "But that isn't what you want and surely it won't be what Vince wants."

"According to Julian, when my father hit Lauren, he virtually gave her a blank cheque. Once my father knows about Lauren's extramarital romantic escapades, that blank cheque will be null and void. Joanne, I know my father. He'll be fair with Lauren. She'll be very comfortable for the rest of her life, but she won't be able to bleed him dry."

"So you invited me to lunch because you want me to pass this information along to Vince."

"I was hoping you'd ask Zack to do it. They're old friends, and Zack is my father's lawyer. My father will need a strategy for dealing with Lauren, and my dad says Zack is brilliant. Will you talk to him?"

"Of course," I said. "I hope Vince appreciates how deeply you love him."

"I keep hoping that, too," Celeste said.

The server brought our gyoza and the bowls of dipping sauce. Celeste had her father's hands, graceful and long-fingered, and she was adept at handling chopsticks. The business of eating and praising our food was a welcome distraction.

When the server cleared our plates and brought the yakitori chicken and kushiyaki, Celeste seemed finally to relax. She picked up the hot sauce and sprinkled it on her food. "You know, for the first time in a long time, I'm actually hungry."

After we'd finished our meal and had our final cup of tea, Celeste took care of the bill, and we put on our jackets and left the restaurant. On the street, Celeste touched my arm. "I'm so glad you came today," she said. "And thanks for agreeing to talk to Zack."

She began to turn away, but I stopped her. "Celeste, what kind of man is Julian Zentner? I'm not just asking out of curiosity. Julian is getting close to our daughter, and it's starting to seem that he wants to get closer. Taylor is just turning fifteen, and Zack and I are concerned."

Celeste's ice-blue eyes, so like her father's, flashed. "You should be concerned," she said. "I have no idea what kind of man Julian is. I doubt if he even knows himself. He changes. Last night when we were talking about the Lauren situation, Julian was all boyish awkwardness – not quite sure how he got himself into such a mess but trying finally to do the right thing. He was very charming. And when he's working with the rest of the staff, he's just Joe Ordinary – a young guy trying to get through the shift. But when he's working a table, especially if the customers are all women, you can just about hear the panties drop."

"He becomes the man he needs to be to make the situation work for him," I said. "A shapeshifter."

"And an accomplished one," Celeste agreed. "Convincing an innocent fifteen-year-old girl that she needs him in her life would be child's play for Julian." On that unsettling note, Celeste jammed her toque over her butterscotch hair, lit her cigarette, and strode to her car.

As soon as I got into the Volvo, I turned my cell back on. It rang immediately. It was Zack. "Where have you been?" he said. "I was getting worried."

"I was having lunch with Celeste Treadgold," I said. "With my cell turned off. You should try it some time."

"I wish I'd tried it today," Zack said. "Margot phoned half an hour ago. Riel has resigned from Racette-Hunter."

"Well, I guess we could see that one coming," I said. "Has anybody talked to him?"

"Oh, yeah," Zack said. "Riel delivered his resignation verbally."

"To you?"

"No," Zack said. "To Margot. He came to her condo. Margot says he was higher than a kite."

My heart sank.

"Margot thinks he'd done a few lines of cocaine. According to her, his behaviour was textbook. He was euphoric, energetic, and eager to talk and talk and talk. Margot said if she hadn't asked him to leave, he'd still be at her place praising his amazing talents as a community organizer and railing about Brock and the rest of us."

"Shit," I said. "Has anyone called Mieka?"

"No," Zack said. "Margot wanted to alert her, but I thought you and I should tell Mieka face to face. That's not a message to deliver over the telephone."

"Agreed," I said. "So, I'm ten minutes from Halifax Street. Shall I just come home and we can take it from there?"

"That makes sense," Zack said. "I'm at Margot's."

I arrived at Margot's *in medias res*. I had concerns of my own: Celeste's observations about Julian were unsettling, as were her revelations about Lauren's plans. However, it was clear that Margot and Zack had been debating the appropriate response to Riel's situation for a while, so I bit my tongue and listened.

"We all know that Riel has used in the past," Zack said. "But he'd been clean for three years and he said he was finished with drugs. It's possible that today was a one-shot deal. It's also possible that the last few weeks have been stressful for Riel and he's opted for better living through chemistry."

Margot's face was distressed. "I hate this," she said.

"So do I," Zack said. "We'll offer Riel whatever support he wants, but we have to make certain the public knows that Riel has resigned and is no longer on the Racette-Hunter payroll. If it gets out that our poster boy has a very expensive habit, we're going to have trouble with fundraising."

I felt completely exhausted. "This is all wrong," I said. "Since Riel and Mieka got together, I've considered him part of the family. It hasn't been perfect, but we can't just cut him loose."

Margot nodded. "I agree. And Leland said if Riel hadn't been willing to sit down with him and work out a compromise, the Village Project would have been finished before it began." Margot picked up a glass of milk on the table beside her and took a sip. "After Leland died, working on that TV show was the last thing I wanted to do. I felt like my brain had shattered into a thousand pieces. But Riel was there. He told me he'd read that grief literally stops thought. Then he shepherded me through all those interviews and meetings. I'm grateful to him, especially if *For the Common Good* has the potential Jo thinks it has."

"The potential's going to be shot to hell if the public learns that one of the principals is a cokehead," Zack said. "I know that sounds harsh, but we can't let our concern about Riel jeopardize Racette-Hunter. This can't get out. I'll talk to Riel."

"Can you hold off until we tell Mieka?" I said.

Zack covered my hand with his. "Okay, but, Jo, we don't have the luxury of waiting for the right moment. This has to be dealt with fast."

CHAPTER

7

At any hour of the day, in any season of the year, UpSlideDown is a good place to be. The idea behind the business is simple. There are times when all parents deserve to get out of the house for an hour or so, kick back with a cup of joe, and watch their kids play with other kids in a bright, safe space filled with toys. UpSlideDown was located in an affluent area very different from the North Central neighbourhood where April's Place would soon be opened. Here, the hour after lunch seemed always to be the father's hour. That November day, the dads were out in force: hunched over laptops, sipping coffee, and casting an occasional look around the room to make certain that Ethan or Chloe or Moses or Zenaya were still present and relatively content.

Several kid-sized tables had been pulled together and set up for a birthday party. I took off my jacket, picked up a pack of paper plates decorated with dinosaurs, handed Zack the matching napkins and paper cups, and we began to set the table. It didn't take us long.

Mieka came from the back with two shopping bags full of toys. She eyed the table. "Well done," she said. "Thanks."

She handed both Zack and me a shopping bag. "We have to get these Dino-Roars out of their boxes before the kids arrive," she said. "The birthday boy's mother doesn't want her son's friends to be frustrated."

Zack shook his head sadly. "Kids today. 'Soft as boiled turnips.'"

"Where did you pick up that nugget of folk wisdom?" I said, handing him a box.

Zack began freeing the dinosaur within. "From a former client. She'd hired a strapping young man to beat her husband to a pulp. When the young man blew it, my client took care of the matter herself."

Zack pulled out a plastic *T. rex*. The box said his name was Monty, and he was about the size of a small cat. Zack held the *T. rex* in the air, rotated it, and examined it with interest. "So what does Monty do?

"Put him on the floor, push the sensor button, and see for yourself," Mieka said. "When you touch him, Monty walks. When you make a noise close to him, he roars."

Zack touched the button and Monty began to walk. Then Zack roared at Monty, and Monty roared back. Zack was delighted. "Where did you get these?"

"Toys "R" Us," Mieka said. She turned to me. "They're intended to encourage active imaginative play."

"Zack already excels at that," I said.

My daughter and I exchanged grins. Then she pulled out two of the little chairs at the birthday table. "I guess play-time is over," she said. "I know you two didn't just happen by to help me set tables. What's up?"

"Riel resigned from Racette-Hunter this morning," I said.

"I was afraid of that," Mieka said. "He's so jealous of Brock Poitras. I tried to tell him that he and Brock aren't competitors, they're colleagues. They bring very different skills to the project and their responsibilities are different."

She straightened the already-straight fork next to the dinosaur plate on the table in front of her. "Zack, is there any way you could just forget about the resignation? I could call Ernest Beauvais and ask him to talk to Riel."

"It's too late for that, Mieka," Zack said. "I'm sorry. We all are, but Riel burned his bridges this morning. When he went to Margot's to resign, he was high."

The news hit Mieka like a blow. For a beat she seemed to fold in on herself. "He'd fought so hard to stay clean," she said finally.

"Then you didn't know he was using again?" I asked.

"No. I haven't heard from him since Thursday night. After you told me about how he stomped out of your meeting, I started calling and texting. I must have left a dozen messages. I invited Riel to come to the house for coffee or to see the girls, but he hasn't responded." Mieka rubbed her temples with her fingertips. "He was supposed to call to tell me where he's living, but he hasn't even done that."

"But Riel did agree to see a doctor and talk to Ernest," I said.

"He agreed, but that doesn't mean he followed through," Mieka said. "Riel is proud. He can't admit he needs help."

"But he *does* need help," Zack said firmly. "And he has to understand that if he's involved with drugs, he's jeopardizing not just his own future and the future of your family, but the future of the centre. I can arrange to have someone track Riel down. When we find him, I can explain the gravity of the situation to him – unless you'd prefer to handle it yourself."

Mieka chewed her lip. "I can't do it, Zack. I've tried. I get nowhere. He just lies to me or makes excuses. I can't make him realize how much is at stake."

Zack wheeled closer to Mieka. "I'll take care of it," he said. "I've known a number of people who had a nice little recreational drug habit that ended up biting them in the ass. Many of them were lawyers, and they lost everything, including their families. But the smart ones got help. Riel has options."

"He doesn't believe that he has options," she said.

"Well, he does," Zack said. "There are excellent twelve-step programs in the city. If he thinks he needs a resident addiction program, I know the names of some good ones. Joanne and I will gladly cover the cost. Most of the addiction centres have a couples program and a family program, so if you want to, you and the girls can be part of Riel's recovery."

Mieka was close to tears. She shook her head. "I'm not there yet," she said. And then none of us had any more time to think about Riel because the birthday party arrived. Eight little boys, each of whom spied the Monty on his place at the table simultaneously. They didn't bother to remove their outside jackets. Within seconds, eight Montys were roaring around the floor with their new owners in hot pursuit.

The noise was already ear-splitting. I put my arm around my daughter's shoulders. "Are you going to be all right?" I said. "I can stay and help."

"There's nothing to do," Mieka said. "I'm going to call the school and have Riel taken off the list of people who can pick up the girls." She gazed at the melee of little boys and Dino-Roars. "After that," she said, "it's business as usual."

Taylor's birthday is on November 11 and in our province that means that her birthday is always a holiday. This year her birthday fell on a Monday. The Remembrance Day services at the legislature were on Friday, so after attending them, we had the entire long weekend to try to put problems behind us and make merry.

Taylor had vacillated about how best to celebrate her birthday. At one point she wanted to invite twelve of her closest friends for a sleepover at our condo, then she floated the idea of a dinner dance at the Hotel Saskatchewan. The dinner dance gave way to a plan for an evening of paintballing and pizza at Prairie Paintball Storm. Finally, Taylor settled on a weekend at our cottage with Margot and Declan; her two best friends, Isobel Wainberg and Gracie Falconer; her family, including her brothers and their significant others; and a birthday dinner featuring all her favourite dishes.

Neither Zack nor I was really into paintball, so we applauded her choice. I was particularly glad that Isobel and Gracie were still front and centre in Taylor's life. The three girls had always been anchors for one another, but that fall Taylor had been so busy with Julian and her art that she had drifted a little from her old friends.

I was, of course, relieved beyond measure that Taylor hadn't asked that Julian be included on the guest list. We had been living with tension since the beginning of the month, and we all needed a break. Riel wouldn't be joining us either. Zack had located him. He was living in the basement apartment of the home of a community worker in North Central. Zack had arranged to meet Riel at our condo. When he didn't show up and didn't offer an explanation for his absence, Mieka said that the next move would have to be Riel's, and Zack and I didn't argue the point.

We had all the ingredients for a good weekend. We would have a full house. The ice on the lake wasn't safe to be on yet, but Isobel's father, Noah, had been building a rink on the flat area between our cottages, so in addition to hiking, we could skate. The forecast called for snow, so if we were lucky, we'd get in some cross-country skiing.

Zack and I had busy lives, but from the start of our relationship we had carved out as much time as possible to be at the lake. I loved Lawyers' Bay at any time of year, but in November when the heraldic colours of autumn faded, trees dropped their leaves, and bare branches became brush-strokes of ink against the grey sky, I experienced a peace that was as rare as it was welcome.

That Friday when we pulled up in front of our cottage, the deep honking calls of Canada geese split the air. We let the dogs out of the car, and then Taylor, Zack, and I watched silently until the last skein of geese flew above us, heading south on their long migration.

Taylor released her cats from their travelling cage, and then we began carrying in the laundry hampers filled with groceries, wine, and sundries. When we'd taken in the last hamper, Zack inhaled deeply. "This is the life," he said. At that moment, he looked five years younger than he had since the night Vince came to our condo to say he'd hit Lauren. I decided that Celeste's revelations about Lauren's romantic history and her future plans could wait till the weekend was over.

Mieka, Madeleine, and Lena were already at work in the cottage. Mieka was in the kitchen grating cheese to top the chili and the girls were setting the long partners' table in the sun porch. Zack counted the places. "Could you ladies possibly squeeze in one more setting?"

Madeleine's brow furrowed. "Did we count wrong?"

"Nope," Zack said. "Your counting was perfect. I invited a friend to join us."

"Will your friend mind if he has a different placemat?" Madeleine asked. "We've used all the orange ones."

Lena sighed heavily. "If Granddad's friend has a different placemat, he'll feel like an outcast."

"Where did you hear the word *outcast*?" I said.

"From Riel," Lena said.

Mieka moved towards her daughters quickly. "Let's use

some of the brown placemats, too. They'll look pretty with the orange."

Mieka and the girls began resetting the table. The brown placemats did indeed look pretty with the orange. "The situation appears to be in hand," I said to Zack. "Come into the kitchen with me while I check on the chili."

There were two very large pots on the stove. Mieka had brought the vegetarian chili that I favoured, and I brought the chili con carne that Mieka had liked since she was a child. I turned up the heat under both pots, picked up a spoon, and began stirring. "So who's your friend?" I asked.

Zack's expression was innocent. "Brock Poitras. His partner is going to a wedding or something in Calgary, and Brock didn't have plans for the weekend."

"And you thought some time at the lake would give you a chance to convince him that his move to Racette-Hunter should be permanent."

"No flies on you, Ms. Shreve. Racette-Hunter is going to need a managing director. Especially now, with Riel out, we'll need someone to provide leadership, decide on strategy, and make sure we achieve our objectives. If Brock comes on board at the beginning of the year, he'll have time to put together the management team he wants and establish Racette-Hunter's presence in the community by Labour Day when we open our doors."

"Are you still planning on being out of R-H by August 1?" I said.

Zack nodded. "Yep, if Brock agrees, I'm sure the transition will be complete by then."

"And we'll have a month at the lake before you go back to Falconer Shreve."

"We'll have our month at the lake," Zack said. "But I might not go directly back to Falconer Shreve."

I stopped stirring. "Thinking of taking a gap year?" I said. "You and I could have a lot of fun backpacking across Tibet with Taylor, Willie, Pantera, and the cats."

Zack chortled. "Actually, I've been thinking about running for mayor."

I started to laugh and then something in Zack's face stopped me. "You're serious," I said.

After a lifetime in politics, my expectations for public officials were minimal, but since he'd become involved in the start up of Racette-Hunter, Zack had taken the chicanery of our mayor and city council to heart. All week he'd been fulminating about the bait-and-switch land deal Howard Dowhanuik had told us about the night of the auction, but fulminating is one thing and running for office is another.

"I've been giving it a lot of thought," Zack said. "Of course, I didn't plan to do anything until you and I talked about it. It would be a three-year commitment for both of us, Jo, but if we got the right city council we could do a lot in those three years."

"Agreed," I said. "But first you'd have to get elected."

"You don't think I could win?"

"Truthfully? No. I don't. Zack, you have several closets full of skeletons, and the opposition will make certain they all come tumbling out: the women, the drinking, the gambling, the times you crossed the line when you were practising law. We're not going to be able to shoot all that down with a nice family photo."

"I have committed many sins but no crimes," Zack said.

"There's a campaign slogan with traction," I said. I turned down the heat under Mieka's chili and handed Zack the spoon. "Give this a stir, would you? I should get started on the salad."

Zack began stirring. "I've never stepped away from anything because the odds were against me," he said.

"I know, and I know you'd be a terrific mayor. You're always the smartest guy in the room, and you're a quick study, but I understand politics, and I'm not sure political life is a good fit for you. You're used to winning, and this city is filled with people who won't want you to win. If you do win, they'll link arms to block everything you try to do. And there will be more of them than there are of us. The ugly little secret of civic politics is that the only people with any sustained interest in what happens at city council are the people who can profit from the decisions the mayor and the council makes."

"So what do we do?" Zack said. "Just stay out of it?"

"That's my first impulse," I said. "But I need time to think. There's not a doubt in my mind that you could change this city for the better, but without breaking a sweat I could give you a dozen reasons why you shouldn't run for mayor. The first one is me. Election campaigns are punishing and I want you around forever."

Zack put his arms around me. "Okay," he said. "That settles it. If you don't want me to do it, I won't."

"I didn't say I didn't want you to run. I just said I needed time to think." I took the ingredients for the salad out of the refrigerator. Cherry tomatoes were Zack's favourites, so I washed them first, put some in a bowl, and handed it to him.

He popped one in his mouth. "You make me very happy," he said. "And that's not just the tomatoes speaking."

Mieka and I had been getting dinner on the table together for many years. We worked together smoothly, and that night we were both careful not to mention the fact that Lena had learned the word *outcast* from Riel.

Dinner was relaxed and filled with laughter. Both chilis were a hit, the cornbread didn't crumble, and Zack urged everyone to help themselves to the cherry tomatoes. Brock was an ideal guest – one who was both interested and interesting. And Maisie Crawford was always fun. She and Peter, our eldest son, had been together for three months and we were all hoping the relationship would last. When Maisie was in the room, Peter couldn't stop smiling. That was good enough for me.

Zack had his own reasons for wanting the romance to continue. Maisie's move from Falconer Shreve's Calgary office to Regina was classified as temporary, but Zack was eager to have Maisie stay in Saskatchewan. She was a gifted trial lawyer whose passion for lacrosse meant that she often showed up in court with a split lip or a bruise. According to Zack, Maisie's injuries melted hearts and proved she was tough. Juries loved her. And to put the cherry on the cheesecake, that night when the talk turned to music, Maisie said that her Uncle Roy taught her early that the Beach Boys' *Pet Sounds* was, bar none, the Greatest Album of All Time. Zack, the world's most fervent Brian Wilson fan, looked as if he would spontaneously combust with joy.

When Zack and I went in to say goodnight to Taylor, we were both in high spirits. Zack wheeled close to Taylor's bed. "You have to admit that was one terrific kickoff for your birthday weekend," he said.

Taylor's expression was distant. "It was really good," she said. "I just wish Julian could have been here." Her eyes travelled between Zack's face and mine. "I asked him to come with us this weekend, you know."

I hoped my relief wasn't too apparent. "Did Julian have other plans?"

Taylor's eyes were still watchful. "No. He wanted to be with me on my birthday, but he said it was a family party and he didn't want to intrude."

"That was very sensitive of him," Zack said.

"Julian and I have been talking a lot lately," Taylor said.

"I'm really getting to know him. He's a very sensitive person." Her voice was challenging.

"I'm glad to hear that," Zack said. "Because you mean the world to us, Taylor. Don't lose sight of that."

Zack's words seemed to disarm our daughter. "I won't," she said softly. "You and Jo mean the world to me, too."

When I kissed Taylor goodnight, I held her close and wished I could hold her like that forever.

The weekend unfolded smoothly and happily. The promised snow never arrived, but the days were bright and cold enough to keep the rink in shape, and we made good use of it. Madeleine and Lena had both taken skating lessons so they were confident skaters. Zack had a Sit-Skate, a sled-skate invention for paraplegics that could be manoeuvred with the strength of the upper body. On ice, as on land, he was a force to be reckoned with.

Saturday morning Maisie got up a game of shinny. The traditional method of forming teams was followed. Everybody threw his or her hockey stick into a pile that Maisie divided into two smaller piles. Everyone picked up his or her stick and joined the others whose sticks had been in their pile. The two teams wound up evenly matched, and it was fun for the rest of us to sit, cheering them on and drinking hot chocolate.

Taylor's family birthday dinner was planned for Saturday night. Zack had to meet with a potential Racette-Hunter donor on Monday morning, so we were celebrating early. Mieka and I made Taylor's favourite dish, paella, and Margot, Declan, Brock, the Falconers, and the Wainbergs joined the rest of the family. The table was filled, and Taylor was beaming. After we'd cleared away the dishes from the main course, Angus turned to Mieka. "Time for the Pogues?"

"You bet," Mieka said. "The candles are on the cake waiting to be lit."

Brock raised his hand in a Halt sign. "Okay, roll it back," he said. "What do the Pogues have to do with Taylor's birthday?"

Angus pulled out his MP3 player. "When Taylor came to live with us, she used to follow me everywhere."

"I'd never had a brother," Taylor explained.

"I was totally into the Pogues," Angus said. "So, of course, Taylor was totally into them too. She was four years old. Her favourite Pogues' song was 'Fiesta.' By the time her fifth birthday rolled around, she knew all the words to 'Fiesta' and she insisted that we sing it when we brought in her birthday cake." He rolled his eyes. "Of course, the Kilbourns being the Kilbourns, it is now a tradition."

He turned on his MP3 and the room exploded with the sounds of the Pogues singing "Fiesta," their raucous celebration of the lusty joys that erupt when willing boys meet willing girls. Mieka brought in the cake, candles blazing. Those who knew the lyrics to "Fiesta" sang along, and those who didn't, clapped.

After Taylor had blown out the candles, we went into the family room and sat in front of the fire while Zack played the piano. He played by ear. He wasn't as good as he thought he was, but he was very good. One night we'd had guests, and a woman who had drunk well but not wisely asked Zack how he could be such a bastard in the courtroom and play piano so beautifully. Zack had drained his brandy snifter and given her his Cheshire cat grin. "You know what they say about Miles Davis. He played the way he'd have liked to be."

As holiday weekends inevitably do, ours wound to a close. After the hockey players had one last game of shinny on

Sunday, we had soup and sandwiches, cleaned up, and said our goodbyes.

Angus was catching a ride to Saskatoon with a friend whom he had to meet by two o'clock, so Peter and Maisie drove him back to the city. Taylor and her cats went back to the city with Margot and Declan. Zack wanted to talk to Brock, so after a heartfelt plea from Madeleine and Lena, Mieka and I took the girls down for a final skate on the rink.

As the girls circled the rink in their jackets and helmets, the snow we'd been promised began to fall in slow, fat theatrical flakes. It was a perfect moment, and Mieka and I both felt it. Then Lena shouted, "Watch this. I saw it on television. It's called the Salchow." Mieka jumped to her feet. "Don't, Lena! You need to learn how to do that."

But it was too late, Lena's toe-jump with her pick in the ice propelled her into the air, but she lost control when she landed. She extended her arm to break the fall, but when she came down hard and screamed with pain, Mieka and I were already running towards the centre of the rink. Madeleine knelt beside her sister.

The moment I looked at Lena's face, I knew the injury was serious. She was pale, shivering, and I feared teetering on the edge of shock. Mieka had dropped to her knees.

"I'll get our car," I said. "We need to take Lena into the city." Madeleine was clearly terrified. I squeezed her shoulder. "This is going to be okay," I said. "Your sister has broken her arm, but we'll get her to the hospital. They'll put a cast on it, and she'll be good as new."

As I ran towards the house, I could hear Lena sobbing. Zack and Brock were in the family room. "Lena fell on the ice. I'm certain her arm's broken. We have to get her into town."

Brock was on his feet. "How's your ambulance service here?"

"We've never used it," Zack said.

"Now's the time," Brock said. "If it's a bad break, Lena needs attention as soon as possible. An ambulance will get her back to the city faster than you can drive. More significantly, if she's in an ambulance, she won't get stuck in the ER waiting room."

Zack was already calling 911. As he gave instructions about how to find our place, his voice was steady, and my pulse slowed. Lawyers' Bay was a gated community, and Zack said he'd stay at the cottage and buzz in the ambulance when it arrived. I grabbed some blankets, then Brock and I went to the rink.

Brock was adamant about not moving Lena. She'd stopped crying, and Mieka covered her carefully with the blankets and was rubbing her legs and murmuring words of reassurance to both her daughters. The ambulance only had to come from Fort Qu'Appelle, an easy ten-minute drive, but it arrived in seven.

The EMT personnel were thorough and efficient. Within five minutes, Lena and Mieka were on their way to Regina. Brock volunteered to drive Mieka's station wagon and the dogs back to the city. We gave him the security pass for the condo, told him where the dog food was, and called Taylor to fill her in on the situation. Then Zack brought our car around; I slid into the back seat with Madeleine and put my arm around her. There was nothing to do now but wait and worry.

By the time Zack, Madeleine, and I arrived at the hospital, Lena was already being examined. The three of us sat in the waiting room. Madeleine climbed onto Zack's lap, and he held her tight. When Mieka came out, her face was strained, but she was in control.

"The doctor says Lena broke her olecranon – her elbow. But pieces of the bone have cut through her skin, so she'll need surgery."

Zack winced. "Is she in much pain?"

"They've given her some medication that seems to be helping. The orthopedic surgeon's on his way to the hospital. His name is Mike Kelly." Mieka tried a smile. "Here's irony for you. Dr. Kelly graduated from Luther the same year I did. We went through high school together. When we processed into the chapel to get our diplomas, we were paired alphabetically, Kelly and Kilbourn. All I remember is that I had on those stupid stilettos I insisted on wearing, and I towered over him." Mieka shook her head at the vagaries of life. "Now that boy is operating on my daughter." She exhaled. "Enough of that. I have to go back in there to talk to Dr. Kelly and to the anesthesiologist." She bent down and hugged Madeleine. "This is going to be all right. We just have to wait and see what's next." She looked at me. "Mum, why don't you and Zack take Maddy home with you. Hospitals are no fun. Plus they're full of germs."

"I'll take my chances," I said, "but I agree that Zack and Madeleine should go back to the condo. The dogs need a run. And we have to figure out something for dinner."

"What do you think, Maddy?" Zack said. "You and I can take the dogs for a run in the roof garden and order a pizza from the Chimney."

"I'm not very hungry," Madeleine said, and her voice was small and scared.

"Neither am I," Zack said. "But let's order an extra-large pie with the works, so we can bring Lena a feast for breakfast."

Zack held his arms out to Mieka and then to me. His message to us both was the same: *I love you.*

A nurse came to tell Mieka that Dr. Kelly had arrived, and he wanted to explain the procedure and get her signature on some papers. Not long after Mieka left with the nurse, Brock Poitras appeared.

"We never talked about where I should drop off Mieka's car," he said. "So I thought I'd track you down and get an update. How's Lena?"

"They're getting her ready for surgery."

Brock groaned. "I was afraid of that. There was something about the angle of her arm." He peered closely at me and frowned. "Are you okay?"

"I will be."

"It's always worse for the family," he said. "There's a Robin's Donuts downstairs. Why don't I get us coffee?"

"Coffee sounds good," I said. "Could you get some for Mieka too? We both take it black."

When Mieka came back to the waiting room, she collapsed into a chair and buried her face in her hands. "They put Lena in a hospital gown," Mieka said. "Mum, she looks so little."

I put my arms around her, and she rested her head on my shoulder. Neither of us moved when Riel Delorme arrived. "Taylor left me a message," he said. "How's Lena?"

"They're taking her into surgery," Mieka said.

Riel took the empty chair next to Mieka. Clearly ill at ease, he stared at the floor. Finally, he said, "If there's any way I can help, just ask. I've done some stupid things, but I love those girls."

Mieka's voice was soft. "I never doubted that," she said.

"Being with you and Madeleine and Lena was the best time of my life," he said. There was real sadness in his voice. Mieka turned towards him. It was a nice moment.

Then Brock Poitras came into the waiting room, and the adage that "life turns on a dime" was once again proven true. When Riel saw Brock, he leapt to his feet and balled his hands into fists. "So you're the replacement," he said. He glared at Mieka. "It didn't take you long," he said. "I'm not surprised. When a woman like you gets a chance to trade up, she trades up."

Mieka crossed her hands in front of her breasts, as though protecting herself against the verbal onslaught.

Riel stared angrily at Brock. "Congratulations, brother," he said. "She's a great woman – in every way, but you've probably already discovered that."

Brock put down the cardboard tray that held the coffee and moved slowly towards Riel. Riel had always been lean. Now he was gaunt, and Brock dwarfed him. "Time for you to leave, brother," Brock said. "I'll give you to the count of three."

Riel was out of the room on one. Brock handed around the coffee and we sat, shaken, sipping our coffee and waiting. It wasn't long before Zack phoned to check on Lena, and to tell us that Vince was back in the city. He said that Vince was full of praise for Dr. Mike Kelly, and that Lena was in good hands.

Two hours later, when a balding young doctor whom I presumed was Mike Kelly came into the waiting room, the three of us leapt to our feet. When he smiled, my heart began beating again.

Dr. Kelly's voice was deep and reassuring. "The surgery went well. It was a little more complicated than we'd hoped, but Lena's fine. When she's in her sixties, she may have a twinge in that elbow if the weather's changing, but apart from that, she'll be good as new in a few weeks. We'll keep her here for a couple of days to make sure there's no infection and her elbow is healing the way it should. You'll have her back home in no time."

"Can I see her?" Mieka asked.

"Better than that," Dr. Kelly said. "An orderly's bringing in a reclining chair and some bedding, so you can sleep in Lena's room."

Mieka slumped with relief. "I was so scared," she said.

"Occupational hazard of being a parent." Dr. Kelly said crisply, then his professional manner softened. "My wife and I have four sons. We're not strangers to the ER. Kids take chances. Sometimes it seems like a miracle that any kid makes it to high school. And Mieka, speaking of high school, that night at Luther when I was paired with you for grad, I thought I was the luckiest guy on earth. Kelly/Kilbourn – talk about alphabetical Fate."

"And here we are again," Mieka said. "Now it's my turn to feel like the luckiest person on earth." She extended her hand. "Thank you."

Dr. Kelly took it. "I'll see you when I make rounds in the morning."

Mieka called Zack with the news. After she'd talked to Madeleine, Mieka handed the phone to me. "How are you doing?" he said.

"Fine, now that we know Lena's all right. I'm just going to peek into her room to reassure myself, then I'll come home."

After I handed the phone back, I turned to Brock. "I guess we can all call it a night."

Mieka turned to him. "Thanks for being here, Brock – and I'm really sorry about Riel. This can't have been the way you wanted to spend the evening."

"I didn't have any other plans," Brock said.

We all walked down to Lena's room. She was still sleeping, and she had a Day-Glo pink cast from above her elbow to her wrist. I kissed her forehead, then hugged Mieka hard. I turned to Brock. "I might as well take Mieka's car and drop you off at your place."

"Fine with me," Brock said.

Brock led me to Mieka's car in the parking lot and handed me the keys. I unlocked the doors. "Is your car still at Lawyers' Bay?"

"For the time being," he said, settling into his seat. "Delia Wainberg's going to drive it back to the city."

I started Mieka's old Volvo. "So where do you live?"

"Broad Street – in the Warehouse District."

"So we're neighbours," I said. "So what do you think of The Village – or what will someday be The Village?"

"It's going to be good for everybody. Let's face it, ours is not a safe neighbourhood. I weigh 260, but when I run after dark, I'm relieved to get home. And the plans for The Village are exciting. The idea of a well-designed community where a fair percentage of houses are within the reach of low-income families is long past due, and I'm impressed with the training programs Racette-Hunter is putting into place. Building a city within a city is going to take a lot of workers. If North Central can supply them, we can change everything."

"You sound like Zack," I said.

"He and I spent a lot of time talking over the weekend. Zack is very persuasive."

"Did he persuade you to work full-time for Racette-Hunter?

"I'm giving it serious thought," Brock said.

When I got home, Zack had the fire going and a bottle of Old Pulteney single malt and two glasses waiting on the coffee table in front of the fireplace.

"I see we're going first class tonight."

"Lena's surgery went well. We have reason to celebrate."

"I know we do," I said. "I'm just going to run upstairs and see if the girls are still awake, and then I'll be back to curl up with you and the Old Pulteney."

A weekend of fresh air had worked its magic. Despite the traumatic event on the rink, the girls were both asleep, but there was a little pile of tissue on Madeleine's pillow. She'd been crying, and her small hand rested on the pulse in Taylor's neck – reassurance that she wasn't alone. I adjusted their covers, kissed them both, and went downstairs.

Zack had our drinks poured. He handed me my glass and took his own. I raised mine. "To Dr. Mike Kelly."

"I'll drink to that," Zack said. "By the way, when you were upstairs, I called Mieka and volunteered to take the first shift tomorrow."

"You're a good guy."

"No, just a guy who's very thankful that everything turned out all right. When you told me that Lena had been hurt, I was as scared as I've ever been in my life."

"Sir Francis Bacon said, 'He that hath a wife and children hath given hostages to fortune.'"

"Sir Francis was right. Before I met you, I wasn't afraid of anything." Zack sipped his Scotch meditatively. "Probably because I didn't have anything to lose."

"Do you ever long for the old carefree days?"

Zack took a last pull on his Scotch. "Nope. Not for a single second."

CHAPTER

8

The plans for the next morning had the precision of a military operation. After breakfast, Madeleine and I would stop by the hospital to see Lena. Remembrance Day is a stat holiday in Saskatchewan, so the schools were closed. Madeleine would be able to spend a good part of the day with her sister, and Zack and I could give Mieka a chance to go home, shower, change, and then drive over to April's Place and make sure everything was on target for the grand opening. Zack would come to the hospital after his donor meeting. At that point, Mieka would join us and we'd take the rest from there.

Like most well-laid plans, ours went awry. Zack had already left and Madeleine and I were just going out the door when Lauren Treadgold called. She wanted to talk to Zack, and there was an unsettling edge of hysteria in her voice. When I explained that our granddaughter was in the hospital, Lauren was dismissive. "I hope she gets well soon. Look, Zack has to get Vince to talk to me. It's urgent. He won't take my calls. Zack has to explain—"

I cut her off. "Lauren, I don't mean to be rude, but Lena's

accident is about all we can deal with at the moment. Zack and I have done what we could to help you and Vince, but right now Lena has to be our priority."

"Look, let me come over, just for five minutes. You'll understand then," she said. Her voice was ragged. "This isn't just about Vince and me any more. Something's happened that could affect the Racette-Hunter project."

"All right," I said. "I was just on my way out the door. Could you come over now?"

"I'll be right there," she said.

After I got Madeleine settled with a book upstairs in Taylor's room, I came down to wait for Lauren. She arrived in less than fifteen minutes. She was wearing a form-fitting red wool coat, a black cashmere scarf, and knee-high leather boots with six-inch heels. As always, Lauren's makeup and hair were immaculate, but even the most skilful application of concealer couldn't hide the bruising around her eye. When Willie and Pantera came to check her out, Lauren patted them absently. Then, still wearing her coat and boots, she followed me into the living room and sat on the couch.

"Have you opened your e-mail this morning?" Lauren asked.

"No," I said. "With Lena in the hospital, it's been a little busy around here."

"So you haven't seen the video," she said. "It was sent to every member of the Racette-Hunter working team. I'm amazed no one has called to ask me to resign yet."

"Lauren, I can't imagine what kind of video—"

"Just take a look."

I went to our room and got my laptop. When I came back, Lauren patted the place beside her on the couch and I balanced the laptop on my knees and opened my e-mail. I scrolled down the list of senders and found only one unfamiliar name: Supporters of Racette-Hunter. The subject line was "Serving the Community?" There was no message, only an attachment. I opened it and watched for a few seconds. It began with a close-up of a man's erect penis. The camera travelled slowly up his body, lingering on his navel and nipples. I was hoping that when I saw the face it would not be one I recognized. But of course the man was Julian. He was sleepy-eyed and incredibly erotic. He reached up languidly, took the camera, and began filming Lauren, starting with her genitals, circling her breasts, finishing with a close-up of her mouth as she bent, laughing softly, to fellate him.

"Do you think Julian sent this to the members of the working team?" I said.

Her headshake was vehement. "No. Not a chance. Julian wanted me to erase it as soon as we were finished."

"Well, if Julian didn't, who else would have had access to your camera?"

Lauren's lovely face was knifed with pain. "It must have been Vince," she said. "I don't remember where I left the camera. But if Vince found it, he would have wanted to see what was on it."

"That doesn't make any sense," I said. "Why would Vince want people to see you having sex with another man? He was devastated when he found out."

"Maybe," Lauren said wearily, "but from the moment he walked into that bedroom, it was game on. Vince caught me having sex with Julian. Point for him. Vince punched me. Point for me." Her fingers touched her cheekbone. "Vince sends people whom I respect a sex video of Julian and me, and thus scores the winning point. Now anyone who looks at my face will think I got what I deserved. My whole life is crumbling," she said. "Zack has to convince Vince to talk to me."

"Are you hoping for a reconciliation?" I said.

"No. I only want to be with Julian. He's the only man I've ever loved. The night of my birthday party at the club, I knew that Julian was my last chance. I'm forty-five years old."

"Lauren, numbers are just numbers. I'm fifty-seven. The best years of my life have been since Zack and I met. I was fifty-four then."

"And Zack was rich," Lauren said. "Don't leave that particular factor out of your equation. Julian will never earn the kind of money Zack and Vince do. I need Vince to take care of me the way I've been taking care of him."

"I don't understand," I said.

"And I can't explain," Lauren said. "Zack *has* to convince Vince to talk to me."

"Okay. I'll talk to him. That's all I can do," I said.

I walked Lauren to the elevator. She was a wan figure. I searched for words of comfort. "Lauren, this will pass," I said. "You're in for a couple of weeks of misery, but after that people move on to their own concerns. Nothing lasts forever."

"Let's hope," she said, but she didn't sound convinced.

When I went back inside to get Madeleine, I noticed that Lauren had left behind her scarf. I picked it up and folded it. The scent of her perfume clung to the cashmere. Lauren was a woman who had everything and nothing. I was worried about her and I was grateful she'd left her scarf behind. Returning it would give me an excuse to check up on her later in the day.

When Madeleine and I arrived in Lena's hospital room, Zack was already there, in full flourish, reading *Charlotte's Web*. He had an actor's voice, large and warm, and he brought genuine feeling to Fern Arable's plea that her father spare the life of the runt of the piglet litter.

Zack greeted us with mock formality. "We have visitors, Lena," he said. "We'll have to resume our story later."

Lena's face pinched with concern. "Does Fern's father kill the piglet?"

"The piglet lives," Zack said.

Lena beamed. "Cool." Her cast looked very large and she looked very small, but her colour was good, and she was obviously excited to see her sister. "I've been thinking. Tomorrow when you take Maddy to school, can you go to my classroom and tell Madame LePage and everyone in my class what happened to me? They'll probably want to make me a giant card. That's what we did when Emily H. broke her leg."

"I'll tell them." Madeleine went to her sister and touched the cast tentatively. "Does your arm hurt?"

"Sometimes. The doctor says it'll hurt less every day and I'll be doing cartwheels by summer." She looked into her sister's face. "Maddy, could you get into bed with me?"

Madeleine climbed up next to her sister. "You can keep reading now, Granddad," Lena said contentedly. And so, side by side, the girls listened as Zack read the story of Wilbur the pig and his amazing journey. When Lena's eyes grew heavy, she wriggled farther under the covers and fell asleep. Madeleine slid out of bed. "Let's go back to the condo for a while," I said. "Your sister needs her rest. We can come back later."

"Okay," Madeleine whispered, and she picked up her coat.

"Granddad and I need to talk for a minute," I said. "We'll just be out in the hall."

Zack followed me into the corridor. "What's up?"

"Lauren Treadgold paid me a visit just before Madeleine and I left for the hospital."

"Did she tell you about the video of her getting it off with Julian?"

"We watched it together on my laptop."

"That must have been grim."

"It gets worse," I said. "I asked Lauren about the chance of reconciliation. She was adamant. She's in love with Julian."

"He's, what? Nineteen."

"Yes, nineteen – young enough to be Lauren's son. Zack, the day we had lunch Celeste told me that Julian is just one of many very young men with whom Lauren has been involved. Celeste wanted me to tell you so that Vince would have leverage when the time came to discuss the terms of the divorce."

"And you decided to wait so we could have a nice weekend."

"Yes," I said. "But now it's time to face facts. According to Lauren, Julian is the only man she's ever loved, and she's determined to have a life with him. This morning Lauren was frank about the fact that she's going to need a very generous settlement from Vince to subsidize her life with Julian."

"Jesus Christ," Zack said. "Vince is a fair guy, and I know he's planning to offer Lauren a decent settlement, but if she's expecting a bundle she's not going to get it. Especially now that the video of her and Julian having sex is making the rounds."

I shook my head. "Lauren seems to think she has a secret weapon. She's desperate to talk to Vince. She said, and I quote, 'I need Vince to take care of me the way I've been taking care of him.'"

"Meaning?"

"Lauren said she couldn't tell me. Zack, I promised her I'd ask you to have Vince get in touch with her."

"I can do that," Zack said.

Lena was awake when we went back into the room. "Maddy's going to stay with me, Mimi."

"That's good. Now I'm going back to the condo, is there anything I can bring for any of you?"

Zack slapped his forehead. "Margot called. She has a present for Lena."

"And, Mimi, we were wondering if you could please bring us some of those banana milkshakes you make."

"I'm partial to those milkshakes, too," Zack said.

"Duly noted," I said.

Margot met me at the door with a gift bag. "This is a regift. Lena will understand. Make sure you tell her it's for keeps."

"Gotcha," I said.

"I guess you heard the latest about Lauren Treadgold."

"She came to see me this morning."

"How's she doing?"

"About as well as could be expected."

"Between *BlueBoy21* and Lauren's home movie, there's not much of Julian Zentner we haven't seen," Margot said dryly.

"Agreed," I said. "But I have a feeling that there's a lot about Julian that we still don't know."

Margot sighed. "Poor Lauren. My mother used to say that there are people who are like broken glass. Get close to them and prepare to bleed. It seems Lauren is in that category. Tell Lena I'll come by and see her tonight."

"No, you won't," I said. "Hospitals are full of nasty bugs. Wait till Lena's home and you two can visit to your heart's content."

Margot yawned. "Sold. I am pretty tired these days. Jo, I have a huge favour to ask. Could you and Zack handle this business with Lauren? I think she's savvy enough to distance herself from the project for a while, but someone should talk to the other members of the team and make sure nobody does anything indiscreet with the video."

"Of course," I said. "We'll keep you posted."

—

It was close to eleven when I arrived at the hospital carrying a large thermos of banana milkshake, four thermal glasses, and a pretty gift bag containing Lena's surprise from Margot.

I handed Lena the bag. "So how's everybody doing?"

"Good," Lena said. "Except, Maddy, can you help me with my present? This cast is heavy." Maddy took the gift bag, dug through the tissue, and pulled out the plainest doll I'd ever seen.

Lena was beaming. "That's Poor Pitiful Pearl. She was Margot's doll when she was little."

"Well, now she's all yours. Margot said to make sure you knew that Poor Pitiful Pearl is yours for keeps."

Mieka had e-mailed Lena's teacher to let her know what had happened and Mme LePage had replied with a list of the assignments her class would be completing during the week ahead. After the milkshakes were finished, Zack began organizing the assignments. Math was first. When Madeleine was in Grade One, Zack had read the Ministry of Education's curriculum goals. The primary goal was to make every student believe he or she was capable of making sense of mathematics. Zack taught Madeleine how to play blackjack, and she aced Grade One math.

Math was Zack's strong suit and no one could argue with success. Zack explained the rules of blackjack to Lena, welcomed me to the game, and the four of us began to play.

We played for Cheerios. Madeleine was good with cards and Lena was a quick study. Zack and I both lost Cheerios bigtime, but Zack was gracious in defeat, commending the girls on their brilliance and warning me to be wary of card sharks.

Lena decided it was time for a real nap, so I tucked her in with Pearl and Madeleine, and Zack and I moved to the corner of the room where we could talk. "Vince stopped by while you were at the condo. He hadn't seen the video, and he didn't want to see it. However, he was curious about who could have, and would have, sent it out."

"Lauren believes Vince did," I said. "She thinks Vince was redressing the balance, making himself the injured party."

Zack scowled. "Vince doesn't think like that. Besides, he seems to be handling the situation with Lauren well. He told me his AA sponsor reminded him to hang on to the line about acceptance in the Serenity Prayer."

"'God grand me the serenity to accept the things I cannot change,'" I said.

"That's the one," Zack said. "Vince seems to have filed Lauren's infidelity under the category of things he cannot change. He had no reason to send around that video."

"Julian did," I said. "This morning Lauren told me that she has to get a substantial settlement from Vince to subsidize her life with Julian."

"And Julian doesn't want to share his life with Lauren?"

"No. According to Celeste, he wants to end the affair. I imagine that video strengthens Vince's hand when it comes to discussing alimony."

"It does indeed," Zack said. "But if Vince pays minimal alimony and Julian slips from Lauren's clutches, you and I will have a problem."

"Julian will be free to pursue Taylor," I said. "And we can't let that happen."

"No, we can't. But let's take it one step at a time. I called Vince and told him Lauren was desperate to talk to him. He said he'd think about it. Vince is a proud guy. He's not going to jump just because Lauren tells him to."

"I realize that she's brought a great deal of this misery on herself, but I feel sorry for her. Lauren left her scarf at our place this morning. I was thinking that I'd take it to her.

Whether Vince responded to her request or not, she might be glad to have someone to talk to."

Zack rubbed the back of his neck. Instinctively, I moved behind him to measure the tension there. His muscles were like rocks. "Tonight's a long-swim, mutual-massage night," I said.

Zack covered my hand with his. "How did we manage to catch the brass ring?"

"I don't know," I said. "But I never stop being grateful."

At noon, Mieka arrived with sandwiches and drinks and we had a picnic. She volunteered to take the afternoon shift, but Zack said that he and the girls were at a pivotal point in *Charlotte's Web* and besides he was growing fond of Poor Pitiful Pearl. After Mieka left, I kicked back in the recliner, put unfaithful wives and troubled young men out of my mind, and listened to the rain and my husband's deep, lulling voice. It wasn't long before I drifted off.

I left the hospital around three-thirty. We were having Madeleine's favourite macaroni and cheese for dinner, and the casserole was already thawing in the fridge. There was a neighbourhood grocery store not far from the Treadgolds that sold vegetables and fruit that were truly fresh, and I planned to shop before I went to Lauren's. I had tried calling her from Lakeview Fine Foods to tell her I was coming by with her scarf, but when there was no answer, I decided to take my chances, hoping I wouldn't walk into an uncomfortable scene between her and Vince.

The rain had grown heavy enough to slow traffic on Albert Street. By the time I approached the Treadgolds I was barely moving. When I glanced towards their large, modern house, I knew immediately that there was a problem. The front gate was wide open. So was the door. I pulled over and began walking towards the open gate. At that moment, the salukis streaked out of the house and headed for freedom. I stepped up my pace and made it into the yard just in time to close the gate behind me. "Take it easy," I said to the dogs. "Slow down. You can have a run, but you're not going anywhere."

I walked up the steps and through the open door into the entranceway. When I called Lauren's name, there was no response. I kicked off my boots and walked into what realtors would call "the great room." It was a cold and imposing space: two stories high with a cathedral ceiling. The colour scheme was stark and dramatic: black and white with accents of red. The fireplace and the floor tiles were black marble. Lauren was lying on the hearth. *BlueBoy21* was propped against the mantle, so close to Lauren that if she had been alive, she could have touched it. Her head was haloed with blood. I knelt beside her and felt for a pulse. I wasn't surprised when there was none.

I took out my cell. My hands were trembling so badly that I dropped the phone. When I picked it up, I dialled 911. Then I called Zack, told him that Lauren was dead, and he needed to get hold of Vince and break the news. Zack was adamant about coming to meet me. I was equally adamant about him staying at the hospital. Vince needed him, and there was nothing he could do at the Treadgolds. The weather had turned ugly. Driving conditions were terrible, and the thought of Zack trying to navigate his chair through the freezing rain scared me. After I finally convinced him to stay at the hospital, I went to the doorway to wait.

The EMT crew was first through the gate, followed closely by two young police officers. "We had a report that a woman at this address has been assaulted," one of them said.

I stood aside. "She's in the living room," I said. "I found the body."

"And your name is . . . ?"

"Joanne Shreve."

"Stay where you are, Joanne," the young cop said. "We'll have questions."

Another squad car pulled up. The officer who'd asked my name came out of the house, spoke to the officers who'd just arrived, then walked over to me. "We've called Animal Control to get the dogs," he said. "They can't go back inside. It's a crime scene. Inspector Haczkewicz from Major Crimes is on her way. She'll want to talk to you about your connection with the dead woman."

It didn't take Debbie Haczkewicz long to show up. Despite her closeness to Zack, when she was on the job, Debbie was all cop. Nonetheless, when she spotted me there was real concern in her eyes. "Are you all right, Joanne?" she said.

"I will be," I said.

"Good. I have your contact information on file, so why don't we sit in my car where it's quiet and you can tell me what happened here."

When we got into Debbie's car, she sighed. "Ah, that's better," she said. "We're dry, we're warm, and nobody's going to interrupt us."

Debbie listened without comment as I explained what I'd found when I walked into the living room of the Treadgold house.

"Were you and Lauren Treadgold close?" she asked.

"No," I said.

Debbie's gaze was level. "Yet you stopped by her house. Had she invited you over?"

"No. Lauren called this morning and asked if she could come by our condo. She was upset and she wanted to talk. When she left, she forgot her scarf. I was concerned about her, and returning the scarf seemed like a reasonable excuse for checking up on her."

"What was Ms. Treadgold upset about?"

"A sex video that someone had e-mailed to the Racette-Hunter working team. Lauren and Vince Treadgold were both members of the team. It was of Lauren with Julian Zentner, the young man who modelled for the painting that's propped up against the mantle, near Lauren's body."

"Curiouser and curiouser," Debbie said evenly. She finished the entry in her notebook and marked it with a star. "Joanne, could you come back inside with me for a few minutes. We'll need a formal identification of the body so we can get in touch with Ms. Treadgold's next of kin."

As I walked with Debbie towards the house, my legs were leaden. More police had arrived. All were wearing their slickers. Debbie and I were pushed through the front door by a powerful wave of yellow Gore-Tex.

Everyone's attention was centred on the area in front of the fireplace. The police were photographing the body from every angle, bagging and labelling evidence, dusting for fingerprints. As they changed positions, I caught glimpses of Lauren's body on the floor. She, too, was in yellow – the yellow Mondrian-patterned tunic she'd worn the morning of our meeting after the art auction. Bloody pawprints patterned the black marble tiles.

It took an effort of will to look down again at the woman on the floor. "That's Lauren Treadgold," I said, then looked quickly away.

Debbie led me to the edge of the area where the police were working and pointed out a bloodied rock on the marble tile near Lauren's head. "That appears to be the murder weapon," Debbie said. She pointed to a large glass bowl filled with rocks not far from the fireplace. "We can't be certain, of course, but logic would suggest that the rock came from that bowl."

"Lauren's stepdaughter told me that Lauren brought home rocks from all the places where she and Vince vacationed,"

I said. "Apparently, Lauren wrote the rock's origin on each rock. If the rock that killed Lauren has a place name on it, I guess you can assume it was one Lauren brought back as a souvenir."

"That's useful, Joanne. Does anything else strike you as noteworthy?"

"The position of the painting," I said. "I doubt very much that Lauren would have placed the painting of Julian against the mantle. She was hoping to speak to her husband today."

Debbie pounced. "About what?"

"I don't know," I said.

"So many questions," Debbie said. "For example, why would Vincent Treadgold buy a painting of his wife's naked lover in the first place?"

"It's complicated." I turned so that Debbie and I were facing each other. "Debbie, I'd better not say anything more until Zack's with me."

Debbie's blue eyes bored into me. Finally, she realized that I wasn't about to be swayed. "All right," she said.

"May I go now?"

"Of course." She walked me to the door, and for a moment we stood together gazing out at the pounding rain. "No matter how often I see cruelty like this, it still makes me furious," she said.

"That's why you're good at your job," I said.

CHAPTER

9

The streets were a skating rink. By the time I got into the hospital parking lot, my already frayed nerves were raw. I was cold, wet, and miserable.

Zack was waiting in the corridor outside Lena's room. He held out his arms to embrace me.

"I'm soaked through," I said.

"I don't care," he said. He folded me into his arms. "I'm so sorry you had to go through this. Do you want to talk about it?"

"Is someone with Lena and Madeleine?"

"Mieka's in there playing Crazy Eights with them. What's the situation?"

"Lauren was murdered. Someone hit her skull with a rock and placed *BlueBoy21* near her body."

"Oh, Jesus."

"Debbie was there. Zack, I told her that Julian was Lauren's lover. I figured she'd find out anyway, and I thought it was best to be open about what we knew."

"But not too open."

"No, when Debbie started asking me about why Vince purchased the painting of his wife's naked lover, I told her I couldn't say anything more until I was with you."

"Smart call. But Debbie's shrewd, she'll see the juxtaposition of Lauren's body and the painting of Julian as a message from the murderer."

"I killed her because of this boy," I said.

"And we know where that arrow points," Zack said.

"Straight at Vince."

"Right," Zack said. "But we could catch a break. The police *could* discover evidence of forced entry or theft," Zack said. "Then they'd have to shift their focus to their database and start hauling suspects in until they find the murderer."

"And you could start believing in Santa Claus again," I said. "Zack, I don't think the story's going to play out that way. The door to the Treadgolds' house was wide open, and except for the area where Lauren was found, the living room appeared to be in order. Nothing was overturned or broken."

"Okay," Zack said. "For the time being we'll rule out 'person or persons unknown.' What about Celeste? I know you like her, but Celeste has a short fuse and her relationship with Lauren *was* turbulent."

"Celeste is a troubled young woman who acted impulsively and recklessly." I said. "But you're the one who says we're all better than the worst thing we do. That's certainly true of Celeste. I don't know her well, but I do know that she's a better person than the text message to her father would indicate. As soon as Celeste realized the consequences of what she had done, she accepted responsibility and sought to make amends."

"And that leaves Julian," Zack said. "The one person neither of us wants to consider. But no matter how we rearrange the cards, Julian is at the centre of this. Much as we hate it, that means Taylor is involved. Lauren was determined to hold on to Julian, but he wanted something more. If Lauren threatened to go to Taylor, Julian might have been desperate enough to kill Lauren."

Zack made a fist and punched the palm of his other hand. "The idea of Taylor being connected with this in any way makes me sick."

"I don't want Taylor anywhere near this mess either," I said. "But we have to tell her about Julian's involvement. She won't make it easy. Taylor's loyal. She'll find excuses for him."

Zack turned his chair towards Lena's room. "Let's go home. You need to get out of those wet clothes and into a hot shower. After that, we'll talk to Taylor."

"What about Vince?" I said. "Shouldn't you be with him when the police tell him that Lauren's been murdered?"

"I should be with him, but I can't find him. I'm hoping that means the cops can't find him either. I've been leaving messages, but so far no response."

"In that case, let's say goodbye to Mieka and the girls and head for home. Vince has your cell number."

Vince called just as Zack and I were waiting for the elevator. When he broke the connection, Zack turned to me. "Vince didn't mention Lauren, so I'm guessing the police haven't talked to him. I'm going to meet him in the doctors' lounge. I can be there in two minutes. Jo, I may be a while. You know I want to go home with you and towel you off after your shower, but Vince can't afford a misstep."

"I'll be fine," I said. "Taylor's probably up in her studio painting; Margot's right across the hall, and I think I can figure out the towelling-off thing."

Taylor had left a note on the table. She and Declan had gone to a movie. She'd be back to help with dinner. A long hot shower and dry clothing helped me feel human again, and I'd just made tea when Taylor walked through the door. I poured us both a cup, then we sat at the butcher-block table and I told her about Lauren Treadgold's death. Taylor hadn't known Lauren well. She was saddened, but her concern shifted quickly to me and to Julian. I assured her that I was fine, but that the police would probably be interested in Julian.

Taylor's face was pinched with concern "Why would they want to talk to Julian?"

There were a dozen reasons, and my mind raced through them all. Finally, I settled on the most innocuous. "Lauren and Julian were friends," I said finally.

"Has anyone told him what happened?"

"I don't know," I said.

"I'm going to call him," Taylor said.

When she went up to her room I finished my tea. The weight of the day's events pressed down on me. I wanted nothing more than to crawl into bed with Zack and pull the covers over our heads, but it seemed escape was not an option.

Taylor was sombre when she came downstairs. I was still sitting at the table and she took the stool opposite mine. "Julian's not doing very well," she said. "I guess he really cared about Lauren Treadgold. He phoned Kaye to see if he could go over to her place, but she has a migraine. I don't think Julian should be alone." She paused. "I asked him to come here for supper. I hope that's okay."

My heart sank. I'd counted on Zack, Taylor, Madeleine, and me sharing a quiet meal and then, after Madeleine was asleep, having a serious talk with Taylor. I was not eager to break bread with Julian. But Taylor's impulse had been a generous one, and I was afraid that saying no might push her into spending the evening with him rather than with us. "Sure," I said, trying to mean it. "The dogs need a run, and I need some air. I won't be long."

"I'll put the mac and cheese in the oven," Taylor said. "350, right?"

"Right," I said.

"I could make a salad."

"A salad would be nice," I said. "Thanks." I put the dogs on their leashes and headed out. As I waited for the elevator my spirits sagged. The image of the blood pooling around Lauren's head was sharp-edged. I had hoped that if I moved fast enough, I might keep that image from dominating my thoughts. But Julian's presence at the dinner table would bring Lauren into our home. It was not an auspicious beginning to the evening.

When Zack and Madeleine arrived, Zack was clearly exhausted. Taylor took one look at her dad and scooped up Madeleine. "Why don't you guys kick back and relax before dinner. Madeleine and I will go upstairs and watch some TV."

I touched one of the deep creases that bracketed Zack's mouth like parentheses. "I think I hear a martini calling," I said.

Zack grinned. "Hey, a martini and mac and cheese. The day just started looking better."

"Don't break out the balloons and confetti yet," I said. "Julian is joining us for dinner."

"You're kidding."

"No. Taylor said he was upset and so she invited him for dinner. Would it help if I told you I'll make the martinis doubles?"

"It would be a start," Zack said.

For all of us, Zack's health was a huge concern, but it was one about which we seldom talked. Before Zack and I were married, we met with Zack's family physician. Henry Chan held nothing back in laying out the problems that come with paraplegia, and the list was daunting: Paraplegia compromises everything, including the working of internal organs, the blood's ability to flow without clotting, and the skin's ability to heal. As a paraplegic, Zack was vulnerable to respiratory ailments, renal failure, pulmonary embolisms, and septicemia. As Henry Chan explained the problems, Zack's eyes never left my face. When Henry Chan was finished, I took Zack's hand. "We're all going to die of something," I said. "And I want to die married to you."

My bravado didn't preclude worrying. I worried about every detail of Zack's life and I worried about letting him know how much I worried. As a trial lawyer, his hours and stress level were horrific. My hope when he volunteered for the Racette-Hunter project was that, although he would be working hard, there would be limits, and Zack would be able to follow the regimen for a healthy life. Until recently, we'd done just that.

Our building had both an outdoor and an indoor pool, and we swam regularly. Zack and I massaged each other daily, so I could check for pressure sores that might prove problematic. We exercised, ate healthily, and established a sane sleep pattern. Every day, I counted my blessings, but as I looked at Zack that night I knew that, for a while at least, all bets were off.

We took our drinks into the living room. Zack regarded his martini thoughtfully. "What do we drink to on a day like this?"

I lifted my glass. "How about drinking to no more days like this," I said.

"Perfect," Zack said. He sipped his martini.

"Vince and I had a chance for a quick talk before Debbie called asking if I had any idea where he was. As you know, I never lie to the cops."

"I know you never lie to Debbie," I said.

"Not much gets by you, does it?" Zack said. "Anyway,

the cops were Johnny-on-the-spot, so Vince and I didn't have much time alone. But we caught one break. The cops weren't there when I told him about Lauren, and that was lucky because I wouldn't have wanted the police to have heard Vince's reaction."

"How did he react?"

"At first he didn't react at all. I thought maybe he hadn't processed the news. So I tried again. I told him that Lauren had died from a blow to the head and that from what I'd heard, she would have died quickly, and she wouldn't have suffered. When he heard that, Vince gave me a blank look and said, 'She's always been lucky.'"

"Holy mackerel."

"Exactly," Zack said. "At that point, Debbie and another cop showed up. Being confronted by the police seemed to snap Vince out of his trance. Suddenly he became very voluble."

"That doesn't sound good."

"It wasn't. I hadn't had time to prep Vince, but I did manage to tell him to keep his mouth shut. He chose not to heed my wise counsel and volunteered a veritable shitload of information about the problems in his marriage."

"It's probably best Vince told the truth." I said. "The police won't have to dig very hard to discover that the Treadgolds' relationship was a troubled one."

"In retrospect, I have to agree, but sitting there, watching Vince open up to the cops was scary."

"What did he say?"

"He filled them in on the meeting he and Lauren had this afternoon."

"So he did heed Lauren's plea to talk?"

"He did," Zack said. "According to Vince, Lauren was very emotional, but they were civil until Vince told Lauren that given the video and other proof of her affair, he was going to consult a divorce lawyer. Vince told Lauren she could have the house, but there'd be minimal alimony. Apparently, Lauren flew into a rage. Vince didn't want the situation to get out of hand, so he went upstairs, packed a suitcase, and took off."

"He's leaving something out," I said.

Zack frowned, then the penny dropped. "All that stuff Lauren said about Vince owing her because she'd taken care of him. Shit. I must be losing it." He took out his cell. "Better late than never," he said. "I don't want that hanging over my head."

When his call went straight to voicemail, Zack rubbed his eyes. "I'll call him after dinner. Incidentally, Vince doesn't have an alibi. As soon as I told him about the video this morning, he booked off at the hospital and went to the Senator. He didn't have to check in because apparently he'd never checked out. He showered and met Lauren as planned at 2:15. He said he left around 2:45. He came back to his room at the Senator, made himself coffee, and read a medical journal until 4:15, when he went back to the hospital."

"How did Debbie react to Vince's story?"

"You know Debbie. She doesn't reveal much. She gave Vince the usual warning about staying in town, and after she left, I gave him the usual warning about not talking to the cops without me by his side, and here I am."

"So you're going to represent Vince?"

"It may not come to that, Jo."

"But if it does, you will."

"I'm his closest friend, remember?"

"I remember."

Lauren Treadgold's murder was going to be a red meat case, and I could see the old fire in Zack's eyes. He leaned towards me. "I won't overdo it," he said.

"I'm going to hold you to that."

At that point the buzzer from downstairs sounded. Taylor flew down the stairs and buzzed Julian in. The evening was underway.

Julian was dressed like a nineteen-year-old having dinner with his girl's parents: leather dress shoes, dark blue jeans, a light-blue-striped cotton dress shirt, and a fawn sport jacket. He'd brought a bottle of wine, which he handed to Zack. The perfect beau, but the perfect beau had been the lover of a married woman, and now that woman had been brutally murdered. Celeste Treadgold's assessment of Julian flashed through my mind. "He can be whoever he needs to be to make the situation work for him."

I didn't trust this boyishly handsome shapeshifter, but Taylor's expression was anxious, and her eyes were filled with hope. Like Julian, I had a vested interest in making the situation work. I went to him and in a voice soft with sympathy said, "How are you doing?"

"Not great," he said. "But better. Thanks for the invitation to dinner. I wasn't looking forward to spending the evening alone."

He held out his hand to Zack. "And thank you, sir."

Zack's eyebrows rose, but he shook Julian's hand manfully. "You're welcome," he said.

Dinner wasn't as awkward as it might have been. Taylor lit the candles, and as always, we ate family-style with the casserole and the salad in the middle of the table and everyone helping themselves. Noticing that the adults were restrained, Madeleine had apparently decided to carry the conversational ball for all of us.

Between forkfuls of macaroni, she filled us in on highlights of life at St. Pius XII. Last week the parents of a boy in Grade Six had won a house in the Hospital Sweepstakes. On Friday, Rome and Paris, identical twins in Grade Two, had switched classrooms and neither of their teachers caught on until lunchtime. Two girls in Grade Eight had dyed each other's hair green. "And," she said before digging into her second helping of macaroni and cheese, "we have a new boy in our class. He's really shy. He doesn't say anything at all."

"It's not easy to change schools in November," I said. "Kids have already found their groups."

"Your grandmother's right, Madeleine," Julian said. "When I was a kid we moved a lot. I was always starting at a new school."

"We don't know very much about you, Julian." Zack's tone, low and insistent, was the tone he used in court with a slippery witness. "Taylor wanted us to get to know you, so why don't you tell us about yourself."

"There's not much to tell," Julian said. "I don't remember my mother. She took off when I was a baby. I guess she couldn't stand my father. I couldn't stand him either, but when you're a kid you don't have many options." There was something practised about Julian's recital of the facts that made me uneasy. "My father and I moved around a lot. He was a plumber – good at his job, but he had lot of crazy religious ideas and he was always getting fired. That's about it, except I did well at school, and when I was fifteen, my Grade Ten English teacher asked my father if I could move in with her. He said yes, so I finished high school in La Ronge."

"So this teacher was like a parent to you," Zack said.

Julian hesitated before answering. When he spoke it was obvious he was choosing his words with care. "Not exactly," he said. "She gave me a nice place to live. She fed me. She bought me clothes. She helped me with my schoolwork."

"And she expected nothing in return?"

"No, she had expectations," Julian said softly, "and they were met. Everything comes with a price. You know that, Zack."

There was an edge in Julian's voice, and Taylor jumped in to change the direction of the conversation. "Julian, tell Dad and Joanne about how important your drawing was to you when you were growing up."

"It pretty much saved me," Julian said. "I never seemed to have time to make friends, but I liked to draw and that was always enough."

Taylor touched Julian's arm. "Making art has always been enough for me, too," she said.

A shadow crossed Julian's face. "The art you make is incredible," he said. "The art I made was a joke. At the end of term last year I took my entire portfolio to the dump."

Taylor eyes were still fixed on Julian. "You never told me that," she said. "I'm sorry."

"Don't be," he said. "Nothing of value was lost."

In the flickering candlelight the intimacy between our daughter and Julian was unmistakable. Zack felt the connection, too. He leaned forward, blew out the candles, and began piling his dishes. "Great meal, Jo," he said. "And, Taylor, your salad was dynamite." When Zack wheeled over to the sink and began rinsing his plate and cutlery, we all followed suit.

And with that, mercifully, dinner was over.

When I went upstairs to give Madeleine her bath, Taylor and Julian went into the living room and Zack left for Margot's. Lauren Treadgold's murder was a tragedy, but it was also a public relations disaster for Racette-Hunter and Zack wanted to make certain Margot didn't get blindsided.

It had been a long day. I had decided that Madeleine and I were ready for *Anne of Green Gables*, but as I read about Mrs. Rachel Lynde "sitting at her window, keeping a sharp eye on everything that passed from brooks and children up," my eyes grew heavy.

I awoke to Madeleine's gentle nudge. "Mimi, you're sleeping and we haven't even finished page one."

"I'm sorry, Maddy. Why don't you choose one of your books and read to me?" And so, listening to *Hide and Sneak*, I drifted off.

When I awoke, the house was silent and Madeleine was curled up beside me. I slid out of bed, tucked in my granddaughter, turned on the nightlight, and started downstairs.

When I reached the landing, I saw Julian and Taylor standing by the door. After Julian buttoned his jacket, Taylor reached up and adjusted his scarf. When he took her in his arms, I tensed. On more than one occasion, Taylor had told me that she felt sick when boys pawed at her, but she welcomed Julian's kiss. When the kiss was over, Julian and Taylor held each other, reluctant to part. Finally, they kissed again, and Julian left.

Taylor was smiling a private smile as she walked towards the stairs. The smile vanished when saw me on the landing.

"How long have you been standing there?" she said.

"Long enough," I said. "Taylor, we have to talk about Julian."

She came up the stairs slowly. "Not tonight. Please. Something really great just happened to me. Let me think about it for a while."

"We love you so much."

"I love you, too, but this has nothing to do with you and Dad. This is about me and Julian." Taylor's voice was both tender and defiant. "Can we just let this wait till I've had a chance to figure out what's happening?"

We were both tired and on the point of tears, but I couldn't walk away. "I'm sorry, Taylor, but there are things you need to know about Julian. Your father and I made a terrible mistake in hiring him as a model for your life study. We trusted Kaye's judgment, but Julian is not the boy we thought he was. He had an affair with Lauren Treadgold. And she paid him to have sex with her. Julian might even be implicated in her murder."

"Julian and I already talked about this," Taylor said tightly.

"When?"

"This afternoon when I called to tell him that Ms. Treadgold was dead. Julian knew everything would come out, and he wanted to make sure I understood the circumstances."

"What were the circumstances?"

"Ms. Treadgold was lonely. Dr. Treadgold was at the hospital all the time. When she met Julian at Diego's, she asked him to stay after his shift and have a drink. Julian felt sorry for her, and they . . . they had sex. It didn't mean anything to Julian. It was what kids call mercy sex. You have sex with a person because you feel sorry for them."

"Julian and Lauren were together for more than a month," I said.

"Julian stayed with her because he didn't want to hurt her."

"He took her money, Taylor."

"Julian doesn't earn that much at the restaurant. Ms. Treadgold wanted him to have nice things."

"And Julian paid for those nice things with his body. Everything comes with a price. That's what Julian said tonight at dinner, and he was willing to pay Lauren's price."

Taylor stepped past me on the stairs. "I'm not going to listen to this. Tonight Julian told me that he loves me. He said that we belong together. He had a serious fight with Ms. Treadgold because she taped them having sex and said she was going to send me the video. Julian says he'd do anything to keep me from being hurt, and I believe him."

When Taylor ran up the stairs to her room, I followed her. Madeleine was asleep in the Taylor's bed, so I took Taylor's arm and drew her out into the hall. My heart was pounding. "We've never gone to bed angry at each other," I said.

"I guess there's a first time for everything," Taylor said. She turned the door handle. "Jo, please wait until tomorrow to tell Dad about what just happened. He looked really tired tonight."

When Zack came back from Margot's, he came straight to our bedroom, where I'd been pretending to read a magazine.

"How did it go?" I said.

"Margot says we have to hire a public relations firm to handle this."

"It would be a waste of money," I said. "They'll just tell you to get out in front of the story. First thing tomorrow call a press conference. Explain what's happened. Be brief and be generous when you talk about Lauren's contribution to the Racette-Hunter Centre, send R-H's condolences to Lauren's family, and ask the press to respect them in this time of grief. Then get out of the room – no questions. Margot should do it. The press won't hound her. She's pregnant and sympathetic."

Zack rubbed the back of his neck. "Well, I'm neither pregnant nor sympathetic, but I'm the one on deck. As of this afternoon Margot is on enforced R & R. Her blood pressure is a little high, so her doctor says she has to take it easy until the baby comes. She's pretty well out of the game until Christmas."

"But she and the baby *are* okay?"

"They're fine. Margot says the doctor's just being careful because of her age and because this is the only baby she'll ever have."

"I'm glad Margot's doctor is being cautious," I said, "but

her absence will mean another hole in the Racette-Hunter working team. Zack, I don't want all the extra work to land on your lap."

"It's not going to," Zack said. "We've got Brock, Howard, Blake, and you and Ernest. Norine has some ideas about potential team members. I called her from Margot's and she's going to set up meetings with some of them tomorrow."

"I've got an idea, too," I said. "Why don't you come to bed?"

Minutes after his head hit the pillow, Zack was asleep. His breathing was deep and even, and I was glad I hadn't shared my burden of worry. There was trouble ahead, and at least one of us needed to get a good night's sleep.

The next morning after I came back from taking the dogs to the roof garden, I crawled back into bed with Zack. "We need to talk," I said. "Last night when I came down from getting Madeleine settled, Julian was leaving," I said. "He and Taylor were by the door. She was in his arms."

"So the vibes we picked up during dinner were for real," Zack said.

"Yes," I said. "Julian and Taylor were kissing and it was a serious kiss. I stayed on the landing until Julian left. Taylor saw me, and we quarrelled. I broached the subject of Julian's sexual relationship with Lauren. Taylor said the only reason Julian had sex with Lauren was because Lauren was lonely and he felt sorry for her."

"And Lauren felt sorry for Julian, so she gave him money."

"Something like that," I said. "He told her about the video and that he argued with Lauren because she was threatening to show it to Taylor."

Zack raised an eyebrow. "Julian's no dummy. Getting all the cards out on the table before we had a chance to talk to Taylor was a shrewd move. Jo, Why didn't you tell me about this last night?"

"Because Taylor asked me to wait until morning. She thought you looked tired at dinner."

Zack's face softened. "She is such a good kid."

"Agreed," I said. "But our good kid is facing a big adult problem."

"So what do we do?"

"Well, I know what we don't do," I said. "We don't come down hard on Taylor, and we don't forbid her to see Julian. From the moment I met Peter's first girlfriend, I knew she was trouble. She was manipulative and far, far too experienced for Peter, but I handled the situation badly, and Pete was so angry I almost lost him. I learned my lesson. No raised voices. No ultimatums."

Zack sighed. "So we just play it as it lays."

"Unless you can think of something better."

"It depends," Zack said. "Would you think I was a jerk if I got a private investigator to check Julian out?"

"No. I'd think you were a father who's looking out for his daughter. While your detective is checking out Julian's life, have him look into the story about the teacher in La Ronge."

I turned my pillow over and smoothed it. I'd had a restless night. Julian's brief biography at dinner had evoked my sympathy, but it had also frightened me. If his Grade Ten teacher had been the beginning of Julian's pattern of latching on to a woman who could give him what he needed, he was more damaged and perhaps more dangerous than we realized. "Another thing," I said. "After Taylor goes to school, I'm going to get in touch with Kaye Russell. I think she owes us some answers about Julian."

"You bet she does," Zack said, and his tone was caustic.

As soon as she heard us in the kitchen, Taylor came downstairs. She was barefoot and in her robe. She poured herself a glass of juice and joined us at the table. Her eyes were anxious.

"I told your dad about you and Julian a few minutes ago," I said.

Taylor's focus shifted to Zack. "And . . . ?"

He held out his arms to her. "We love you. We trust you. And we'll talk about this when you're ready to talk."

Taylor dove into his arms. "Thank you," she said. She turned towards me. "Jo, I'm sorry I got mad last night, but when you get to know Julian, you'll understand why we're so important to each other."

Kaye Russell was teaching until 10:30 so we agreed to meet at her office at 10:45. Mieka had phoned to say that Lena would be released later in the day, and that she'd stay at the hospital until then. That meant that after I drove Madeleine to St. Pius, I had an hour free.

When Margot called asking if I could stop by, her timing was perfect.

She answered the door in her pyjamas and she was wearing a pair of fuzzy pink slippers.

"I remember when you wouldn't be caught dead without your Manolos," I said.

Margot patted her belly. "The times they are a'changing. Come have a cup of tea with me and tell me what's happening. But start with the good news. I could use some."

I followed Margot into the kitchen and watched as she filled the kettle. "Lena's coming home from the hospital around lunchtime," I said. "Mieka is crazy busy with UpSlideDown and the opening of April's Place, so Lena and Poor Pitiful Pearl will be spending the days with us till the end of the week. Lena could probably go back to school, but the doctor says better safe than sorry."

"That seems to be the accepted medical protocol these days," Margot said dryly. "I guess Zack told you I'm on enforced R & R. Feet up, and no more meetings in my house. The doctor says I have to draw boundaries between work and leisure. For a lawyer who habitually put in sixteen-hour days, that's a novel idea."

"Please tell me the meetings aren't going to be at our place."

"No, you're off the hook. The condos downstairs that are being converted into offices are apparently close to being ready. Norine's having furniture and office supplies delivered today. You, Zack, and I are supposed to go down and choose offices when we have some time."

"So we'll be living over the store," I said.

Margot laughed. "Look on the bright side. We'll save on parking."

When the chamomile had steeped, we took it into the living room. I always felt at home at Margot's. Like our condo, it was an open-concept plan with a vaulted ceiling and skylights. Two storeys of light, hardwood, granite, and glass. But Margot had decorated her place herself and the effect was stunning: spectacular oversized rugs in shades of cream, ochre, and beige; soft pale leather couches and chairs, bronze lamps that cast a gentle glow; huge ornamental jars filled with dried grasses.

The fireplace was lit, and Margot and I sat in front of it on deep chairs of buttery leather.

As we sipped our tea, Margot surveyed the room. "I'm going to have to do some serious redecorating," she said. "I never thought a baby would be living here."

"You have plenty of time before your little girl starts throwing pureed carrots at the wall."

"I can hardly wait," Margot said. "I just wish Leland were with me to see the carrots fly."

I took her hand. "I know it's not the same, but by the time your daughter starts throwing carrots your condo is going to be SRO. We're all so excited about this baby – especially Zack. He's never been around a newborn."

Margot grinned. "Zack and a newborn: now that's going to be worth the price of admission." Her face grew serious. "I don't know what I would have done without you two in the last few months. And I'm very grateful to you both for handling the fallout from Lauren's death. I called Vince to tell him how sorry I was. Given the fact that he and Lauren were estranged, it was hard to know what to say."

"It is," I agreed. "It's also hard to know what to do – not just with Vince but with the R-H working team." A shadow of concern crossed Margot's face, and I was quick to reassure her. "We can handle this, Margot. Zack's all over it, and so am I."

Margot sipped her tea. "Thanks. Those jackals that I fired from the Peyben board are waiting for me to fall on my face. As one of our former board members was exiting the Peyben office for the last time, he shook his finger at me and told me that focusing Leland's company on community building was idealistic claptrap."

"Well, it isn't. Those jackals you fired may want to spend the rest of their lives locking their car doors, rolling up their windows, and looking the other way when they're forced to drive through North Central, but Leland had a reason for changing the plans for The Village. He knew the people of North Central had to be a priority. Racette-Hunter is just part of the larger picture. You're not alone, Margot. You and Declan have the support of the new board. And right across the hall, you have Taylor, Zack, and me."

Margot's cornflower blue eyes were serious. "Like a family," she said.

"Right," I said. "Like a family."

Margot put her teacup back on its saucer. "Okay," she said. "As members of a family, there's something we have to talk about."

I felt a shiver of apprehension. "Go ahead."

"It's Taylor. Declan is worried about Julian Zentner's influence on her." Margot cocked her head. "Do you want me to stop?"

"No," I said. "Zack and I are concerned about that, too. Especially because last night Taylor told me that Lauren and Julian had quarrelled about the sex video. Apparently, Lauren was threatening to send the video to Taylor if Julian ended the affair."

Margot whistled. "Wow. Declan says that Taylor is out of her depth with Julian. Obviously Declan is right."

"Zack and I had been hoping that since the painting was finished, Julian and Taylor would go their separate ways, and we wouldn't have to interfere."

Margot put her feet up on the ottoman and gazed critically at her fuzzy pink slippers. "But Julian and Taylor haven't gone their separate ways," she said finally.

"No," I said. "And that baffles me. The two of them worked together for weeks, and Taylor hardly ever talked about Julian. A couple of times they came downstairs and had lunch together, but usually Taylor did her homework and Julian leafed through an art magazine. Sometimes he talked to Taylor about an article he was reading, but it was all very casual."

"But now Julian is front and centre in Taylor's life."

"He is, and I don't get it. There's a piece missing here."

"I may be able to supply it," Margot said. "Despite the lack of romance, Declan and Taylor are close. One of the things that drew them together at the beginning was that they both felt overshadowed by a parent. Declan felt that no matter what he did he would never measure up to what Leland accomplished, and until she painted *BlueBoy21*, Taylor felt the same about Sally."

"And *BlueBoy21* changed that," I said.

"Yes," Margot said. "Taylor told Declan that when

BlueBoy21 sold for such a high price, she knew she could finally shake off Sally's shadow."

"I get that," I said. "But what does this have to do with Julian?"

"Julian has apparently convinced Taylor that he is her key to making serious art," Margot said. "He keeps trying to get her to watch the Sally Love documentary with him. Taylor is still refusing, but according to Declan, Julian is making a big deal about Sally's comment that sex was the catalytic force in her art – that when she was in a relationship with an exciting partner, she had the juice to paint, and when she wasn't, she dried up."

"And of course, Julian is volunteering to be the exciting partner," I said.

"He's convinced Taylor that the energy she had when she was painting *BlueBoy21* came from him," Margot said softly. "And Declan's afraid that Taylor is buying his argument and Sally's."

I slammed my hand against the arm of the leather chair. "What a great legacy for a mother to leave her daughter," I said.

Margot was pensive. "I've never once heard you criticize Sally."

Taylor's anger the night before was a fresh wound. "Well, I'm criticizing her now," I said. "I loved Sally, but she really did believe that her talent excused everything. She used people, and when she was through with them, she walked away and left other people to clean up the mess." I stood and started pacing. "For eleven years, I've tried to help Taylor realize her value. Then Sally sends a message from the grave telling her daughter that all that matters is her art and that she can't make great art unless she has sex."

Margot stood and put her arm around my shoulder. "To be fair, in the documentary, Sally talked about other sources that powered her art – seeing the world, meeting all kinds of people, going to galleries and museums."

"I know. When *The Poison Apple* was telecast, I wanted Taylor to watch it with Zack and me. I knew some of Sally's comments would be troubling, and I thought we could give context to what Sally was saying."

"But Julian is the one supplying both the comments and the context," Margot said.

I pivoted to face her. "And he's manipulating Sally's words so that Taylor will give him what he wants – sex."

"What Julian wants is more than sex," Margot said. "He's feeding on Taylor's insecurities about Sally. Julian is telling Taylor that if she wants to make the kind of art her mother made, she needs him."

"You're sure about that?" I said.

"Very sure. Declan agonized about breaking Taylor's confidence, but in the end, he realized he had no choice. Jo, I think Julian is trying to convince Taylor that they can't exist without each other."

"Romeo and Juliet," I said. "Two against the world. Also two who died. That slimeball."

I was still boiling when I walked into the university. I crossed the atrium and down the hall that led to the fine arts department and found Kaye's door open. She looked pale, and her hand seemed to tremble as she motioned me to the chair across from her. I wondered if there'd been lingering effects from medication she might have taken for her migraine.

"Julian said you had a migraine yesterday."

"You saw Julian?"

"Taylor invited him for dinner last night. Actually, that's why I wanted to see you. Kaye, Zack and I aren't happy about Taylor's relationship with Julian."

Kaye's face hardened. "Why? She's painting better than she ever has in her life and it's because of him. He has a great deal to offer her."

"And he's putting a price on it. Did you know that Julian's encouraging Taylor to have sex with him?"

"It has to be someone," Kaye said. "Why not Julian?"

I felt my gorge rise, but I kept my voice even. "For starters, Taylor just turned fifteen. She's still forming ideas about who she is."

Kaye looked at me blankly. "Taylor knows who she is. She has an incredible gift and she has you and Zack. Taylor will be fine. It's Julian I'm worried about." Behind the thick lenses of her glasses, Kaye's eyes were huge and filled with pain. "I blame myself for the turn his life has taken. When I knew him first, Julian was sweet and hopeful and idealistic. The day I told him that it was unlikely he could succeed as a visual artist, I destroyed all that. It was as if he decided that if he couldn't make art that people wanted, he'd become an object that people wanted. Now he sees himself as a commodity."

I was silent for a moment, collecting my thoughts. "Julian is a very disturbed young man, Kaye. You were supposed to be our friend. You were Taylor's teacher. Why would you expose her to a boy with such serious problems?"

"Because I knew he and Taylor could help each other." Kaye put up her hand in a Halt sign. "You're angry now, but hear me out. Julian is not 'a very disturbed young man.' Except for the occasional beer, he doesn't drink. He doesn't do drugs. He's not violent. Life dealt him a blow, and he took a wrong path. I believe we're allowed to do that at nineteen."

"I agree," I said. "But being kept by an older woman – that's a pretty major wrong path – and his involvement with Lauren Treadgold—"

She cut me off. "Julian was always selective. He's probably had fewer partners than most undergraduates."

I was furious. "You mean Lauren wasn't the only one? Taylor has just turned fifteen. What possessed you to offer her up to a man like Julian?"

"I didn't 'offer Taylor up.' You asked me to recommend a model. As someone familiar with Taylor's work, I knew Julian was what she needed. She and I had agreed on a goal before she began the painting. She wanted to produce a competent piece that showed an understanding of anatomy. Of course, the piece she made went well beyond 'competent.' There was something in Julian that Taylor saw and responded to."

"His grief over the family he never had, the art he'll never make," I said.

"Exactly, and that was the other reason that I suggested Julian. Taylor is a very young fifteen. You and Zack have protected her. If she's going to make the kind of art of which she's capable, she's going to have to experience more, feel more. My hope was that Julian would awaken something in Taylor."

I counted to ten. "Her sexuality?"

"Awareness of her sexuality will open up an entire range of feeling that Taylor still hasn't tapped into."

"Because she's a virgin. Damn it, Kaye, Taylor will 'tap into' that range of feeling when she's ready. Forcing Julian upon her could have done irreparable damage."

"If Sally were alive—"

"But Sally isn't alive," I said. "Luckily for Taylor, she wasn't raised by someone who would never see anything more in Taylor than her talent. No one is more aware of my shortcomings as a parent for Taylor than I am, but from the time I brought her home I at least saw the whole child. Taylor suffered an unimaginable loss when she was four years old. She was a very damaged little girl when she came to us, but my children and I did everything we could to let her know she was part of our family. And, of course, Zack thinks the sun rises and sets on her. Taylor's worked hard to become the girl she is today. I'm not going to stand by and let Julian ruin her life."

When I picked up my coat, I was shaking. I didn't say goodbye.

Lena was dressed and ready to go when I got to the hospital. With her Day-Glo pink cast on one arm and Poor Pitiful Pearl in the crook of the other, she was clearly prepared to rock and roll.

"Lena's discharge papers are signed," Mieka said. "We have reams of information about how to care for a young grasshopper with a cast, so I guess we're set."

"We're having leftover macaroni and cheese for lunch today," I said.

Lena beamed. "My favourite – well, one of my favourites."

"Your mum always says it's better the second day."

"I didn't have it the first day, so I won't know," Lena said with impeccable logic.

When we got home, Zack had already set the table. At Lena's place there was a handmade welcome-home card, a DVD of *Charlotte's Web*, a bag of gummy worms, and a mug with the words *SOME GIRL* spelled out in spidery calligraphy.

After a round of hugs, Mieka started getting lunch on the table. When I offered to help, Mieka waved me off. "You and Zack have done enough. Just relax and get caught up on your mornings."

So Zack and I went into the living room and sat together on the couch. "So," I said. "How *was* your morning?"

He stretched lazily. "Not bad at all. James Loftus, the CEO of Blackwell, has agreed to set up a mentoring program."

"So Mr. Loftus succumbed to your charm," I said.

"Yeah, that, and the fact that I told him Margot was looking into pooled fund management for Peyben and she was leaning towards Blackwell."

"Is pooled fund management a big deal?"

"Depends on your perspective. Blackwell recommends that any investor considering pooled fund management bring a minimum of $20 million to the table. Peyben will be bringing considerably more than that. Anyway, it's a good deal for everybody. We get a stellar corporate partner and excellent fund management, and Blackwell gets a whole whack of money to invest."

"A win–win situation," I said.

Zack gave me a cat that swallowed the canary smirk. "Yep. So how was your morning?"

"A dead loss," I said. "We can talk about it later. Right now, I think I could just use a strong arm around my shoulders and some comfort food."

Lena was an enthusiastic eater. She polished off two helpings of macaroni and cheese, asked for more milk in her *SOME GIRL* mug, ate a handful of gummy worms, and then, saying that it was hard to sleep in the hospital because people were always waking her up, declared she was ready for a nap.

When Mieka came back from tucking in Lena, she seemed weary. "You look like you could use a nap yourself," I said. "Why don't you crawl in with Lena for a while?"

Mieka stretched and yawned. "That bed certainly looked tempting, but I have to get back to work. Between UpSlideDown and trying to find a manager for April's Place, I'm going full out these days."

"Sure you're not overdoing it?" I said.

"I go to bed when the kids do. Except for Lena breaking her arm, all's well."

"Have you heard from Riel?"

"No, not since he stormed out of the hospital. He's still among the missing. I had called him last week about putting in some shelves at April's Place – you remember how great the ice cream stand he built for the girls was. Anyway, he seemed interested, but I haven't heard from him this week at all."

"Have you tried calling him?" I said.

"I left him a message this morning saying that Lena was getting out of the hospital today and coming here. Maybe he'll have the courage to call you. But I'm not going to run after him, Mum. At the moment, I've got my hands full taking care of the girls, keeping my business running, and getting April's Place off to a good start." Mieka slipped into her coat, bent to kiss Zack, and then embraced me. "Thanks for spoiling my ladies, and for the mac and cheese," she said. "It really is better the second day."

After Mieka left, Zack turned to me. "Time for show and tell," he said. "And it's your turn. How was your meeting with Kaye?"

"Unsettling," I said.

As I gave Zack an account of my talk with Kaye, his gaze never left my face. "So Julian is just a nice boy who made a bad life choice," he said. "Jesus, Jo, if you knew how often I've heard trial lawyers, including me, use that defence, you'd know that 99 per cent of the time it's bullshit."

Zack's lips curled in disgust. "I always thought Kaye was a sensible woman. What the hell's the matter with her?"

"Guilt? I don't know, and to be honest, right now, I don't care. There's more. Margot and I had a talk this morning, too. Declan told her that Julian is playing some serious mind games with Taylor. He's trying to convince Taylor that the only way she can make art that's as significant as Sally's is through a relationship with him."

"And Taylor's buying it."

"Declan's afraid that she might be."

"So where do we go from here?"

"I honestly don't know. All I know is that our daughter is being torn apart. She loves us."

"And Julian's telling her that's not enough – that all she really needs is him. God, I'd like to clean his clock."

"I know the feeling, but any hostility on our part will just drive Taylor into Julian's arms. For the time being, all we can do is stick close to Taylor, try to get her to open up to us, and pray that she doesn't do something irrevocable."

Zack was meeting Vince Treadgold at Falconer Shreve at two-thirty. He was still hoping that Vince would be in the clear about Lauren's death, but he was hedging his bets by introducing Vince to Maisie Crawford and Chad Kichula, another associate of whom Zack thought highly.

I walked him to the door. "I'm glad you're arranging for Vince to have backup," I said.

"You think he's going to need a lawyer," Zack said.

"I don't know. Just make sure you get Vince to tell you what Lauren meant when she said she was going to ask him to protect her the way she was protecting him."

As soon as the words were out of my mouth, I saw the worry in Zack's eyes. I put my hands on his shoulders. "Hey," I said. "You're the one who always says it's better to know that not know."

"Yeah," Zack said. "But not knowing makes it easier to sleep nights."

—

Lena had just awakened from her nap when the buzzer sounded from the lobby. It was Riel, and he avoided an awkward moment by letting me know that he had gotten back to Mieka and that she had okayed a visit with Lena.

I poured Lena a glass of juice. "That was Riel," I said. "He's on his way up. He wants to see you."

"Will Mummy mind?"

"No, she's the one who told him you were here. Lena, Riel loves you and Madeleine, and that love doesn't stop just because he and your mum have problems."

"So I can just be the way I always am with Riel?"

"Absolutely," I said.

"Good, because I miss him. Maddy does too."

"Be sure and let Riel know that," I said.

Riel was looking better. The hectic glitter was gone from his eyes and his hands were steady. He was carrying a jigsaw puzzle, which he handed to Lena. "I didn't have a chance to wrap this," he said, "but I thought it might be something we could do together." He checked to see my reaction.

I nodded. "Are you up for a puzzle, Lena?"

"You bet," she said.

"Then get to it," I said. "And I'll start dinner."

Lena and Riel set up their puzzle on the large round coffee table in the living room. Lena was normally a chatty child, but she and Riel worked quietly. Occasionally, they murmured something to each other or exclaimed with delight or disappointment, but they worked diligently, their heads bent to the task at hand, both with dark braids that shone under the overhead light.

By the time they called me in to see the finished puzzle, the chicken was in the oven, the potatoes were peeled, the salad was made, and I was reading a Colm Toibin novel. The puzzle was a picture of the creatures of the rain forest, and it glowed with the vibrant colours of the tropics: a toucan with a bright yellow chest and an oversized beak; a glistening greenish-brown anaconda; a butterfly with electric blue wings, two brilliantly marked poison dart frogs; a gorilla with a sadly human face – all against a backdrop of lush green foliage.

"Well done," I said. "Let's leave it there for Maddy and Taylor and Granddad to see."

"I'm never going to take it apart," Lena said.

"If you never take it apart, we'll never have the fun of putting it back together again," Riel said.

"Good point," I said. "Margot sent over some brownies from Evolution this morning, can I interest you two in a snack?"

"You can interest me," Lena said.

Riel stood. "I'd better get going."

"Thanks for the puzzle," Lena said. "It's really neat."

Riel hadn't taken off his jacket. Now he zipped it and reached over and touched Lena's head. "It was fun spending the afternoon with you." He turned his eyes to me. "Thanks for letting me stay."

Lena's voice was bright. "You can come back."

"I'll do my best," he said.

I walked him to the door. "Any time you want to talk, I'm here."

Riel's smile was poignant. "There's so much I need to say." He took a step towards me. "Joanne, I've dug myself into a hole, and I don't know how to climb out."

"Could you talk to Ernest?"

"I've started to call Ernest almost as many times as I've started to call Mieka," Riel said. "I never have the guts to get to that last digit." He gave me a small wave. "See you around."

Zack picked up Madeleine from school, then they swung by Luther to get Taylor. Mieka had managed to get away from work early, so they all came up in the elevator together.

Lena claimed them immediately. The minute everybody had their coats off, Lena led them into the living room to admire the puzzle.

Zack, Mieka, and I were having tea and the girls were at the butcher-block table having their after-school snacks when Taylor finally came back from looking at the puzzle. She was thoughtful. "That's a cool puzzle," she said. "And it's really cool that it came today." She poured herself a glass of milk and sat down on one of the kitchen stools. "Darrell texted me this morning, and I called him when I was on my lunch break. The man who bid against Dad for *Two Painters* is offering me a commission. I said I'd talk to you about it."

"What do you want to do?" I said.

"I wasn't sure, and then I saw Lena's puzzle, and I had an idea about something I might do with Julian."

I wanted to take Taylor in my arms and plead with her not to involve Julian, but I forced myself to remain silent and continue chopping vegetables.

Zack made a quicker recovery. "Julian in the rain forest?" he asked.

"Julian in the rain forest surrounded by creatures that are endangered, dangerous, and beautiful," Taylor said. "I think I could do something good."

"So you want to accept the commission," Zack said.

"Yes. I really do," Taylor said, and I could feel her excitement. "Dad, would you mind talking to Darrell about the money?"

"Not at all."

"But I'd like to be there when you talk to him. I'm going to need to learn the business side of this." Taylor whipped out her iPhone. "I'd better text Julian and see if he's interested. We're having dinner together tomorrow night, so we can talk about it then." She took a large sip of milk.

I knew Zack was no happier about this development than I was, but he didn't miss a beat. "If you're having dinner with Julian tomorrow night, I guess he won't be able to go to the Pats game with me."

Taylor did a double take, then she laughed, sputtering her milk. "As if . . ." she said. "Sorry, Dad, just the idea of Julian at a hockey game."

Taylor's iPhone beeped. She read her message. "Julian says, 'Go for it.'"

"In that case, we'll call Darrell after supper," Zack said. "Right now, I have a suggestion. Nobody wants to wreck Lena's puzzle. Why don't we load up our plates, go into the living room, and watch *Charlotte's Web*?"

Like all good lawyers, and actors, Zack had mastered the art of the cool vibe, but as he wheeled his chair into place I could see the tension in the set of his shoulders. It had been another tough day. I drew a chair up beside him and put my lips to his ear. "I'll go to the Pats game with you." He gave my hand a grateful squeeze, leaned over, and whispered, "I don't actually have tickets," then turned back to the opening credits.

Every adult in the room had private worries. Mieka was concerned about Riel. Zack was burdened with the knowledge that Vince's situation was worsening, and he and I were both apprehensive about Taylor's relationship with Julian. But the story of Wilbur and Charlotte worked its magic. When Wilbur carried home Charlotte's magnum opus, the sac of eggs she laid at the fair before dying, we were all in tears.

CHAPTER

10

After Mieka and the girls left, Zack and Taylor called Darrell Bell. When Zack told me the size of the commission Cole Dimitroff was proposing, my jaw dropped.

"Did Taylor seem fazed by Mr. Dimitroff's offer?"

"Not a bit," Zack said. "All she said was that she and Julian better get started."

I sighed. "Not exactly the news I was hoping for."

The day demanded a massage, and as soon as I poured the oil into my hand and began kneading Zack's neck muscles, I knew I had my work cut out for me.

"Do you want to talk about the situation with Vince?" I said.

"Might as well," Zack said. "I took your advice and asked Vince if he understood what Lauren meant when she referred to protecting him . . ."

I dug my fingers in more deeply. "And . . ."

"And I'm glad I asked. I wouldn't want to get blindsided by this. According to Vince, on Sunday of the Remembrance Day weekend, Lauren got a call from a man telling her that he saw her driving her Land Rover erratically the night of the auction. He said she ran a red and then hit a lamppost."

"Hence the damage you noticed on the headlight when we picked up the car," I said.

"Right. But the caller went on. He said a homeless guy was sleeping under the lamppost and the Land Rover ran over his leg. That the guy was okay but is going to need a lot of help . . ."

"So was the street person the one making the phone call?"

"No, the caller identified himself as 'a friend of justice.' Whoever it was muffled his voice. Lauren told Vince she couldn't connect it with anyone she knew. The salient point is that the friend of justice asked for $20,000 to keep from going to the cops. But Vince is positive he hit a post, and that's all. No matter how drunk he was, he couldn't have missed running someone over."

"How did this man know it was Lauren's car?"

"Only one answer for that – he had to be someone who knew the Treadgolds well enough to know she usually drove the Rover."

"Someone who knew them and was prepared to blackmail them."

"So it would seem. Lauren agreed to pay the caller. He was going to pick up the money the next afternoon."

"The day Lauren was murdered," I said.

"Yes. But when Lauren and Vince had their confrontation, the friend of justice still hadn't turned up. Lauren told Vince that if he agreed to a generous divorce settlement, she had the cash and was ready to pay the blackmailer. If Vince didn't agree to alimony, she'd send the friend of justice to the police with the information that Vince had been driving her car – drunk – and she'd tell the cops how she got her black eye."

"What did Vince do?"

"He caved," Zack said. "He agreed to pay Lauren substantial alimony. If Lauren made good on her threat, Vince would be charged with assault and with leaving the scene of an accident. And that's just for starters. He could lose his medical licence."

I felt a chill. "That's a pretty powerful motive for murder," I said.

Zack ran his hand over his head. "Tell me something I don't know. But it's possible that the friend of justice killed Lauren. She could have reneged on their deal or he could have decided he wanted more money and she refused."

"Was the cash in the house when the police arrived?"

"I don't know. I'm going to call Debbie and see what's shaking."

"What about the fact that Lauren had the Land Rover repaired?"

"Not germane," Zack said. "Vince didn't learn about the repair until I told him about it. The only other people who know about the repair are you and me and I'm Vince's lawyer."

I pressed hard on the base of Zack's spine and he groaned. "Don't try to bully me," I said.

"I'm not bullying you," Zack said. "The repair really is not relevant. What matters are Vince's actions the night of the art auction. He was drunk. He was driving recklessly. He honestly doesn't remember hitting anything, but he knows he ran a red. Anyway, it scared him, and he parked the SUV and walked to the Senator. Somebody took the car for a joyride, and the next day Lauren picked up the car. End of story."

I stopped massaging and sat back. "Zack, do you think Vince killed Lauren?"

"No. Debbie has the holy trinity in this one: means, motive, and opportunity, but that doesn't make Vince guilty. I always try to put myself in the client's place. Sometimes, I can actually feel that crazy anger clients must have felt when they crossed the line. But when I put myself in Vince's place, I don't feel crazy anger. I'm a successful surgeon; I'm respected in the community; I was furious when I witnessed my wife having sex with another man; but I'm not really in love with her any more and I can afford the best divorce lawyer in the country. Yes, she's blackmailing me about something I didn't do, but if it comes out, I'll fight it. I feel pretty much in control."

"Vince wasn't in control when he hit Lauren's eye."

"No, and he wasn't in control the night of the art auction. But buying your wife a painting of her naked lover is a long way from killing her. In the end, Vince didn't care enough about Lauren or the money she wanted to risk his life and career. And another thing. When a husband kills his wife, there's almost always gratuitous violence. There are far more blows or wounds than were necessary to get the job done, and a signature wound. Often a husband severs his wife's ring finger."

I shuddered. "And Lauren died of a single blow to her temple."

"Yes. My guess is that the murder wasn't premeditated. I think the killer lost control, picked up the rock, hit Lauren once, and really connected. A crime of anger but not of passion. Anyway, if Vince is charged, he now has a defence team." Zack picked up the bottle of massage oil. "Your turn, Ms. Shreve."

"Let me give you a little more attention," I said. "You're still as tight as you were when we started."

"Nope, this is a mutual massage. Fair's fair. Off with your pyjama top."

Zack's hands were powerful, and as he kneaded the area between my neck and shoulders, my muscles began to unknot. "You handled the latest episode of life with Julian well," I said.

Zack chuckled. "I'm glad Taylor thought so. What the hell are we going to do about that situation, Jo?"

"I don't know. Taylor really wants to accept that commission, and she believes Julian is her muse – or whatever the male equivalent of a muse is."

Zack ran his thumbs in circles down my spine. "I guess the male equivalent would be Apollo. He reigned over all nine muses."

I turned my head. "You know the most surprising things," I said.

"I wish I knew how to make Julian disappear. If he's going to be Taylor's Apollo, he'll be here all the time."

"That could be an advantage," I said. "We'll be able to keep an eye on him. I wish they were at least planning to have dinner here tomorrow, but Taylor says they're going out."

"And if wishes were horses, beggars would ride," Zack said, wrapping his arms around me from behind. "I'm too tired to think positively. Let's hit the sack."

The next morning when the dogs and I went up for our run around the roof garden, the city was shrouded in fog. I hadn't thought much about the pathetic fallacy since high school, but given the number of things in our lives that were uncertain, it was difficult not to read significance into the morning's weather.

Nothing in my own high school experience gave me insight into the push–pull that Taylor's life had become. I'd read once that when an adolescent is close to her family, she has to find some way to justify the break she must make with them to become her own person. I had never been close to my mother, and my father died the year I graduated from high school. My break with my family had been effortless. When I moved from boarding school to university, the only change in my life had been my address.

The boys I dated in high school had been boys from other private schools who were like me: studious, nerdy, socially awkward. I was pretty enough to take to a dance or a party, I was a good listener, and I accepted wandering male adolescent hands as part of the rite of passage.

My parents had not loved me as Zack and I loved Taylor, and none of the nice interchangeable boys I dated had wanted from me what Julian wanted from our daughter. Julian had led us into uncharted territory, and I was desperate to find our way back to safety.

By the time the dogs and I finished our run, the fog was beginning to lift. As the familiar landmarks of our neighbourhood emerged and the lights of downtown became visible, I felt an unreasonable optimism. Taylor was, at heart, a loving and sensible girl. Everything in her history with me suggested that, ultimately, she would make the right choice.

When the dogs and I came back from our run, Zack was in his robe, making porridge.

"I'm starving," I said. "Can you stand sitting next to me before I have a shower?"

Zack breathed deeply. "It will be pleasure. I get a contact high from your endorphin rush."

We were just finishing breakfast when Zack got a phone call. He mouthed, "Debbie," so I went to shower.

Zack was clearing the kitchen table when I came back.

I began rinsing the dishes. "Any news?" I asked.

"The police have been through the Treadgolds' house with the proverbial fine-tooth comb. Debbie didn't mention the money."

"So the friend of justice did show up."

"We live in hope," Zack said.

It was a little after nine the next morning when Mieka brought Lena to Halifax Street. I had some errands to do that

I thought Lena would enjoy, and in my opinion, Lena had spent enough time indoors. Our first stop was Toys "R" Us. According to Mieka, Dino-Roars were going to be a hot ticket for Christmas and I didn't want Zack to be disappointed if I couldn't get one for him. Once I had the Dino-Roar in my shopping cart, Lena and I gave ourselves over to the pleasures of browsing.

Like all lucky browsers, Lena and I discovered some treasures. At seven, Madeleine had just embarked on chapter books, and I spotted a copy of Judy Blume's *Tales of a Fourth Grade Nothing,* a book that had been a favourite of my kids. Then since I was Christmas shopping, I bought the other three books in the series to put under the tree. Lena found a *Charlotte's Web* jigsaw puzzle and I spotted a gorgeous on-sale book of photographs of the rain forest for Taylor. I doubled back to get another Dino-Roar as a gift from Zack for Margot's baby, and we were done.

Our next stop was Pawsitively Purrfect to get food for Willie, Pantera, Bruce, Benny, and the feral cats that Taylor and I fed. Lena and I were exclaiming over birthstone charms for dogs' collars when I heard Celeste Treadgold's smoky contralto. "People are full of surprises, Joanne," she said. "You never struck me as a woman who would buy her dog a bone-shaped birthstone charm."

"We own a bouvier and a mastiff – both male," I said. "I can't see either of them sporting a bone-shaped birthstone charm. My granddaughter and I are just having a shopping day. Lena, this is Celeste Treadgold. Celeste, this our granddaughter Lena Kilbourn."

"I'm pleased to meet you, Lena," Celeste said. She touched the Day-Glo pink cast. "What happened to your arm?"

"I was skating and I tried a Salchow."

Celeste grimaced. "Let that be a lesson to you. Forget physical activity. Take up smoking."

Lena looked questioningly from Celeste to me. "That was a joke," Celeste said.

Lena nodded gravely. "I thought it must be."

There was a rack of dog mugs a few feet away. Celeste took Lena's hand and steered her towards them.

I was on edge and Celeste's move jarred me, but Lena was already happily inspecting a mug. "Mimi says we're starting our Christmas shopping today," she said. "Maybe I can find something for somebody."

"I'll bet you can," Celeste said. "This store is chock-full of gifts with a very large WOW factor."

When Celeste rejoined me, she picked up a birthstone charm. "Maybe I should buy a couple of these as welcome-home presents for the salukis. The cleaners are finished with the house, so I'm picking up Darius and Dalila from the kennel today."

"Your father is going to move back in?"

"For the time being, and I'm moving back into my old room for a while, too," Celeste said. "Life's funny, isn't it? After all these years, I finally have my father all to myself, but I don't know how to treat him, and he doesn't know how to treat me. We're like solicitous strangers, always tip-toeing around each other, fearful of saying the wrong thing." She gave herself a shake. "Anyway, moving back to the house seemed like the simplest solution, if only because of the dogs." She fell silent. Clearly she had something on her mind that wasn't easy to say. Finally, she cleared her throat and began. "Joanne, I can't believe we just ran into each other. I've been trying to get up my nerve to call you."

"Kismet," I said. "An old friend of mine used to say, 'Fate leads the willing and drags along the reluctant.'"

Celeste's laugh was short and sardonic. "I'm certainly reluctant, but I had to do something. I heard an ugly rumour today. Apparently, some people are saying my father sent the video of Lauren and Julian so he wouldn't have to pay alimony."

"That is ugly," I said. "But I thought it was sent only to the R-H working team."

"It was." Celeste rubbed her temples. "Jo, I hate involving you yet again in the black hole of my life, but Zack needs to know that I was the one who sent out the video. It wasn't premeditated. I went over to the house to borrow my father's digital camera. There was no one there, so I looked around. I found a camera. I knew it wasn't his because his had been a gift from me a couple of Christmases ago. I don't think he's ever used it. Anyway, I figured this one was probably Lauren's. The memory card wasn't empty, so I decided to see what might be on it."

"And you found the video of Lauren and Julian."

"I did, and I wish I hadn't. I have my father's temper. I get these blind rages. I wanted to punish Lauren for what she'd done to my father. And I needed to ease my own guilt for sending my father the text that started the whole disastrous chain of events. When I saw the video I thought I'd found a way to make it right. "

"But you hadn't," I said.

"No. Yet again I screwed up. I overheard Lauren telling my father once that my presence in the house just made everything worse." Celeste regarded the dog charm in her hand pensively. "It turns out Lauren was right after all," she said.

Lena came back carrying a mug with picture of a mastiff on it. "Do you think Granddad will like this for Christmas?"

"You know how much he loves Pantera," I said. "This mug will be perfect." I turned back to Celeste. "I'll tell Zack about the camera, and the video. But you should tell your father yourself, Celeste."

She took a step closer to me. "Joanne, you have to believe that I didn't intend for any of this to happen. Things just took on a life of their own." Her azure eyes were troubled.

"I believe you," I said. "But, Celeste, you'd better prepare yourself because I think the repercussions have just begun."

When we got back to Halifax Street, Lena and I stopped in the alley beside our building to feed the feral cats. I pulled a bag of kibble onto the tailgate, carried the bag to a sheltered place near the abandoned furniture factory next door to us, slit open the bag with my pocketknife, and dumped the kibble onto the ground. I repeated the process three times.

Lena was fascinated. "Do you ever see the cats, Mimi?"

"No, but I know they're there because by tomorrow morning all that food will be gone."

"And then what will the cats do?"

"Wait for us to bring more kibbles," I said.

After lunch, Lena decided to take a nap. I lay down beside her and drifted off. We awoke to see Zack in his chair beside us. "You two were both smiling in your sleep."

I sat up. "We had a good morning, didn't we, Lena?"

"Mimi and I got you Christmas presents."

"That sounds promising," Zack said. "My morning was less festive."

"Have you eaten?" I asked.

"I had a sandwich at the office, but I wouldn't mind a cup of tea. How about you, Lena?"

"Can you fix it my special way?

"Half milk and two teaspoons of sugar," Zack said. "Consider it done."

When we slid the rain forest puzzle out of the way to make room for the new puzzle, Lena pointed to the toucan's beak. "Did you know the beak helps keep the toucan comfortable? It's like a thermal window. When it's too cold outside, the beak keeps the heat inside the toucan and when it's too hot, it lets the heat out."

"Where did you learn that?" Zack asked.

"From Riel," Lena said. Then she opened the new puzzle, dumped out the pieces, and began.

"We're not needed here, Ms. Shreve," Zack said. "Let's take our tea into the living room."

We settled into our new favourite place – me in one of the reading chairs by the window and Zack beside me in his wheelchair.

"I have news," I said. "Lena and I ran into Celeste Treadgold today at Pawsitively Purrfect, and she had a confession to make. She was the one who sent the video of Lauren and Julian to everyone."

"Well, I'll be damned," Zack said.

"Apparently, Celeste came upon it by accident—"

"So she decides to humiliate her stepmother and, incidentally, give her father yet another motive for murdering his wife." Zack stirred his tea. "Boy, the shit just keeps piling up, doesn't it?"

"Seemingly," I said. "So where do you go from here?"

"Well, the cops are on it, of course, and we have private investigators looking into Lauren's life – trying to figure out who hated, or loved, her enough to kill her. Vince and Julian are at the head of the line, but Celeste isn't far behind."

"Celeste is carrying a heavy burden of guilt," I said. "Today she told me that she 'didn't intend for any of this to happen – that things just took on a life of their own.'"

Zack grimaced. "That sounds perilously close to a confession," he said. "Maybe I should give her a little lawyerly advice."

"Celeste said she was going to talk to Vince," I said. "Zack, I'm tired of all this uncertainty, and suspicion. I would be so grateful if somebody flushed out the friend of justice."

"Better yet would be if the friend of justice had a suitcase full of cash, a solid motive for wanting Lauren Treadgold dead, and no alibi," Zack said. "If that happened, I'd tell Santa he could take my name off his list."

Lena had just awakened from her nap when Mieka and Madeleine came by to take her for a Dilly Bar at the DQ. Not long after that, Taylor called to share her own immediate plans. She had an appointment with Chantelle at Head to Toe. She'd take a cab home from the salon, but Julian was picking her up for dinner at six, and she'd probably be a little late.

When I passed the message along to Zack, he rolled his eyes. "If I have to sit chatting with Julian for an hour, I'll go bug-fuck nuts. Is it too early for a drink?"

"Yes, but you can make me one, too."

Watching Zack do anything gave me pleasure. He was always completely focused on whatever he undertook. When he handed me my glass, he said, "Do we have anything planned for dinner?"

"Nothing," I said. "I thought maybe we'd order in."

"We haven't gone out to eat for a while. We could go to a restaurant."

"The same restaurant Julian and Taylor are going to?" I said.

Zack's face was innocent. "Coincidences happen."

"If we showed up at the restaurant where Taylor and Julian were having dinner, she'd never speak to either of us again. Zack, I'm no happier about this situation than you are, but if we start putting up barriers, we'll make Julian irresistible to Taylor."

"Forbidden fruit," Zack said gloomily. He took a large sip of his martini. "So what do we do?"

"We continue to welcome Julian in our home. We watch

him like a hawk, and we hope for the best. Now why don't I call Margot and ask her if she and Declan want to join us for Chinese tonight."

"You win," Zack said. "But let's get extra almond shrimp. They're Taylor's favourite."

"So we're going to show her what she missed by not staying home with us?"

"No, we're going to show her that we love her."

Dinner with Margot and Declan was pleasant. Peking House never disappointed, and we somehow managed to keep the conversation light and lively.

Zack and I cleaned up and were in bed before eight-thirty. We were still curled up, half dozing, when there was soft knock on our bedroom door. It was Taylor. She came in and sat on the edge of our bed.

"How was your evening?" I said.

"Good," she said. "We were planning to go LaBodega – that's always fun – but Julian said he needed some place quiet to unwind, so we went to Table 10."

"Lauren Treadgold's death must be hitting him pretty hard," I said carefully.

"It is," Taylor said. "There's so much going on inside Julian. Tonight he was talking about how there's a finite amount of water on the earth and how every drop of water has been here forever. The water evaporates and falls to earth as rain or snow or sleet. It moves around, but the amount of water never changes. Julian says it's the same with talent. There's a finite amount of talent and it moves around, and I was lucky because the talent fell on me."

"And Julian wasn't lucky," I said.

"He used to think he wasn't," Taylor said, "but now that he has me, Julian thinks his luck has changed." She stood, bent to kiss us both goodnight, and started for the door.

I wanted to call her back, but her revelation about Julian had stunned me.

Zack reached under the covers for my hand. "Taylor, there's a carton of almond prawns from Peking House in the refrigerator for you," he said.

For a second or two, Taylor seemed frozen. "Is something wrong?" I said.

Taylor half turned. "Not with me," she said. "I was just wondering what Julian's life would have been like if he'd had someone who remembered he liked almond prawns."

Zack waited till Taylor closed the door behind her. "This can't go on, Jo."

"I know," I said. "I just don't know how to make it end."

CHAPTER

11

In its earliest days, the office of the Racette-Hunter project was housed in the same glass tower as Zack's law firm. The optics were bad, and Norine began searching for a space that reflected what Racette-Hunter was about: access, opportunity, and equality. The place Norine found was ideal: a restaurant that had, by turns, been a greasy spoon, an Italian bistro, a barbecue joint, a deli, and a noodle house. After the noodle house folded, the owners of the building offered the space for rent, and Norine snapped it up.

For our purposes, it was ideal. It was in North Central, it had been retrofitted to meet the accessibility code for public places, and it was clean and spacious. The kitchen still functioned, and that meant there was always soup and bannock for hungry volunteers.

The morning after Taylor's dinner with Julian at Table 10, I had an early morning meeting with Norine about a program called Public Allies that I thought might be a good fit for North Central. Zack had some items he wanted to run by Norine, so the two of us were at the Racette-Hunter office by a little after eight.

There were already a half-dozen volunteers there. Norine led us to the one private place in the building: the kitchen. She offered us coffee and then reached into her briefcase, pulled out a bulky envelope, and handed it to Zack. "Someone left this in our mailbox during the night," she said

Zack opened the envelope. It was filled with hundred-dollar bills, neatly bundled. Zack counted them. "I know what this is about," he said.

Norine raised a nicely shaped eyebrow. "Really?"

Zack and Norine had never had secrets. Zack moved his chair closer. "Someone was shaking down Lauren Treadgold for $20,000," he said quietly. "The blackmailer was supposed to meet Lauren the day she died. Until this moment, we weren't certain whether the blackmailer actually showed up that day."

"Why would the blackmailer drop the money off here," Norine said.

"Guilt?" I said. "Maybe whoever blackmailed Lauren had second thoughts and decided to donate the money to a good cause."

"Or maybe they just didn't want to have all those crisp hundred-dollar bills in their possession if the police came calling," Zack said. "Whatever the mystery donor's motivation, that money is going to have to go to the cop shop for a while. I'm not crazy about Debbie learning about the friend-of-justice angle, but I can't hold this back. That money is evidence in a murder case."

Norine's expression was troubled. "I found something else this morning. There was a glove on the sidewalk by the front door when I came to work. I didn't think anything of it. I put it in our Lost and Found box, but if our anonymous donor dropped it, it could be evidence, too." She stood. "I'll get it."

The glove Norine brought back was a man's tan winter glove. She handed it to me. It was thickly lined leather and had a Velcro strap round the elasticized wrist to keep out the cold. As I turned it over in my hands, I felt a sickness in the pit of my stomach. "Zack and I gave gloves like this to Riel for his birthday in October."

"We gave Riel a pair of gloves *like* this glove," Zack said. "For all we know, one of the volunteers could have dropped it."

Norine shook her head. "I was the first one here this morning. It started snowing a couple of hours ago. Mine were the first footprints on the path."

Zack examined the glove. "Triple insulation," he said. "Nice, but, Jo, this glove really could belong to anybody."

I took the glove from Zack and checked the size inside. "Size 8," I said. "These gloves were expensive and I didn't want to make a mistake about Riel's glove size, so I called Mieka. Riel's a size 8."

"I locked up at seven-thirty last night," Norine said. "The snow started around five this morning. Riel must have dropped the envelope in our mailbox sometime during the night."

Norine's distress was obvious. She was fond of Riel and had always been his champion. She was a realist, but even realists cling to the wisp of hope. "This is all just speculation," Norine said. "But *if* Riel was involved, he at least tried to make amends."

"And if he was at the Treadgolds' house the day Lauren died, Riel might have information that would identify her killer," I said.

"That's presuming that he isn't the murderer," Zack said.

"Riel is not a killer." Norine's tone was sharp. "You'll have to look elsewhere, Zack."

"I'm prepared to do that, but when I look elsewhere, I don't like the options: Vince? Celeste? Julian?"

"Let's not make ourselves crazy by speculating," I said. I picked up the glove. "I'll see if I can track Riel down and talk to him about this."

"He's doing some carpentry at April's Place," Norine said. "He called yesterday to tell me he was working there."

"That's good news," I said, "and April's Place is only a few blocks from here. I can go over and talk to Riel right now."

"Do you want me to come with you?" Zack asked. "If Riel feels cornered, he might lash out."

"Riel shouldn't feel as if everyone he cares for is against him," I said. "When he came over with the puzzle for Lena, he and I connected. I think he'll talk to me."

"Do you really believe you'll get a straight answer from him?" Zack said.

I stuffed the glove in my jacket pocket. "There's only one way to find out."

Fresh snow blanketed the streets and more was falling. It was a day for a bracing walk, but my sense of well-being was eroded by memories of times when I had seen Riel lose his temper. He was gentle by nature, but when he was on the receiving end of what he perceived as prejudice or witnessed an injustice, he snapped. Once when I'd told him about a heartbreaking encounter I'd had with a child who was working the streets, he brought his fist down on Mieka's wooden kitchen table with such force that I thought he had split the tabletop. Lauren's life was privileged and her sense of entitlement was strong. If she said something that triggered Riel's temper, it was conceivable that he would pick up a rock and strike her.

By the time I arrived at April's Place, I was regretting my decision to confront Riel. My regret deepened when I saw that he was in the children's coat and boot room, painting boot racks in bright primary colours. His sunny greeting was a surprise. "As you can see, I'm back on the job," he said.

"Norine told me," I said. "That's great news."

"Mieka won't be in till after lunch, but if you want to warm up, take a seat." Riel gestured to the benches that lined the room. "I painted those yesterday, and I've checked – the paint is dry." He dipped his brush into a can of paint the colour of a tangerine.

"Actually, I came to see you," I said. I reached into my bag and took out the glove. "I brought this back."

He took the glove with his left hand, placed it on the floor next to him, and began painting one of the slats of the boot rack. "Thanks," he said. "I was wondering what happened to that."

"Norine found it. It was on the step outside the Racette-Hunter office. She also found an envelope containing $20,000 in cash."

Riel kept painting, his face expressionless. "And the envelope is connected to me how?" he said finally.

"You tell me," I said. "Here's what I know. Someone phoned Lauren Treadgold on Sunday night claiming to have seen her driving her Land Rover dangerously the night of the art auction. The caller said that Lauren drove into a lamp-post and over the leg of a homeless man sleeping beside it. He asked for $20,000 in cash. In exchange he promised not to go to the police. Lauren said the voice was muffled, and she couldn't place it. The next day she was murdered. Before she was killed, Lauren told her husband about the blackmail threat and assured him it would be taken care of. The police found no cash in the Treadgold house. This morning Norine found $20,000 in cash in the R-H mailbox and this glove on the walk."

Not until he'd finished painting the boot rack did Riel decide to tell the truth. "I was the one who made the call. I was coming down off a high the night I came to the hospital and saw Brock Poitras with Mieka." Riel closed his eyes at the memory.

"That was a tough night for everybody," I said.

"I didn't make it any better by totally losing it in front of you and Mieka. When I left the hospital, I was sick about the way I'd behaved. I just wanted to forget myself, turn off my mind and my emotions. It's easy to score drugs in that neighbourhood, so I did. After I'd done a couple of lines I felt better. I also had one of those brilliant insights cokeheads have. I knew that if I was going to keep using, I was going to need money, and since my prospects for a paying job were nil, I had to find a source of income. The night of the art auction I'd seen something that I knew I could use. I was downtown and I'd seen Lauren Treadgold's Land Rover come out of nowhere, run a red, bump up onto the curb, ding the corner of a mailbox, and speed off."

"And the homeless man?"

"There was no homeless man. The incident was over in seconds. But I knew it was Lauren's car. I've driven it, and of course, that yellow is distinctive. Anyway, I was the one who called her."

"And it didn't worry you that Lauren would recognize you when you came to pick up the money?"

"No, because coke has a way of blurring reality. I made up a story in which I would present myself as an intermediary – someone who made sure that a homeless guy got his due, and after doing a couple of lines, even I believed it. I had no problem calling Lauren, and she seemed to have no problem believing me."

"And she continued to believe you when you showed up at her house to claim the money for the homeless man."

Riel put the lid back on the tin of tangerine paint. "I thought she'd bought the story, but when I turned to leave with the money, she said, 'Joanne must be so relieved that you're out of her daughter's life.' She might as well have kicked me in the stomach.

"I walked straight out the door. It was pouring rain. I kept walking. And the more I walked, the madder I got. Here's this rich white woman who's had everything handed to her from the day she was born treating me like something she stepped in on the sidewalk. Lauren Treadgold was hardly a saint. I'd seen that video of her getting it on with Julian Zentner, a guy who's not even half her age. I don't know how long I walked. Finally I decided that I'd walk back to Lauren Treadgold's house and tell her she could take her money and shove it. I was really looking forward to seeing her face when this piece of scum showed that he had pride.

"When I got back to the Treadgold house, the outside door was open, and I went into the vestibule. The door to the house proper was closed, but I could hear people talking. I didn't want anyone but Lauren Treadgold to hear what I had to say, so I left. Jo, you have to believe that Lauren was very much alive the last time I saw her."

"I believe you. But you have to go to the police with this, Riel," I said.

Riel's lips curled in derision. "You think the cops will actually believe that a guy from North Central was returning $20,000 in cash to a woman like Lauren Treadgold."

"This isn't about you, Riel," I said. "You have information relating to a murder. If you want a lawyer with you when you go to the police, Zack will make the arrangements."

Riel stood. "I'm going to have to think this over, Joanne."

I zipped my jacket. "Understood," I said. "But you don't have much time. You have my cell number. If you don't call me within the hour, I'll go to the police myself."

My feet were leaden as I walked back to the offices. Riel's account of his two visits to the Treadgold house had been credible, but I kept adding another frame to his description of the final scene between Lauren and him. In this version, when Lauren told Riel that I would be relieved to have him out of Mieka's life, Riel picked up a rock and brought it down on her skull.

Norine and Zack had been quiet when I recounted what happened. "I'm going to talk to Riel," Norine said finally. She was already pulling on her coat when my cell rang. It was Riel. He sounded tired but resolute. "I'll go to the police," he said.

"Do you want a lawyer?"

"I probably should have one. Can she or he meet me here at April's Place? I really would like to finish those benches."

"I'm sure that can be arranged," I said. I hesitated. "Riel, be proud. You're doing the right thing." I broke the connection.

I turned to Zack. "Riel would like a lawyer. Can you get somebody to April's Place as soon as possible?"

Zack already had his cell in hand. "Consider it done. I'm going to have to go outside the firm, but I know just the person. Mildred Thill is a lawyer, but she's also an expert on addiction. She can offer Riel the kind of help he needs."

"I'll go with Riel to the police," Norine said. "He's writing himself off as a loser and he's not. Our community needs him, and Riel needs to hear that we need him."

The fact that Norine was now working in the inner city hadn't changed her mode of dress. She never wore anything but Max Mara, and that morning as she finished buttoning her elegant double-breasted camel hair coat and knotted her navy, cream, and khaki scarf, I remembered Taylor describing Norine as a tribal princess. She was close to six feet tall with the broad shoulders and long limbs of some Northern Cree. She looked like what she was – a woman to be reckoned with. She walked back inside to tell one of the volunteers that at ten o'clock she'd be back at the office for the weekly meeting of the Racette-Hunter working team, but until then, she could be reached by cell. Then she left to let Riel know she was standing by him.

Zack and I decided to stay at the office and get caught up on e-mails. I'd called Ernest Beauvais to tell him about Riel, and he'd agreed to come to the meeting early so we could talk.

Ernest arrived wearing the jacket he had worn at Lauren's birthday party. The leather on the old ironworkers jacket was faded and cracking. When he came over to where Zack and I were sitting, he noticed me looking at it. "I'm going to see Riel after our meeting," he said. "I thought I'd wear this jacket to remind myself that four generations of my family have made mistakes, paid for them, and gone on to live useful lives."

"That's exactly what Riel needs to hear," I said. "Ernest, we're all on Riel's side."

Ernest's voice was a low rumble. "I know, and that's exactly what I'm going to tell him."

At the meeting, Brock Poitras delivered the report that covered the areas for which Lauren had been responsible, and I was glad Ernest was there to say the words that acknowledged Lauren's contribution and her passing. Ernest explained that Lauren's funeral would be private – family only – and he asked that we keep Vince in our thoughts during a difficult time in his life. He also said a short prayer for Riel. As always, Ernest's presence in the room seemed to strengthen us all.

The reports were all positive, and for the first time a team of landscape architects and an elder knowledgeable about planting indigenous grasses and traditional healing plants joined the meeting. The project was starting to come together as Leland Hunter had envisioned it would. When Zack and I stepped into the cold November air, I could feel his excitement.

"It's fun to be able to do something that will change the city, isn't it?" Zack said.

"It can be," I said. "That's part of the allure of politics."

Zack gave me a sidelong look. "Have you given the matter of *my* political future any further thought?"

"I have," I said. "The election's in October, so if we decide to go for it and start now, we have eleven months to work behind the scenes – assemble a slate of progressive councillors, run a solid campaign, win, and clean house."

"You sound like you're leaning towards a 'yes' vote," Zack said.

"Just thinking out loud," I said. "And not all my thoughts are positive. Our best issue is the fact that the mayor and the councillors are puppets of the developers, but you and I have a significant amount of stock in Peyben Developments, and Margot owns Peyben."

"And Peyben found the partners, the money, and the talent to get the Racette-Hunter Centre built after the city and the province had dicked around for years," Zack said. "We could take the teeth out of that tiger."

"We probably could," I said.

Zack stopped wheeling. "I like the sound of that 'we,'" he said.

"You do realize that if you decide to give the mayoralty race a shot, I'm there."

Zack's eyes met mine. "Just like that?"

"Just like that," I said.

Zack grinned. "I don't have anything on until one o'clock. Can I buy you lunch? Today's Thursday, liver and onions day at the City Hall cafeteria."

I shook my head. "You never miss an opportunity, do you? Okay we'll go down to City Hall, eat liver and onions, then you can shake a few hands and I'll sneak upstairs and measure the windows in the mayor's office for drapes."

"Who has more fun than us?" Zack said.

I leaned down and kissed him. "Nobody. Nobody has more fun than us."

When I got back to Halifax Street, I made split pea soup and then called Margot to ask if she was up for a visit. She said she'd be delighted and not to bother to knock. When I came into her living room, Margot was curled up on the couch with a cup of tea and a bag of Oreos watching *The Young and the Restless*.

I sat on the other end of the couch, but Margot's eyes never left the screen. "It's almost over," she said. She waved the bag of cookies in my direction. "Have an Oreo."

I took two. "I never pegged you for a *Y&R* fan," I said.

"When I was in law school, the female students and two gay guys got together at the pub every Friday to watch."

"That was what – twenty years ago? Do you have any idea what's happening now?"

"None," Margot said, "but it doesn't matter because I have pregnancy brain, and I wouldn't retain the information anyway." The theme music came up and Margot hit the remote and turned the set off. "So what's going on in the big world? I just want to hear the fun news."

"Well, Zack's thinking about running for mayor."

Margot's eyes widened. "You've got to be kidding."

"Nope. He's been talking about it for a while now, and he's dead serious. We had lunch at the City Hall cafeteria so he could press the flesh."

"He's not going back to Falconer Shreve?"

"Maybe not for the foreseeable future."

"Wow! Zack for mayor! Is he not aware that the opposition and the media do background checks on potential candidates?"

"He's prepared to tough it out."

"Zack is the least political person I know. Where did this come from?"

"The Racette-Hunter project has been an eye-opener for him. Now that the centre is moving towards completion, the mayor and city council are busting their buttons over what they've accomplished."

Margot's laugh was short and sardonic. "And they've thrown up roadblocks every step of the way," she said. "I don't blame Zack for being pissed at that."

"Well, the glory-grabbing is a small irritant compared to what's in the works now. Zack's been fuming about how the mayor and the council are trying to relocate the housing intended for Westchester Place to Dewdney Park. And lately we've been hearing rumours of other, even more questionable land deals."

"So Zack's going to be the knight in shining armour for the people who always end up getting hooped," Margot said. "Well, he's got my vote." She narrowed her eyes at me. "But he doesn't have yours."

"I'm still trying to figure that out," I said. I stood up. "I didn't come over here to talk about Zack's next career move. We're having split pea soup for dinner tonight. Do you and Declan want to join us?"

"Declan has a basketball game tonight, and he's going for

pizza with his team beforehand. If you don't mind, I think I'll just stay put and watch back episodes of *The Young and the Restless* – I still can't figure out who slept with whom and when."

"I'll bring your dinner over so you can concentrate," I said. "When you're in labour and you really need distraction, I'll fill you in on the romantic history of the Abbots and the Newmans."

Margot raised an eyebrow. "You watch *Y&R*?"

"Mieka has loved it forever. When she was in high school, it was her reward for doing algebra."

"So you watch it because Mieka likes it."

"No, I watch it because I like it. See you at six."

Taylor had been uncharacteristically withdrawn when she came home from school. She murmured hello and went straight to her room. As the minutes ticked by and her bedroom door remained shut, I grew anxious. Finally, I went upstairs, rapped on her door, and opened it a crack. Taylor was lying on her bed with the comforter pulled up to her neck, staring at the ceiling.

"Is everything okay?" I said.

She pulled the comforter closer. "I'm fine," she said. Then she turned her back to me.

I delivered Margot's dinner early, hoping that I could catch Declan at home before he went out with his teammates for pizza. I was in luck, Declan answered the door. He took the tray. "This looks great," he said. "When I get back from the game, I'll have a bowl."

"Good," I said. "Declan, can I talk to you for minute?"

"Sure. Do you want to come in?"

"No, let's just talk out here."

Declan took the tray inside and returned almost immediately.

"When Taylor came home from school, she seemed upset," I said. "She won't talk about what's wrong. I wondered if she'd said something to you."

For a beat, Declan stared at his runners. Then he opened up. "Julian's telling Taylor that they need each other to survive, I told her that's just bullshit – that she doesn't need Julian. She doesn't need anybody. She can handle her own life."

"Is she listening to you?"

"She's starting to, but she's afraid of what Julian might do if she breaks off with him."

My throat clenched. "Is Taylor afraid he'll hurt her?"

"I'd never let that happen," Declan said flatly. "Julian is threatening to harm himself, and Taylor believes him."

"Then it's time for Zack and me to step in."

"That's the best news I've heard in a long time," Declan said.

"You're a good guy," I said. I reached over and touched Declan's hair. Dreadlocks are hard to tousle, but I did my best.

When Zack got home, Taylor came downstairs as soon as she heard his voice. She hugged him and then she hugged me, but she was quiet at dinner. Split pea soup was a family favourite, and I didn't want to ruin our meal by discussing Julian. So we talked about the Grey Cup events that were springing up all over town like mushrooms after a three-day rain. The Saskatchewan Roughriders were the western champions, and the game against the eastern champion Montreal Alouettes would be played in Regina on November 24. Taylor was going to a party at the Wainbergs. Taylor loved parties, especially themed parties. A Grey Cup party was right up her alley, but even talking about the event at the Wainbergs didn't draw Taylor out of her shell, and I could see the worry in Zack's face.

After Taylor went upstairs with her books, Zack and I took our coffee into the living room.

"Declan and I had a chat tonight," I said. "He says Julian's trying to convince Taylor that they have to take their relationship to a deeper level."

"Sexual," Zack said, and his voice was quietly furious.

"More than sexual," I said. "Symbiotic. Julian is telling Taylor that they can't live without each other. He's apparently threatened to hurt himself if she breaks off her relationship with him."

"That tears it," Zack said. He wheeled to the bottom of the stairs. "Taylor, can you come down for a few minutes."

Taylor was in her pyjamas and slippers. She followed Zack into the living room, but she didn't sit down. Her eyes darted between our faces. "If this is about Julian, I'm going back upstairs."

"Just hear us out, please," I said. "Your dad and I are concerned that you're about to make a bad decision."

She whirled around to face me. "In case you haven't noticed, I've made some very good decisions lately. My paintings brought $43,000 to Racette-Hunter and every decision about those paintings was mine. I decided on a subject. I decided on the approach I'd take. I decided about how I would position my subjects. I decided the colours I'd use and how I'd use light and space. Now I'm making another decision. I'm going to continue working with Julian."

"Taylor, I'm sorry. We just can't allow that to happen," Zack said. "We made a terrible mistake about Julian. We trusted Kaye's judgment, and Julian was not the man we thought he was. He used Lauren Treadgold, and he's using you."

"I'm not listening to any more of this," Taylor said and she raced up the stairs and slammed her bedroom door.

"Go after her," Zack said. "We can't leave it like this."

When I knocked on Taylor's bedroom door, she didn't answer. I went in anyway. She was sitting cross-legged on the bed, breathing hard.

I carried a chair over so I could be close but still give Taylor space. "Taylor, I know that Julian's been telling you that you can't make good art without him – that he can unlock something inside you that's keeping you from being the artist you can be."

Taylor's eyes filled with tears. "Declan talked to you," she said. "I thought I could trust him."

"You can trust him," I said. "Declan loves you. He loves you enough to risk losing you because he knows you need to be protected."

"I don't need to be protected against Julian," Taylor said, and her voice was low with fury. "He wants me to be the best artist I can be. That's what I want, too."

"And that's what your dad and I want for you," I said. "But from the moment Julian came into our lives, things have changed. You've changed. You, your dad, and I have always been open with one another, but for more than a month Julian was here almost every day and you never once mentioned that he was posing naked."

Taylor's face was flushed with anger. "That's because he never did pose naked. He always wore a bathing suit." Taylor leaped off her bed, grabbed her knapsack from the floor, and shook the contents onto her bed. There were sketches and there were photographs. She picked one up and thrust it at me. It was in colour. "This is Julian's penis," Taylor said. "If you want to dig through the rest of my stuff, you'll find pictures of all of Julian's sexual parts. I thought you knew how I felt about boys. I wasn't ready to see Julian naked, so he suggested I work from pictures." She picked up another photo. "This is a scrotum," she said coldly. "Painting it from a photo was as easy as painting a piece of fruit."

"I'm sorry, Taylor."

"I don't care if you're sorry or not sorry," she said. "The

point is you didn't trust me to do what I needed to do. Now, just please get out of here and leave me alone."

Zack was at the bottom of the stairs waiting. "I take it your talk did not go well," he said.

I was still holding the photo Taylor had given me. I handed it to Zack. He stared at it over the rim of his glasses. "That's Julian's penis," I said. "When I went upstairs, the killer point I was planning to make was that Julian was changing Taylor, that she had kept the fact that Julian was posing naked secret." I took the picture from Zack. "As it turns out, Julian never was naked. He wore a bathing suit. When Taylor was painting Julian's genitalia, she worked from pictures. She's furious that we didn't trust her to do what she needed to do."

"Shit," Zack said. "Do you want to ask her to come down to talk to me?

"She's too upset," I said. "So am I. Let's all just sleep on it, and try again tomorrow."

CHAPTER 12

Friday morning we awoke to glorious sunshine and blue skies, but I had stopped believing in the pathetic fallacy. As I took the dogs up to the roof garden, my heart was heavy and the scene that greeted me in the kitchen when I got back to our condo didn't lighten it.

The line of Taylor's mouth was grim and her body language made it clear she didn't want physical contact with either Zack or me. She drank her juice, ignored the porridge in the pot, and made herself toast. When she sat down at the table, Zack wheeled close to her. "Taylor, do you want to talk about this?"

"No. Not now."

"We love you."

Taylor pushed her chair back and stood. "Julian said you'd try to do this. He told me that no matter how many times you tell me you love me, I should remember that this is my life."

She grabbed her backpack and walked quickly out of the room. I saw that the bubblegum pink toque that matched the lining of her boots was still sitting on the kitchen counter. I called out to her as she was opening the front door. She pivoted to face me and I saw that she was crying. I went to her and snugged her toque over her ears the way I had when she was a child. And then, as I had when she was a child, I kissed the tip of my daughter's nose. We looked into each other's eyes, and for a beat, I thought we might be home free. But when I reached out to wipe away her tears, Taylor turned and ran for the elevator.

I shut the door, walked into the living room, and collapsed on the couch. Wordlessly, Zack followed, transferred his body from his chair to the place beside me, and drew me to him. Willie and Pantera came in and flopped as close to us as they could manage. For fifteen minutes, Zack and I held each other in a silence that was broken only by the ticking of the grandmother clock and the breathing of our dogs.

Mieka called just as Zack was cleaning up the breakfast dishes and she had good news to pass along.

She and Riel had talked after he spoke to the police. Riel told her everything he'd told the police about his attempt to blackmail Lauren Treadgold and his painful encounter with her when he picked up the money. He had also recounted how, when he heard voices on his return visit to the Treadgold house, he'd fled.

But there was new information. When the police took him through the sequence of events surrounding his two visits to the Treadgold house, Riel remembered something that he'd blanked on when he talked to me. When he left the Treadgolds for the second time, Riel was physically and emotionally spent. He decided to take the bus home. As he waited in the shelter at the bus stop, he saw someone running down the street in front of the Treadgold house. The rain was coming down in sheets, and Riel couldn't tell whether the figure was male or female. All he knew was that the person was slender, had pulled up the hood of their rain gear, and wasn't much of a runner.

According to Mieka, Mildred Thill, the lawyer Zack had recommended, had handled Riel's police interview well. Ms. Thill pointed out to the police that Riel had come forward voluntarily with information that allowed them to expand their investigation; that he'd attempted to return the $20,000; and that when that attempt failed, he'd donated the money to Racette-Hunter.

"Where's Riel now?" I said.

"Out on the porch, painting the benches," Mieka said. "Mum, I don't know what I'm going to do when he's finished with the painting. I don't want to lose him, but I'm not ready to go on as if nothing has happened. I don't think Riel is either. One good thing: Riel and I are having coffee tomorrow with Mildred Thill."

"That is a good thing," I said.

"It is," Mieka said. "Mum, I'm relieved that Riel's addiction is out in the open. At least now we can see the problem and deal with it."

Zack came into the living room, fooling with his iPad. When I told him that Riel had gone to the police and given the full story, Zack exhaled with relief. "That's promising," he said.

"And there's another glimmer of hope on the horizon," I said. "Mieka and Riel are having coffee tomorrow with that lawyer you recommended. They're going to talk about Riel's addiction."

"Whoa," Zack said. "That's more than a glimmer of hope. Mildred gave a talk on addiction at a trial lawyers' lunch last year, and I was impressed. She had some interesting things to say about the relationship between childhood traumas and addiction."

"Well, Riel's childhood was filled with trauma. He saw his mother's husband murder both his mother and his father."

"He also grew up feeling marginalized – another marker for addiction."

"Did Mildred have any suggestions for approaches that really work in conquering addiction?"

"Actually, she did. She quoted this Vancouver doctor. I forget his name, but he talked about the road to recovery requiring what Buddhists call 'mindfulness.' I'm usually not into that touchy-feely stuff, but what Mildred said about addicts slowing down and focusing on what's happening inside themselves made a lot of sense to me."

"Let's hope mindfulness works for Riel," I said. "Let's hope that for once the universe unfolds as it should."

"Hoping isn't enough. We need to be proactive. Let's go back to bed and fool around. That always gets the universe unfolding in the right direction."

"Sold," I said. "Do you realize how long it's been since we made love?"

"Three days," he said, "but who's counting?"

"There's something I want to try," I said. "It was number one in a *Cosmo* article called 'Ten Sex Tricks That Will Drive Your Man Crazy.'"

Zack wheeled over, put his arm around my hips, and squeezed. "Let's get on it."

Cosmo's Sex Trick Number One involved a serious degree of athleticism on my part. When we were finished, Zack looked at me with new respect.

"That deserves champagne and truffles."

And then the landline rang.

"I guess I'll have to hold off on the champagne and truffles," I said, reaching for the phone

Our caller was Gracie Falconer. Taylor hadn't shown up at school that morning and she wasn't answering her cell.

Gracie was worried. I promised Gracie I'd call her when I heard from Taylor, and then I broke the connection and told Zack.

I could see the tension in the set of Zack's jaw. "Let's not panic," he said. "Taylor was upset when she left here, she might have decided she just didn't want to face school."

"Then where is she?" I said. I picked up the phone and dialled Taylor's cell. A recorded voice told me the cellular customer was not available. "She's turned off her phone," I said. "That's not like her."

"No, it isn't," Zack said. "Let's start at the beginning and take it from there. If Taylor hadn't met Declan at the elevator as usual this morning, he would have been in touch." Zack checked his watch. "He'll be in class. I'll text him and ask him to call."

Declan responded immediately. Zack took the call and outlined the situation. When he hung up, his face was grave. "Declan dropped Taylor off at the usual spot, outside the main door, and as usual he left to park his car. That was the last he saw of her. He's going to ask around to see if anyone saw Taylor inside the school."

"I'll start texting the girls Taylor is tight with at school." I took the list of phone numbers off the zonk board and began. When Declan called back, he confirmed what the texts of Taylor's friends had established. No one at Luther had seen our daughter inside the school that morning.

Zack sighed. "Like it or not, the next call is to Julian."

"Your turn," I said.

Zack dialled and waited. "Shit. Straight to voicemail." He wheeled over to the hall cupboard and got his jacket. "What kind of car does Julian drive?"

"A black vw beetle. Do you think they're together?"

Zack picked up his wallet and car keys. "Probably. Where does Julian live?"

"I don't know. I'll call Kaye. Although given our last encounter, I don't imagine she'll be very helpful."

When she heard my voice, Kaye was chilly, so I got straight to business. "Kaye, I need Julian's home address. Do you have it?"

"I do, but he's not at home."

"How do you know?"

"Because he lives in the bungalow next door to me. I bought it when I moved in here after the accident, and I've let special students live there rent-free for years."

"I didn't know," I said.

"There's a lot you don't know, Joanne."

"Fill me in," I said.

"No. I know how you feel about Julian," Kaye said. "I'm not going to share his plans with you."

"Do his plans include Taylor?" I said. "Because if they do, you should remind Julian that Taylor is fifteen years old. There are laws."

"Perhaps," Kaye said. "But young love will find a way." Then, having scored her blow, Kaye hung up, leaving me sick with anger and fear.

Zack wheeled towards me. "Is she with Julian?"

"Kaye implied that, but she might have been bluffing. Zack, for years I've considered Kaye a friend. Certainly, I always felt she was loyal to Sally. Now I don't know. I think Kaye's feelings for Julian are blocking out everything else for her."

"You mean she's in love with him?" Zack said.

"No," I said. "If she were, Kaye wouldn't be encouraging his relationship with Taylor. Kaye truly has been a mentor to her students. She lost her husband and child and then she did something incredibly brave. She embraced other young people. I think she sees what she did to Julian, denying his talent, as a betrayal, and she's trying to make amends."

"I don't get it," Zack said.

"Neither do I," I said. "But we don't have to. We just have to deal with what's left behind."

Zack and I drove straight to Kaye's. The entrance to the bungalow next door had four stairs leading to a deck – not accessible. As I walked up the driveway, I saw Kaye looking through her front window. I forced myself to wave, but she turned away. I knocked, then pounded at Julian's door, but there was no response. When I got back into our car, I could see Kaye at her window again, watching.

For the rest of the morning, Zack and I drove to places where Taylor would have felt comfortable. Her friends in Old Lakeview were at school, but we checked their homes anyway. We also stopped by the Willy Hodgson Rec Centre where Taylor taught art to at-risk kids, UpSlideDown, April's Place, and Peter's vet clinic. No one had seen Taylor but everyone promised to call if she was in touch. I tried Taylor's cell countless times. It was still turned off. Declan called us every half-hour – "Just checking in," he said. The worry in his young voice touched my heart.

Fortified by coffee and a box of Timbits, Zack and I decided to try Julian's house again. When I saw the black VW in the driveway, my heart leaped. To my surprise, Julian not only answered the door, he invited me in. The house was immaculate; so were Julian's manners. He stood aside so I could enter. Taylor's bubblegum pink toque was on the hall table. "I just made coffee," he said. "Would you like some?"

"No, thank you," I said. "Zack's in the car. As you can imagine we're both very anxious about Taylor."

Julian's green eyes were mesmerizing. "Taylor's fine. She just needed time to think things through."

"Is she here?"

"No."

I pointed to the toque. "But she was here."

"Taylor phoned me when her friend dropped her off at Luther. She was upset. She didn't think she could get through the day at school, so I picked her up and we went for coffee and talked. She hadn't slept well, so I suggested she come back here and have a nap."

"Julian, if you have hurt Taylor—"

Julian's voice was soft. "No matter what you believe, Jo, I'm not a monster. Taylor was very upset. I calmed her down, I stayed with her while she slept, I made her lunch, and then I took her where she wanted to go."

"Where is she now?"

"Someplace safe. She and I had a long talk this morning. You and Zack are treating her like a child, and she's not a child. She's a mature artist who needs to be free to make her own decisions."

"She's fifteen years old, Julian."

"Those are just numbers. The fact that she's fifteen doesn't bother Taylor and it doesn't bother me." His expression was boyishly innocent. The shapeshifter. "You're looking a little tired, Joanne. I think it might be time for you to leave."

"I'll leave if you tell me where my daughter is."

"If Taylor wants you to know, she'll tell you. Why don't you let her make that decision? As she told you last night, she's made some very good decisions lately."

I picked up Taylor's toque and left. As soon as I was outside, I broke into a run, jumped into the car, and slammed the door. "Get me out of here before I do something illegal," I said.

Zack started the car and we took off. "Julian says Taylor's fine," I said. "And we have no choice but to believe him."

"Where is she?"

"I don't know," I said. "She was at Julian's house till after lunch, then he took her somewhere else. He wouldn't tell me where. He's in control, and he's loving every minute. When I reminded him that Taylor is fifteen, Julian told me age is just a number."

"Bullshit." Zack groaned. "I don't suppose there's much point in trying Taylor's cell again."

I shook my head. "Julian made a point of telling me that it's up to Taylor to decide when to get in touch with us. Or *if* to get in touch with us. He actually said *if*."

"If? What the hell?" Zack said.

"I know. Apparently, Julian has convinced Taylor that whatever she needs to do to make art is justified."

"That certainly was Sally's credo," Zack said.

"Yes, and every time I think about Sally's formula for a worthwhile life, I feel sick: 'Fuck and you'll make great art.'"

Zack's laugh was derisive. "No guy on the make has ever been handed a greater line than that."

"And Julian is definitely on the make. He wants our daughter's body *and* her talent." I stared out the window, hoping against hope. Zack reached over and patted my hand. "Why don't you call Debbie Haczkewicz?"

"Taylor's only been gone half a day," I said. "And Julian says she's safe. I can't see Debbie wanting to get involved with this."

"It's worth a try," Zack said. "Taylor's a fifteen-year-old girl who's being pulled apart and doesn't know where to turn. Debbie's son, Leo, was older than Taylor when he reached that point, but when he needed help, I was there, and Debbie will remember that. I think she'll do what she can – nothing major – just maybe have officers who are already on patrol keep their eyes open."

When we called Debbie, we listed all the places where Taylor would have been comfortable. Debbie took down the information and promised to do what she could. She was kind, but she had the Lauren Treadgold murder investigation on her plate and a dozen cases that demanded her attention. When I hung up, I felt deflated.

"Zack, I'm tired of this. Let's just go home. Maybe Taylor is there."

She wasn't. It was one of the longest afternoons I could remember. A dense, steady rain had started just as we came back to Halifax Street. The sky was the colour of pewter, and even with the lights on our condo was a shadowy, gloomy place. Zack and I turned on the fireplace, made tea, attempted to busy ourselves, tried not to call Taylor every five minutes, and waited tensely for the phone to ring.

In Regina in November, sunset comes shortly after five o'clock. Neither Zack nor I broached the subject, but I knew we were both waiting for the darkness to gather. Taylor had always been afraid of the dark. Wherever she was, if she was alone, it was possible that she might get in touch.

But it was Declan who came to our door just as dusk was closing in. Taylor had called him. She was in her studio behind our old house on the creek. Julian had agreed to give her the afternoon to think things through, but he was coming at eight to pick her up, and Taylor was more confused than ever.

"Did Taylor ask you to come and get her?" Zack said.

"No," Declan said. "She just wanted to let us know she was all right."

Zack looked at his watch. "And Julian's coming at eight." He wheeled over to the closet and got his jacket and threw his satchel over the back of his chair. I was right behind him.

Our old house on the creek had lights that were timed to go on at dusk, and when we pulled into the driveway on that rainy evening they seemed like an omen of hope. Zack and I went around back to Taylor's studio. The lights were on there too. We forced ourselves to knock and wait outside.

There was no heat in the studio, and when Taylor answered the door, she was wearing her coat and boots. I reached into my pocket, took out her toque, and handed it to her. She took it, pulled it on, and mumbled, "Thanks."

"We're glad to see you," Zack said. "We were scared."

"That's why I called Declan," Taylor said. She was standing in front of the north wall of her studio. The wall was floor-to-ceiling glass. The rain was coming down in sheets behind her. Taylor was five-eight, but against the wall of darkness she seemed small and vulnerable. "I knew you'd be worried," she said. "I knew he'd let you know I was okay."

"And you knew that we'd come," I said.

Taylor nodded.

"Thank you for thinking of us," Zack said.

"I think of you all the time," Taylor said, and her voice was trembling.

My own throat closed. "Taylor, what can we do to make this better?"

"I don't know," she said.

For a couple of minutes, the three of us were silent, listening to the rain. Then Zack reached back for his satchel. "Taylor, there's something I wanted to show you."

Her brow furrowed. "If it's something ugly about Julian, I don't want to see it."

"It's nothing to do with Julian. It's just something for you and for Joanne. It's a surprise I put together after your birthday party at the lake." Zack reached behind him for his satchel and pulled out his MacBook Air. "Why don't you two get close, so we can all watch together?"

Zack balanced his MacBook on his lap and turned the sound up full blast. Suddenly, Taylor's studio was filled with the voices of the Pogues singing their crazy, raucous, life-gulping song "Fiesta," and we were watching a video called *Taylor Throughout the Years*, a rapid-fire retrospective of photos of Taylor starting with one of her blowing out the candles on her fifteenth birthday and moving backwards at breakneck speed. As the Pogues sang, image piled upon image: Taylor in her condo studio; Taylor at the old house with her cats; Taylor at Christmas giving me an illustrated version of Pablo Neruda's "Ode to Socks"; Taylor at the lake building the inuksuit with Gracie and Isobel; Taylor standing between Zack and me on the wintry day we were married; Taylor with the bishop, the dean, and the other kids in her class on the day she was confirmed; Taylor carving a pumpkin at Halloween; Taylor holding the newborn Lena, with Madeleine proudly by her side; Taylor at age four and a half going to a birthday party wearing a frilly dress and her pyjama bottoms because they were covered in stars.

As "Fiesta" wound down, the last picture appeared on the screen. It was of Taylor the day she came to live with my children and me. The shot brought back that day to me with aching clarity. She was a silent and painfully obedient child who wouldn't let me out of her sight. I gave her a package of crayons and a sketchbook. Then I sat down on the floor beside her. As she began to draw a dazzlingly blue butterfly, she bit her lip in concentration; her small body relaxed and for the first time I could see the girl she was. It took her two hours to finish her drawing of the butterfly. When she finished, she turned to me, her dark eyes filled with questions she was afraid to ask.

"You're going to live with us now," I said.

"For how long?"

"As long as you want," I'd said. Then I'd taken a Polaroid of her with the butterfly drawing and together we put the photo in our family album.

Zack turned off his laptop. The silence among us was electric, charged with unsaid words. Finally, Taylor moved close to me and lay her head on my shoulder. "I want it to be over," she said simply.

"It will be," Zack said. "I can tell Julian."

"No," Taylor said. "He should hear it from me, but you'll have to let me pick my own time."

When we got back to Halifax Street, Taylor went straight to her room. After we heard her door close, I went to Zack. "What made you think of showing Taylor the video?"

"I was planning to give it to her for Christmas," Zack said. "But tonight it hit me that what Taylor needed more than anything was a reminder of the girl she is."

"That was brilliant," I said.

He put his arm around my hips and squeezed. "No," he said. "It was just damn lucky."

CHAPTER

13

Our weekend was very quiet, and during the following days we all seemed to be in a holding pattern. Taylor went to school. Julian came over after school to pose. Taylor had dinner with us, did her homework, and went to bed. She was preoccupied and sad, but she was clearly steeling herself for the task of telling Julian, and true to our word, we had resolved to let her choose her own time.

Taylor spent most of the next Saturday in her studio, but Saturday night she went over to Margot's to talk to Declan. When she came home, she kissed us both goodnight and said, "I'm ready. I'll tell Julian tomorrow afternoon when he comes over to pose."

Everyone in our province becomes a weather-watcher on Grey Cup Sunday. One of my thousand worries about Zack is that he'll catch a cold that will develop into something more serious – sitting three and half hours in a freezing stadium being pelted by rain is the first step to pneumonia. Mosaic Stadium does not have a domed roof, but Saskatchewan has the most dedicated fans in the league, and Zack is the most dedicated of the dedicated. He and I had braved the elements many times for Riders games, but when I checked the weather forecast that morning, it appeared we were in luck. The temperature was going to be a balmy plus ten. There would be no wind or precipitation and plenty of sunshine was headed our way. Zip-a-dee-doo-dah.

Before the Cathedral's ten-thirty service, Taylor had talked to me about the least painful way of breaking off with Julian. We agreed that the best tack was simply to tell the truth – that Taylor was too young for the kind of relationship Julian hoped for.

The prospect of causing Julian pain was eating away at her. It was eating away at me, too. Julian might have been a hustler and a manipulator, but he was also a very troubled nineteen-year-old boy, and my heart went out to him. We were all quiet on the way to the service.

Everyone at the church, including our dean, Mike Sinclair, wore the green and white garb of the Riders fan. When we took our place beside Mieka and the girls, Zack whispered, "I bet a bundle on this game. Can I pray that the Riders win?"

"No," I said. "But you can pray that if the Riders tank today, I never find out how much money you lost."

Zack's expression was cherubic. The music for the processional began. Madeleine and Lena were both altar girls that morning, and as they passed us, angelic in their white robes, Zack was in his glory. It was an auspicious start to the day.

The game started at 5:00 p.m. and except for Taylor, who was going to the Wainbergs' Grey Cup party, the game would be a full-family affair. Peter, Angus, and their respective girlfriends would be joining us at Mosaic Stadium. I was looking forward to the game, but the spectre of Julian loomed.

He arrived at the condo just after lunch. Taylor's sessions with him could last hours, but this one was over in about forty-five minutes. When he came downstairs, he walked past Zack and me like a man in a trance. I followed him to the door. "Take care of yourself, Julian," I said. He just kept on walking.

Taylor came down soon afterwards. Her face was strained, but she seemed calm. "Well, it was awful, but I didn't back down. I told Julian we could be friends, but it couldn't be anything more. He offered to keep coming over until the painting was finished, but I told him it might be easier for both of us if I worked from photographs. He was really nice about letting me get all the shots I needed. I invited him to come over when the painting is finished."

"Did that help?" I asked.

"I hope so," Taylor said. "Julian was really upset. He said I was his only hope."

"His only hope for what?" Zack said.

"Being someone who mattered in the art world," Taylor said. She held out her hand. It was trembling. "I think I need to lie down for a while."

After Taylor was out of earshot, Zack exhaled. "God, I'm glad that's over."

"I feel sorry for Julian."

"So do I," Zack said. "He has what my mother used to call 'hurting eyes,' but he'll be okay. Julian's a survivor."

"I wish I was as sure of that as you are," I said.

Two hours later Taylor came back downstairs dressed for the Grey Cup party: her hair was in a ponytail anchored by a green and white scrunchy, she was carrying pom-poms, and wearing a team sweater, a retro cheerleader's skirt, bobby sox, and green and white runners. She looked the way a fifteen-year-old girl should look on her way to a football party, except that she was pale and her eyes were swollen from crying.

Zack's face mirrored my own concern. "You don't look like you're in a party mood, Taylor," I said. "Why don't I stay home with you? I could use a quiet evening."

"No," she said. "You've been looking forward to the game, and it's not as if I won't know everybody at the Wainbergs. I won't have to pretend that I'm having a blast if I'm not."

When Margot and Declan came over to pick Taylor up, Declan took me aside. "Did she tell him?" When I nodded, relief washed over his young face.

As always, Margot looked smashing. She had draped a Roughriders scarf around the neck of her white sweater, and her green pregnancy leggings showcased her gorgeous legs.

"That's a great outfit," I said. "You're certainly not leaving it in the locker room."

Margot grinned. "I came to play."

"And you're giving it 110 per cent," Zack said. "Three football clichés in a row – nowhere near the world record. Sadly, it's time for us to hit the road. Traffic to Mosaic is going to be murder." He turned to Taylor. "Not too late to change your mind," he said. "Just say the word, and your mum and I will stay home with you."

Taylor kissed the top of his head. "Dad, you've been talking about this game for weeks. Go. Have a good time. I'll be fine."

Zack looked dubious. "Okay, but if you need us, you know where we are."

It was a great afternoon. The Montreal Alouettes and the Riders were evenly matched. Both sides made spectacular plays; both made serious mental mistakes; and both took bone-headed penalties. The Riders won in the last twenty seconds of the game, and, as they say, the crowd went wild. Stoked by popcorn and soft drinks, Madeleine and Lena had been remarkably patient, but as they joined in the high-fiving, I knew that they were celebrating both the Riders victory and the fact that the game was finally over.

Everybody was going back to Mieka's for dinner, but Zack and I asked for a rain check. We were both worried about Taylor. We knew how deeply she had been wounded by the situation with Julian, and we wanted to be at home if she needed us.

It took us forever to get back to Halifax Street. On our way to the car, we ran into a dozen people we knew, all of whom wanted to talk about the game. When we got into the Volvo, Zack snapped his seatbelt and then fumbled around in his jacket. "Shit. I must have left my phone at home. Can I borrow yours?"

"I never take my bag to the game. Just one more thing to lose. Is it urgent?"

"No, I was just going to call a buddy of mine in Montreal and gloat."

"Nice," I said.

When we finally turned onto Halifax Street, an ambulance was just pulling away from our building, siren shrieking, lights flashing. My mind raced. "That can't be for Margot," I said. "If there was a problem, someone would have called us."

"If we'd had our phones with us," Zack said.

"Right," I said. "If we'd had our phones with us." I pulled into the twenty-minute zone at the front of the building. "What do you want to do?"

Zack was already reaching into the back seat for his wheel chair. "Go upstairs and see if there are any messages," he said.

Zack's mind was still on Margot. As the elevator doors closed, he turned to me. "If the baby's born now, will she be all right?"

"Margot's due on Christmas Day, so it will be an eight-month baby. The odds are certainly in her favour, but full-term is always preferable."

Zack took my hand. "I'm glad we went to church this morning."

"Me, too," I said.

When we got off the elevator, the hall was quiet. I knocked on Margot's door, but there was no answer.

As soon as I unlocked the door to our condo, the dogs were upon us. Willie and Pantera were always eager greeters, but that afternoon they were frantic. Zack bent to comfort Pantera and I stroked Willie. "Calm down," I said. "Everything's fine."

But even as I cooed reassurance, I knew nothing was fine. There were boot marks on the hardwood downstairs, a ficus on the landing had been knocked over, and the pot had broken, spilling soil and leaves on the stairs.

"What the hell?" Zack said.

I called Taylor's name, but my voice echoed hollowly through the empty house. As I tore up the stairs, trying to sidestep dirt and shards of pottery, the dogs were at my heels. I called them off, but even to my own ears, my commands sounded thin and unconvincing. Zack positioned his wheelchair at the bottom of the stairs. When I reached the second floor, I smelled the blood before I saw it. At first, all I saw was a red smear in the hall. I was terrified, but I forced myself to continue towards Taylor's studio. I stared through the open door and saw a pool of blood on the floor in front of Taylor's easel. The room began to swim around me. I bent, put my hands on my knees, and tried to take deep breaths. The sickly-sweet smell I inhaled turned my stomach. Willie and Pantera pressed themselves against my legs.

I shouted at them to get out of the studio and slammed the door. I seldom raised my voice to the dogs and the shock sent them running towards Zack.

Zack had always had the power to soothe me, but when I got to the landing and saw the fear in his face, my knees turned to water. I clung to the banister, and finally I made my way to him. "Something's happened," I said. "There's blood in Taylor's studio, but she's not there."

"If she was in that ambulance, we have to get to the hospital," Zack said, and his voice was authoritative.

"We don't know which hospital they've taken her to," I said.

Zack had already grabbed his cell from the table. It was obvious his call had gone to voicemail. "Vince, it's Zack. Joanne and I just came home from the game. An ambulance was pulling away from our building, and we're afraid Taylor's been hurt. We don't know what hospital she'd be taken to. If we call the hospitals, we'll just get jacked around. Can you find out where she is?"

While we waited for Vince to call back, Zack and I held on to each other wordlessly. When the phone rang, we both froze. Zack's face was grey when he picked up, but as he listened to Vince the colour seemed to flow back into his cheeks. "Thank God," he said. "Okay, we'll meet you in emergency at the General."

He took my hand. "It's not Taylor," he said. "The injured person was male, but when he was admitted, there was a girl with him. That's all Vince could tell me."

Regina General was only minutes from our house. Zack drove, and locked in our own thoughts, we were silent until we arrived in the ER. Easily 90 per cent of the wounded in the waiting room were wearing Roughriders garb. The room was a sea of green, but the celebration was over. Alcohol and adrenalin had taken their toll, and reality was setting in.

Vince was waiting for us. "Follow me," he said. He pushed through double doors and down a corridor where cubicle curtains separated patients on hospital beds waiting for further treatment. He stopped at the last cubicle in the hall. "I won't come in with you," he said. "This is an awkward situation. Julian is the patient. He apparently entered your condo this afternoon and slit his wrists."

"Is he going to be all right?"

"He lost a lot of blood. Taylor and Declan did the right things. Taylor called 911 and Declan ripped up an old shirt and made tourniquets, but I don't know. If you need me, someone on staff will have me paged."

"Can we go in?"

"Yes. It would be probably be wise to get Taylor home."

I pulled the curtain so Zack could push his wheelchair in. Taylor was covered in blood. When she saw Zack, she collapsed into his arms. Declan was beside her, also bloodied. Julian was on the bed, hooked up to the machines that measure our mortality. Under the clinically bright light, Julian's always pale face was alabaster. He was alarmingly still. A nurse entered the room behind us. "Are you his parents?"

"No, that's our daughter. Julian is a . . . a friend."

The nurse was brusque. "There are far too many of you in here now, but if any of you can help with next of kin, we'd appreciate it. On the card in his wallet Julian lists his emergency contact as Kaye Russell. He included Ms. Russell's telephone number, but when we tried it the operator said the line is disconnected."

"May I see the number?" I said.

The nurse copied it from Julian's chart onto a piece of scrap paper and handed it to me. I scanned it. "The last digit in the number is wrong," I said. "The number here is 7. It should be 1."

"Thanks," she said. "Now you can all clear out."

Taylor went over and touched Julian's hand. "He's so cold," she said. "Is he going to live?" Her voice was small and scared and when the nurse responded, her tone was kind. "Your boyfriend's young and that's a plus. Is there a relative we can get in touch with?"

Taylor shook her head.

"There are none," Zack said. He took a business card from his wallet and handed it to the nurse. "I'm a lawyer. You can call me if you need a signature."

The corridor throbbed with the muted sounds of suffering and fear. As the four of us pushed through the double doors to the waiting room, no one paid us any mind. Taylor and Declan looked a mess, and Zack was in a wheelchair. We were clearly fellow sufferers. When we got to the door, I turned to Declan. "Have you talked to Margot?"

"No. And she'll be worried. I said I'd call and tell her how Taylor was doing."

My arm tightened on Taylor's shoulders. "You weren't feeling well?"

Taylor shook her head. "I was upset about Julian. I thought the party would help, but it didn't, so Declan took me home." Her voice was a whisper. "If Declan hadn't been there . . ."

The thought, rife with possibilities, hung in the air. "Let's just be grateful Declan was there," Zack said, and his tone, firm and convincing, put an end to speculation.

Our family doctor, Henry Chan, once told me that when an accident involving a number of people arrives in the ER, the directive is always the same: "Salvage what you can."

That night, we tried to salvage what we could. Margot was waiting for us when we got back to Halifax Street. Silent, she shepherded us into her condo. Zack stayed in the hall to wait for the police; I led Taylor down to the guest bathroom to shower, and Declan went upstairs to shower there.

When Zack came inside, Margot pointed to her liquor cabinet. "Help yourself," she said.

"Thanks," Zack said. "Ms. Shreve, what would you say to a martini?"

"I'd say, 'Where have you been all my life?'" The situation was beyond terrible, but exchanging the lines of our old joke was comforting. Zack made our drinks, poured Margot a ginger ale, and the three of us went into the living room.

Zack took a large sip of his drink and sighed. "Well, let's see. The police wanted to talk to Taylor and Declan, but I said no dice till tomorrow. They're checking out the condo now."

Margot frowned. "The police don't suspect foul play, do they?"

"No," Zack said. "Julian knew what he was doing. Apparently, he'd kept the security card for the condo Taylor gave him when they were working together. He came equipped with a box-cutter. He slit both wrists."

"Was there a note?"

Zack didn't have a chance to answer. At that moment, Taylor came down the hall. She was wearing a white terry towel robe, and she had a towel tied round her hair. She looked frail but better. Zack held out his arms to her, and she went to him. "How's it going?" he said.

Taylor's face was buried in Zack's neck and her voice was muffled. "Not good."

When Declan came downstairs, he opened a beer for himself and a soft drink for Taylor and joined us in the living room. Small talk was impossible, and for a few minutes we sat around, occasionally glancing at one another like guests at a bad party.

Finally, Taylor broke the silence. "I want to talk about it," she said. Her voice was flat. "After we left the Wainbergs, I kind of fell apart. When we got back here, Declan came into our place with me. He said I should go up and get into bed, and he'd stay downstairs and watch the post-game shows until you came home.

"When I went upstairs, the door to my studio was open and I saw Julian. He was lying on the floor. He has a robe that he wears when he's not posing." She touched the sleeve of her own robe. "It was soaked with blood. I guess I screamed. I got down on the floor to see if Julian was still breathing, but I couldn't tell. Then Declan was there. I called 911 and Declan ripped up a shirt and tried to stop the blood."

"It didn't do any good," Declan said bleakly.

Like Taylor, Zack and I were not eager to spend the night in our condo. Margot offered us her guest bedrooms. When I went across to get toiletries and clothing for us all, the police were just leaving.

A young female officer addressed me. "Taylor Shreve is your daughter?"

"Yes, but we don't want you questioning her tonight. She's talked to us about finding Julian. I can tell you that much."

"That would be a start." She pulled out her notebook and I relayed Taylor's account.

"Poor kid," she said.

"Poor all of them," I said.

She nodded.

When I got back to Margot's, there was a semblance of normal life. The television was on – still post-game talk. Live reports from the Green Mile and of the crowds downtown.

"I tried to order pizza," Margot said. "The Copper Kettle said there'd be a three-hour wait."

I opened the fridge. "How would everybody feel about bacon and eggs?"

No one said no, so I pulled out the frying pan.

Zack and I sat with Taylor until she was asleep. I was glad our bedroom was next to hers so we'd be able to hear her if she awoke in the night. I hadn't thought that way in years. As he turned down his side of the bed, Zack said, "God, what a day."

"One good thing about this day is that it's over," I said.

Then my phone rang. I checked the caller ID. It was Kaye Russell. I picked up and my ear was seared by the terrible primal mourn of a woman keening. There was nothing to do but listen and wait.

When Kaye was, at last, able to form words, the toxicity of her rage tore at me. "Julian's dead. Taylor did this," she said. "Like mother, like daughter. Sally destroyed people. Taylor's just like her – using people – then throwing them away. Don't think I've forgotten how Sally treated you. She was a selfish bitch and the apple hasn't fallen far from the tree."

I'd had enough. "Kaye, I'm going to hang up now," I said. "We'll talk later."

When I hung up, Kaye was sobbing.

Zack and I spent the next few minutes lying side by side staring at the unfamiliar ceiling. Finally, I broke the silence: "Julian's dead and his suicide has driven Kaye over the edge. She hates Sally and she hates Taylor. I know Kaye has suffered, but so has Taylor. I don't want Kaye anywhere near our daughter, Zack. After we tell her about Julian tomorrow morning, I think we should go to the lake."

"Fine with me," Zack said. "I've got a couple of meetings, but nothing I can't handle by Skype. The grand opening of April's Place isn't till Friday. Apart from that, I can do everything from Lawyers' Bay."

"Good," I said. "We have to deal with some things before we go. Taylor and Declan have to give statements to the police. I'd like Henry Chan to check Taylor out, and I should call the school and arrange for homework assignments."

"You've covered the bases," Zack said. He took off his glasses and rubbed his eyes. The horror of Julian's death seemed to hit us both at the same time. "God, this is terrible, isn't it?" he said.

"It is," I said. "But we can't let this destroy Taylor's life, Zack. We have to get her through."

The next morning Zack and I waited till we heard Taylor stirring, and then we went to her. We'd brought Willie and Pantera and Taylor's cats over to Margot's, and Taylor was in bed stroking Bruce and Benny. One look at our faces and her lips began to quiver. "Julian didn't make it, did he?"

"No," I said. "He didn't. He died last night."

Taylor didn't cry, but she seemed to shrink into her robe. "It's my fault," she said.

"That's not true," Zack said and his voice was steely. "Julian made a decision. It was the wrong decision, but it can't be changed. Your mother and I are very sorry that Julian is dead – believe me, we really are sorry, but, Taylor, Julian's death was not your fault. He died by his own hand."

Taylor nodded. "He was always so alone. It's terrible to think that he was alone last night."

"He wasn't alone," I said. "Kaye Russell was with him."

"She loved Julian," Taylor said. Her eyes had been downcast, now she raised them to me. "Do you think I should call her?"

"No," I said. "And, Taylor, if Kaye tries to call you, don't talk to her. She's very angry right now."

"At me?"

"At everybody."

Taylor had a studio at the lake, and determined to complete the painting of Julian, she created a schedule for herself. She rose early, finished her schoolwork, and then went to her studio, coming back to the cottage only to eat or make tea. It was difficult to read her mood. She was quiet, but Taylor was often quiet when she was absorbed in making art.

Zack and I had our routine, too. In the mornings we walked the dogs and took care of Racette-Hunter business. After lunch we had a nap, took another walk, then worked again till it was time to get dinner ready. Every night just before bed, we sat down together and at Taylor's request we listened to the Pogues "Fiesta" and watched *Taylor Throughout the Years*. She never explained the significance the ritual had for her, but it appeared to give her comfort.

We were living day by day, and it seemed to be working, but at the end of the week a new and ugly possibility had presented itself. When the police searched Julian's home after his death, they'd found a suicide note, buried under a pile of art magazines in his basement. It read, *I did it for you*. Short and sweet.

Debbie Haczkewicz had good cop instincts and the wording of Julian's suicide note had troubled her. There'd been no salutation and no signature – just five words: *I did it for you*. And the note had been hidden. Debbie's reasoning was sound. If Julian were leaving a message for Taylor, why would he have deliberately put the note in a place where she was unlikely to find it?

And there was the troubling use of the past tense. According to Debbie, most suicide notes are written in the present tense. "I am doing this for you" connects the writer's action directly to the loved one. Debbie confided to Zack that her gut was telling her that when Julian wrote *I did it for you*, he was referring not to his plan to commit suicide but to Lauren Treadgold's murder.

Debbie had instructed her officers to look more closely at Julian's activities on the day of Lauren's death, but the search had barely begun before the police handwriting expert determined that the note was not in Julian's hand. The police were now focused on finding the person who had written those five fatal words, but so far they had been unsuccessful.

Julian's funeral was Thursday morning. Kaye Russell was making the arrangements, and although Taylor wanted to be there, Zack and I vetoed the idea. Taylor was painfully vulnerable, and Kaye Russell had become vindictive. She continued to bombard our daughter with poisonous telephone messages that I deleted at the end of each day. After Zack listened to a few, he bought Taylor a new cell and suggested that we consider harassment charges. Knowing Kaye's history, I couldn't bring myself to take that step.

Taylor spent the morning of Julian's funeral in her studio. When she didn't come back to the cottage for lunch, Zack and I went to get her. She seldom let us see any piece she was working on until it was finished, but that morning Taylor led us to her easel.

The portrait of Julian in the rain forest was far from complete, but I could already feel the piece's nascent power. Julian stood naked, facing the viewer directly from the picture's centre line. With his flawless alabaster body and his black curls spiralling against his slender shoulders, he was unsettlingly erotic, but there was an innocence about him that touched my heart. Except for his haunted, hostile green eyes, Julian's face was without expression.

He was surrounded by other creatures of the rain forest: a golden lion, a tamarind monkey, a toucan, a jaguar, a poison dart frog, a Bengal tiger, a harpy eagle. All were extravagantly beautiful; all had eyes that carried the accusation I read in Julian's eyes. *We are moving inexorably towards extinction. This is what you have done to us.*

Taylor watched our faces closely as we examined the painting, but she didn't wait for us to comment. "It's good, isn't it?" she said tentatively.

"It's better than good," Zack said. "Cole Dimitroff made a very wise investment."

Taylor bit her lip. "I wish Julian could have seen it."

Friday, November 30, was the grand opening of April's Place. Lunch was going to be venison stew and bannock. There would be balloons, plenty of media attention, and a giant cake. Mayor Ridgeway, who as Zack frequently noted had done dick-squat to support the building of the play centre, had volunteered to cut the first slice. The joint was already jumping by the time we arrived. Perhaps 90 per cent of the parents and kids there were First Nations, and everybody was having fun.

The building was a deconsecrated synagogue that had become a dance studio. The main room had a gleaming hardwood floor and one mirrored wall. The space had been too small for the activities Mieka and Lisa Wallace had in mind, so they'd doubled the size of the building to include a large, quiet play area and tables and chairs where parents could have a cup of coffee and watch their kids.

As soon as we arrived, Brock Poitras commandeered Taylor to give Mieka a hand in the kitchen. "Tell Mieka I'll be right there," I said. "But I'd like to say hi to Margot first."

"I'm going to have a chat with the mayor," Zack said.

"Watch it," I said. "There are children present."

Zack flashed his shark grin and wheeled off. Margot was across the room in deep conversation with a girl of about three. The child was wearing a pink tutu from the tickle trunk and she was close to tears. When I joined them, Margot gave me a brief wave but kept her focus on the little girl. "You look so pretty," Margot said. "Why are you sad?"

"Because I don't know how to . . . *twirl*," the child said.

"I can twirl," Margot said.

The girl eyed her suspiciously. Margot arranged her arms

and legs in what I recognized from Mieka's ballet days as fourth position; then Margot bent both her legs into a deep plié, turned her head, body, and legs together in a full circle, and finished back in fourth position as gracefully as a very pregnant woman could.

"Now, we'll do it together," Margot said. "Can you tell me your name?"

"Sabrina," the child said.

"All right, Sabrina. Just do what I'm doing."

Slowly, but accurately, Sabrina followed Margot's example and completed a pirouette. Satisfied, she danced across the room so she could watch herself twirl in the mirror.

For a minute or two, Margot and I silently followed Sabrina's progress. "They say that there's a moment in every person's life when they do something that changes another life," I said finally.

"And the twirl was my moment?" Margot said.

I watched Sabrina moving ecstatically in front of the mirror. "You could have done worse," I said.

"How are things with you?" Margot said.

"We're getting by," I said. "Being at the lake is helping. It's peaceful, and Julian was never at Lawyers' Bay, so there are no associations."

"Is there anything I can do?"

"Actually, there is. Zack and I've been talking about the condo."

Margot face grew anxious. "You're not thinking of moving, are you?"

"No. We're committed to the neighbourhood and we want to be nearby when the baby comes. It's just that Taylor, understandably, doesn't want to go back to the rooms upstairs, so Zack and I wondered how you'd feel about us installing a stairlift so he and I could use the second floor."

"Consider it done," Margot said. "I take it you'll need some painting and floor refinishing."

"Yes. I think it might be smart to change the paint colours in the rooms on the second floor – take away their history." I cringed. "God, Margot, listen to us. A boy died and we're decorating."

"I know," Margot said. "But as you have said to me on more than one occasion, ready or not, life goes on. I want you, Zack, and Taylor right across the hall from us for as long as possible. I'll paint those rooms myself if that's what it takes."

I laughed. "What a woman. She twirls, she paints, and she's dynamite in a courtroom." I stood. "Now, I'm going to see if I can give Mieka a hand."

"That stew smells great."

"I'll get you a bowl. You can be my first customer."

Serving stew and bannock to everyone in the room was chaotic, but Mieka and Riel were managing the kitchen and it was a pleasure to watch them working together efficiently and companionably. The women in the community had done all the cooking, and the food was superb. When Ernest Beauvais said the blessing, first in English, then in Cree, I had a good feeling.

After we'd finished clearing the dishes away, Zack said, "Time to hit the road."

I looked around the room. "I'll get Taylor." It was a task that was easier said than done. I looked in the playrooms. She wasn't there. When she wasn't in the boot and coat-room, I felt the first stirrings of panic. I went into the kitchen. Riel was loading the dishwasher. "Have you seen Taylor?" I said.

He shook his head. "Not lately. I saw her a while ago. She was outside talking to her old teacher."

"Kaye Russell?" I said.

"The one with the buzz cut?" he said. His tone was jocular, but when he saw my concern, the fun went out of his voice. "Is there something wrong, Jo?"

"I hope not."

"What can I do?"

"Help me look for Taylor outside, would you? Don't say anything to Mieka. We don't want to ruin the party."

That autumn was the rainiest I could remember, and yet again it was raining hard. Riel scanned the street. "Jo, why don't you go down the street towards Victoria and I'll go up towards 12th. We can square the block and meet in the middle."

As soon as I turned onto Victoria, I spotted Kaye and Taylor. Kaye was wearing her Andy Warhol raincoat, but Taylor was just in her sweater and jeans. Kaye appeared to be frog-marching Taylor down the street. I called Taylor's name. She tried to turn, but Kaye wouldn't let her. I ran until I caught them. "What are you doing?" I said.

Contorted by fury, Kaye's face was transformed. "I have pictures of Julian's funeral that Taylor needs to see. The camera's in my car."

Taylor's eyes found mine. "Kaye just said she had photos of Julian she wanted me to have."

"I do want you to have them," Kaye growled. "And I want you to look at them every day of your life."

Riel was coming down the block towards us. "That's enough, Kaye," I said. I reached over and pulled her arm off my daughter.

Kaye turned and began to run. All Riel had to do was wait for her. Kaye tried to run past him, but her bad leg slowed her and Riel caught her easily. He grabbed her arm and held on.

"You can let her go, Riel," I said. "Kaye lost someone she cared about recently. She doesn't know what she's doing."

Riel tightened his grip on Kaye's arm. "Call the police, Jo."

"We don't need to involve the police," I said. "Kaye is troubled, but she hasn't really hurt anyone."

Riel's eyes were blazing. "Yes, she has. She killed Lauren Treadgold."

My mind was racing. I remembered the note hidden beneath the art magazines in Julian's basement. I looked at Kaye. "You killed Lauren for Julian," I said.

"I saw her running from the Treadgolds the day of the murder." Riel's eyes bored into Kaye. "It was pouring, but I could see the colours of this coat even through the rain. You were limping – like you were just now. Call the police, Joanne," Riel said.

I got out my phone and dialled 911.

"I did it for him," Kaye said, and her face was a rictus of despair. "I did it for Julian. He was trying to get away from Lauren. He thought being with Taylor would give him a fresh start. Lauren was going to show Taylor the sex video, and Julian was afraid that would turn Taylor against him. He called me in despair. I went to plead with Lauren, but she wouldn't listen. She kept saying that Julian was *her* fresh start and she would never give him up. I guess that's when I picked up the rock. I don't remember. I just remember the blood." Suddenly her misery turned again to fury and she glared at Taylor. "I sacrificed Lauren Treadgold for Julian. And then you made the sacrifice meaningless. You're just like your mother. You have no heart."

Taylor's entire body was trembling, but Kaye showed our daughter no mercy. Like the crone in a fairy tale, Kaye spit out a final curse. "Sally didn't want you, you know. For the month after you were born she was unable to paint, so she found a new lover, left you with your father, went to New Mexico, and made some of the best art of her life. She wrote me that giving birth to you had been a mistake."

CHAPTER 14

I asked Zack to stop at our condo before we drove back to the lake. He and Taylor stayed in the car while I took the elevator upstairs and picked up our copy of the Sally Love documentary and the DVDs containing the outtakes. It was time for Taylor and me to lay our ghosts to rest.

On the drive to the lake, Taylor was silent until we got to the turnoff. "Is it true that my mother didn't want me?" she said.

It was the question I'd been dreading since Kaye's outburst, and I hadn't managed to come up with an answer that was both truthful and comforting. "It's true that she went to New Mexico and left you with your father," I said, "but particularly at the end of her life Sally was very glad she had you."

"She just didn't want to live with me," Taylor said.

"That's not true. Just before she died, Sally found a place in Vancouver for you two to live. It was on the ocean, plenty of windows, and a studio big enough for both of you."

"Sally only wanted me when she realized I could make art."

"We don't know that, Taylor," I said. "All we know is that at the end of her life Sally wanted to be with you."

"That's not enough," Taylor said, and the line of her mouth indicated that, for the time being at least, the subject was closed.

Zack made tea when we got to the cottage. There were no safe topics of conversation so Taylor picked up a magazine, I opened the novel I was reading, Zack checked his messages, and we drank our Earl Grey. When she'd finished her tea, Taylor announced she was going to her studio, then she put on her jacket, picked up her two cats, and left Zack and me free to talk.

"It's going to take her a long time to get over this," Zack said. "I really am glad it wasn't Julian. Taylor would have believed that Lauren's death was her fault, too."

"What's going to happen to Kaye?" I asked.

"Short-term or long-term?" Zack said.

"Long-term," I said. "How is this situation going to play out legally?"

"If I were handling Kaye's case, I'd convince the Crown that this was an aberration," Zack said. "Kaye has a solid reputation as a teacher and it would be no problem to round up character witnesses to say she's always been a fine citizen. I'd get a shrink to do whatever she or he could to bring Kaye back from la-la-land, and when Kaye was ready, I'd prepare her to testify. Then I'd warn the Crown that Kaye would be great on the stand; I'd vilify the deceased and I'd try to get the Crown to agree to a joint submission on a low sentence."

"And the Crown would agree?"

Zack raised both eyebrows. "That would depend on many things," he said. "But it would be worth the gamble."

When Zack's cell rang, I picked up our cups and went into the kitchen to start on dinner.

After about ten minutes, Zack came into the kitchen looking relieved rather than triumphant. "That was Debbie. They've taken Kaye into custody. Asia Libke is Kaye's lawyer. Asia's young, but she's good. The police are questioning Kaye now, but she's confessed that she killed Lauren."

"Does Vince know?"

"He's probably already been told," Zack said. "But I'll give him a call just in case."

I went outside to light the barbecue. It wasn't long before Zack appeared at the back door. "What are we barbecuing?"

"Cook's choice," I said. "Pickerel. So how did Vince take the news?"

"Calmly. He thanked me for all my work and said he never doubted that sooner or later he would be found innocent, but it was a relief to have it over."

"Maybe now he'll remember that he has a daughter," I said.

"Actually, Vince did say something about going someplace warm for a while with Celeste."

"A silver lining at last," I said. "Vince and Celeste both need to make amends. Now they have a chance."

On Saturday morning, Taylor was up and at her studio early. Zack and I spent the morning doing what people who are deeply in love and have weathered a crisis together do. We made love. Then we took a long walk with the dogs and thanked our lucky stars.

After lunch Zack went into town for a meeting, and I decided to attack a task I'd been putting off – giving the old partners' table and its twenty-four chairs some serious polishing with beeswax. I'd just cleared off the table when Taylor came out to the sunroom.

She scanned the expanse of the table. "The wood in this table is amazing," she said. "I never really noticed it until now."

I held up the can of polish and my cloth. "My plan today is to give that wood some loving care."

"I can help," Taylor said.

"There's plenty of work for two," I said. "The rag bag is in the cupboard by the back door."

Taylor came back with a rag, dug into the wax, and went to the far end of the table. We worked wordlessly but amiably till we'd almost met in the middle.

Taylor broke the silence. "Why didn't my mother want me?" she said. She leaned closer to the wood she was polishing.

"Do you want to take a break to talk about this?" I asked.

"No," she said. "We can talk while we work."

"I don't really have an answer, Taylor. Sally and I had been estranged for thirty years when we finally got together again, and it was at a terrible time in her life. Her show at the Mendel was causing an uproar. She was getting pilloried in the media. People were pulling pranks that weren't very funny – putting sugar in her gas tank, sending her gross packages through the mail, that kind of thing. She was trying to get custody of you. So she was battling your father and Nina. But despite everything, she was still Sally, fearless and funny and absolutely determined to raise you. I'm glad I had that time with her. I'd been angry at her for so many years."

Taylor dug her cloth into the can of beeswax. "I'm still angry at her," she said quietly.

"I know you are," I said. "And I understand why. All you know about Sally is that she left when you were months old and she went on to make amazing art."

"I know what I've read on the Internet," Taylor said. "She didn't have many friends."

"People were jealous – not just her of her talent, but of her beauty and of the fact that she chose to live life her own way."

"She hurt a lot of people," Taylor said.

"She did, but Taylor, she'd been badly hurt herself. She was different before your grandfather died."

"Too bad I didn't know her then," Taylor said, and her mouth curved into Sally's mocking smile.

"Maybe we can remedy that," I said. "A few weeks ago, Ben Bendure, the man who made that documentary about Sally's life, sent two DVDs of the material he didn't use. He wanted you to have them. Whenever you're ready, we can look at them together."

Taylor polished silently for a few minutes, then she said, "Let's finish the furniture and look at them today."

And so, when the table and all its chairs were gleaming, my daughter and I threw out our rags, put the tin of wax back in the cupboard, washed our hands, and turned on the DVD player.

We started with the scenes that Zack and I had watched – of Sally and Des Love at the beach.

Taylor was transfixed. She was holding the remote and as Sally and Des bent towards each other to smooth the roof of a castle, Taylor hit Pause. "I didn't know that my grandfather and Sally looked so much alike."

"Except for your hair colour, you look like both of them," I said. "And you move your body the way they did – confident and graceful."

Taylor's eyes were still fixed on the screen. "I used to make sand villages like that when I was little," Taylor said. "Remember that cottage on Long Lake we rented for a month every summer?"

"I do," I said. "And I remember your villages. You were never content with just a pail and shovel. You had to have all that paraphernalia Sally and your grandfather had."

"There was no way I could know that Sally and my grandfather needed all that stuff for their villages, too."

"Maybe it was in your DNA," I said. "All I know is that you were insistent, so we got you what you needed. Angus used to say you could have opened your own construction company with the equipment you had."

"You always helped me build," she said.

"I did," I said. "Of course, I wasn't as good as your grandfather and Sally."

"But you were there," Taylor said. She hit Play and watched as Ben and I joined Nina for lunch. When Nina dumped the goblets of pansies that had been at her husband and daughter's places, the venom in Nina's eyes was unmistakable and Taylor cringed. "Why did Nina hate her own daughter?" she asked.

"She was jealous," I said. "She was jealous of Sally's talent and her beauty and of the fact that your grandfather and Sally had a bond that didn't include her."

Gradually the shape of our lives was returning to normal. Taylor had gone back to school and was working again with the Kids at Risk program in the inner city. Except for some grumbling about Declan's hovering, Taylor seemed to be adjusting.

Most mornings, Zack and I drove her into the city, then took care of our separate tasks. I had hoped Zack's ardour for civic politics would have waned, but he had formed a top-secret advisory committee to explore the possibility of him running for a mayor. In Regina, *top-secret* means that pretty much everyone in the city knows what's going on within a week. I was getting plenty of phone calls: 50 per cent offered support; 50 per cent suggested I take Zack out behind the woodpile and slap him around until he came to his senses. Once again, the ground was shifting under my feet.

—

Every night we made time to watch two or three segments of one of the DVDs. Many of the outtakes from the summer of the sandcastles were fun. Sally and me swimming out to the raft with the indefatigable old yellow hound dog that had followed Des home one day and never left. Ben trying to conduct an interview with Sally about her art and Sally responding with monosyllabic answers until she and Ben both started laughing and gave up. Sally and me waterskiing, showing off for the camera and taking some spectacular falls.

Lighthearted moments, but then came a scene that prefigured the darkness that was to come. Nina and Des Love were hosting a dinner party on the deck of their cottage. The sun was setting and the sky and the lake were on fire. The table was set with Nina's usual cleverness – hurricane lamps; a vintage sandpail filled with a summer bouquet of pale pink roses, lavender, and delphinium; a scattering of seashells on the pale blue cloth. The men were in sports shirts and pressed slacks; the women wore sleeveless dresses with silky full-length skirts that undulated with each step they took.

It was the kind of dress-up affair Nina favoured, and she was gorgeous in a gown the colour of seafoam, but all eyes were on Sally, deeply tanned, without makeup, her blond hair in the kind of loose ponytail only the young can carry off. She had pulled a chair up to the table to talk about a Monet exhibit she and Des had seen the week before in Chicago. As she talked about the violent beauty of the brushstrokes in Monet's haystacks, Sally's long arms cut through the air, unconsciously mimicking the painter's movements. When her hand hit a glass of red wine at the place next to her, the wine splashed Sally's T-shirt and Nina's pretty tablecloth. Sally leapt up in mock horror. "Well, I guess I'm banished," she said, laughing. Des smiled at her fondly. "Nonsense. You're the life of this party. Sit back down and tell us about Monet's brushstrokes."

The camaraderie between father and daughter was unmistakable; so was the hatred in Nina's eyes. She remained poised, but as she gazed at the daughter who had ruined her perfect party, Nina's loathing was manifest.

But then we came to an interview Ben Bendure had done with Sally a year later. She was sitting on a couch with Izak Levin, the forty-five-year-old art critic to whom she had turned after Des's death. Sally's untamed hair had been smartly cut, her outfit was boho chic, she was smoking a cigarette, and her eyes had lost their sparkle. Ben had moved the camera close, and when Taylor saw the change in her mother, she leaned forward. "Pause the tape," she said.

Zack did and Taylor turned to me. "How old was she there?" Taylor said.

"About fourteen," I said.

"And the man with her was her lover."

"Yes," I said.

"She doesn't look like herself any more," Taylor said. "What happened to her?"

"Not long after that evening where Sally knocked over the wine at Nina's party, everything went wrong," I said. "Des had a stroke that paralyzed his right side. He was right-handed."

Taylor touched her own right arm reflexively. "He couldn't make art," she said.

"No, he couldn't. He was an immensely physical man and suddenly his life seemed to be over."

"So he didn't want to live any more?" Taylor said.

Zack's eyes met mine, and he nodded imperceptibly, indicating it was time for the truth. "That was Nina's explanation," I said. "She told everyone that Des wanted to die and that he had decided to take her and Sally with him. There was poison in Des and Nina's cocktails and in Sally's soft drink. Nina's story turned out to be a lie. Nina was the one who'd poisoned the drinks, but Sally had no way of knowing that. Des Love had been the centre of Sally's world, and till the day she died, she believed he had tried to kill her."

"Is that why Sally didn't stay with anyone very long?" Taylor asked.

"I'd never made the connection before," I said. "But you're probably right. You saw how much Sally loved Des. When Des died, something in Sally broke. For the rest of her life she was searching for someone who could make her whole again."

Emotion always went straight to Taylor's mouth, just as it did to Sally's, and I could see from the quiver of her lips that she was struggling. "That's why she had sex with all those people," Taylor said. "But it never worked for her."

"No," I said. "It never worked."

The image of the girl with the smart haircut, the cigarette, and the lifeless eyes stared out at us from the television screen. Taylor went up to the screen and traced her mother's features with her finger. "I'm so sorry" she said. "I wish it could have been different for you. I wish you could have had what I have."

Taylor had begun to lay her ghosts, and so had I. In allowing Taylor and me to see that Sally had lived the only life she was capable of living, Ben Bendure had given us a great gift, and when I called to thank him for the outtakes, I told him so.

We moved back to Halifax Street on December 20, Taylor's last day of classes. Students were dismissed at noon on the last day, so the three of us had lunch at a vegetarian place close to Luther and then came home. I had been nervous about how Taylor would react to moving back into the condo, but a coat of paint and some furniture rearranging can work wonders.

Mieka and the girls and Margot and Declan were bringing supper at six, so Zack, Taylor, and I had the entire afternoon to get used to our refurbished digs. Zack and I had dropped the animals by after we took Taylor to school, so when our daughter walked into her new bedroom, her cats, Bruce and Benny, were already curled up on her bed. Their timing couldn't have been better. Cats in arms, Taylor began sizing up her room and the changes we'd made in the other guest bedroom so she could use it as a place to watch TV or use her computer.

Not surprisingly, Taylor hesitated about going upstairs. Several times I noticed her casting her eyes towards the second floor, but she gave the stairs a wide berth. "If you want, I can go up there with you," I said finally.

She shook her head. "You're not going to be able to come up with me every time. I might as well get it over with." As she approached the stairs her stride was determined, but she climbed slowly and when she reached the landing, she stopped and looked down at me. After a beat, she turned, squared her shoulders, and went up to her old studio.

She stayed there for a long time. When she came down again, she moved towards Zack and me. "Well, I did it," she said.

"Next time will be easier," Zack said.

"I hope so," Taylor said. She brightened. "I like the colour you chose for your bedroom."

"It's called Tuscan pear," I said. "We thought it would be nice to wake up to."

She nodded approval. "You have a lot of wall space. Why don't you get some of Sally's paintings out of storage and ask Darrell to hang them for you? If you want, I can help you choose."

"Sounds like a plan," Zack said. "Guess it's our turn to investigate the upstairs, Ms. Shreve." He wheeled towards the bottom of the stairs and glared at the stair lift for his chair. "You know I hate these fucking things," he said under his breath.

"I know," I said. "I also know you'd crawl over broken glass for Taylor."

Zack transferred his body onto the chair of the stairlift and up we went. Zack's old wheelchair was waiting on the second floor. Taylor's studio was now our bedroom. The lights were low and the room was warm with welcome. Zack had never complained about feeling cramped in the bedroom downstairs, but as he wheeled around our new room he seemed pleased. "We can make this work, Jo."

"You mean our lives, or the fucking stairlift?"

He chuckled. "Our lives. The jury's still out on the fucking stairlift."

When we returned to the main floor, Taylor was in the dining area, gazing thoughtfully at *Two Painters.* "I know this is your painting, Jo, but I've been thinking about this space." Her arm swept the area between her and Sally. "There's too much of it. Sally and I don't even seem to be in the same world. I've been looking at some of Desmond Love's work on the Internet – I'd like to put in something like one of his abstracts – bright and joyous. I could prop it against an easel between Sally and me." She turned to face me. "What do you think?"

For the first time in weeks, my enthusiasm was unforced. "I think that's a terrific idea," I said.

Margot went into labour in the middle of the night, just as the first day of winter was beginning. I was her labour coach, and Zack was my ride, so Declan would stay with Taylor in our condo until we got home. Margot had a difficult time. At 11:00 a.m. her ob-gyn decided to do a Caesarean.

When he left the room to consult with the anesthesiologist, Margot groaned and grabbed my hand. "Is it too late to change my mind?"

"About the Caesarean?"

"About the whole thing." She grunted. "God, I sound like an animal."

"Grunting's good," I said. "Moving a baby down the birth canal and out into the world is hard work."

Margot's honey blond hair was dark with sweat and she was clearly exhausted. "I can't take any more of this," she said. "Where the hell is that anesthesiologist?" Suddenly her eyes opened very wide. "It's coming. Get the doctor, and – did I imagine it or did you tell me Zack is here?

"I told him I thought you were close an hour ago," I said. "He's in the waiting room."

"Get him," Margot said. "I want him in here to see there's something I can do that he can't." She groaned. "Quick."

We made it back just in time. As the baby crowned, Margot made a sound that began as a moan and ended in a scream. Zack was visibly alarmed. "It's okay," I told him. "The worst is over. Now comes the good part." The doctor tilted the baby down to release her highest shoulder, then the second shoulder appeared and the baby slid out. When she gave a healthy cry, Zack beamed and gave Margot a thumbs-up. "You win," he said. "That was nothing short of amazing. Now I'm getting out of here."

Alexandra Joanne Hunter, who would be known as Lexi, was a strong and beautiful girl, nine pounds, ten ounces; twenty-two inches long, and blond and fair-skinned like Margot. She was born at 11:11 a.m., the precise moment when the winter solstice occurred. Margot was tired and hungry, but as Lexi latched on to her breast, her face was serene. "Look at that girl. She knows exactly what she needs and she goes after it."

"Just like her mother," I said.

"And her father," Margot said.

"With genes like that, Lexi will be unbeatable," I said. "Time for you to get to know each other." I kissed Margot and Lexi. "Sleep well, Lexi," I said. "You have a whole world to discover."

When the elevator stopped at our floor, the owner of Crocus and Ivy, a local shop that sold high-end children's wear, wheeled out an old-fashioned pram filled with cozy clothing, gifts for the winter solstice baby. A photographer followed close behind, ready to snap pictures of the event.

As Zack and I got into the elevator, we were joined by two nurses. One appeared to be in late middle age; the other was younger, perhaps in her mid-twenties. Both wore the cheerful teddy-bear print uniforms of the obstetrics nursing staff. The women were chatting with the weary intimacy of workers who've shared a long shift.

"Our winter solstice baby was certainly born under a lucky star," the younger woman said. "Her mother is Margot Hunter. She owns some big international company." She shook her head. "It doesn't seem fair that her baby's the one who gets that gorgeous carriage and all the goodies."

The older nurse chuckled. "My grandma had a record that she played over and over again. All I can remember is the opening. 'Them that's got shall get and them that's not shall lose.'" Truer words were never spoken."

The younger nurse nodded. "I was on duty when last year's winter solstice baby was born. He was fetal alcohol syndrome."

Zack and I followed the two nurses out. The lighting on the floor of the Mother-Baby units had been muted, but the overheads on the main floor were pitilessly bright. When we reached the front doors, Zack looked at me and his brow furrowed. "You've lost your glow," he said.

"So have you," I said. "But it's time to put on our game faces and head for home. We have a daughter waiting."

When we got back to Halifax Street, Taylor was asleep on the couch, covered with a quilt. Declan was sitting beside her. He stood when he heard us come through the door. "How are Margot and Lexi?" he said.

We kept our voices low. "Perfect in every way," I said. "You can see for yourself tomorrow morning."

"Thanks for staying with Taylor," Zack said.

"Margot said if I saw her giving birth it would freak us both out and she'd never have any grandchildren. Anyway, I'm always happy to be with Taylor."

"How are you doing?" I said. "We haven't really had a chance to talk lately."

"I'm fine. And Taylor's going to be fine, too." His voice was filled with hope. "It's going to take a while, but Taylor and I have plenty of time. This morning I figured out that Lexi will live to see the beginning of the twenty-second century. That's pretty cool, isn't it?"

"Mega cool," Zack said. He held out his hand. Declan shook it and held on. He had tears in his eyes. "I miss my dad," he said.

"So do I," Zack said.

After Declan left, I bent to smooth Taylor's hair. "I'd better get our girl into bed. She was probably awake until dawn."

"Why don't we wait awhile?" Zack said. "Taylor's comfortable where she is, and you're still upset about that old Billie Holiday line."

"'Them that's got shall get?'" I said. "I didn't realize that was Billie Holiday."

"'God Bless the Child,'" Zack said. "I've got it on my playlist if you want to hear it."

"I'm depressed enough," I said.

"That's when you're supposed to listen to the blues," Zack said. "Let's give it a shot. We have a bottle of champagne in the refrigerator, we have a roof garden, and we still have our coats on. Let's go up, check out the city, and listen to Billie."

"Why not?" I said. I took down the champagne flutes, and Zack picked up his MP3 player and the champagne. The dogs, sensing good times ahead, raced to the door.

The day we stepped into was cold and grey. The evergreens wintering on the roof garden had been decorated with red ribbon, and as we moved towards the edge of the garden Zack and I puffed little clouds of breath. Somewhere the safety alarm of a car blared, then stopped.

Zack loved dramatic moments, and few moments are more dramatic than popping the cork on a bottle of champagne. He opened the bottle and poured some into the flutes I was holding. The contents of one of the glasses overflowed onto my mitten.

"Hey, suck that mitten," Zack said. "A client sent the champagne, and it's the good stuff."

"You're such a classy guy," I said.

"I'll take that as a compliment," Zack said. "So what shall we drink to?"

"How about to those we've lost and those we've gained," I said.

"That seems to cover it," Zack said, and his voice was husky with emotion.

We touched glasses and took our first sip. Zack wheeled close to me. "Time to listen to Billie." He touched Play and the quiet night was filled with Billie Holiday's warm, intimate, and heartbreakingly wise voice. She was a storyteller, and as she sang about how the strong get more while the weak ones fade, my throat closed. By the time "God Bless the Child" finished, I'd come to a decision.

Zack peered at me carefully. "Still no glow," he said. "Let's take in the lights. That will cheer you up." He pointed to the star the construction crew had hung on the scaffolding of the Racette-Hunter Centre. "I really like that star," he said. "Let's come up with some sort of snazzy lighting to mark the R-H Centre when it's finished. We want to remind everyone – especially the people of North Central – that we're there."

"Snazzy lighting is always a crowd pleaser," I said. "That can be your first official act as mayor."

"Whoa," Zack said. "What happened to the dozen reasons why I shouldn't get into the race?"

"They're still with us," I said. "But they're overridden by the one reason you should. We can't have kids hurling rocks at strangers' cars because they know that nothing good will ever happen to them, and we can't have FAS babies whose lives are over before they've begun."

"And you think we can change that?" Zack said.

"I don't know. I just know we have to try."

Zack turned his chair to face me. "You're one helluva woman, Joanne."

I leaned down and embraced my husband. "And you're one helluva man."

Zack's lips were cold and so were mine, but a kiss is still a kiss.

When the kiss ended, I straightened. "Let's listen to Billie Holiday again," I said. And as Billie Holiday sang the final hopeful verse of "God Bless the Child," Zack and I joined our gloved hands, looked down at the city together, and dreamed our separate dreams.

ACKNOWLEDGEMENTS

Thanks to:

Lara Hinchberger, my editor, and her associate Kendra Ward, for giving me the kind of collaborative editing experience writers dream about.

Heather Sangster for her eagle eye.

Ben Bowen-Bell, my seven-year-old grandson, for the cover concept, and Terri Nimmo for making Ben's concept a reality.

Barbara Weller, LICSW, for reading the manuscript and for giving me expert advice about psychology.

Rick Mitchell, retired Staff Sergeant in Charge of Major Crimes Section, Regina Police Service, for his insights into the lives of the people of North Central.

Darrell Bell for great conversations about art.

Najma Kazmi, M.D., for her sensitivity and professionalism.

Hildy Bowen for sharing her knowledge about the many things I don't know.

Ted Bowen, my love of forty-four years, for making all things possible.

Finally, thanks to the City of Regina, which has provided me with such rich material over the years. I have always tried to portray our city truthfully, but my novels are fiction and in *The Gifted* I have envisioned a dream outcome for the un-played (at the time of writing) 2013 Grey Cup. As well, I invented out of whole cloth a mayor and city council who served my narrative purposes. My civic scoundrels bear no resemblance to our real mayor and city council, all of whom are dedicated public servants.